STAR TREK®
ACTION!

"IMPULSE ENGINE

C.S. ④
THIS POINT

TOP

STAR TREK®
ACTION!

TERRY J. ERDMANN

creative consultant Paula M. Block

P O C K E T B O O K S
New York   London   Toronto   Sydney   Tokyo   Singapore

for Florence and Hattie

CONTENTS

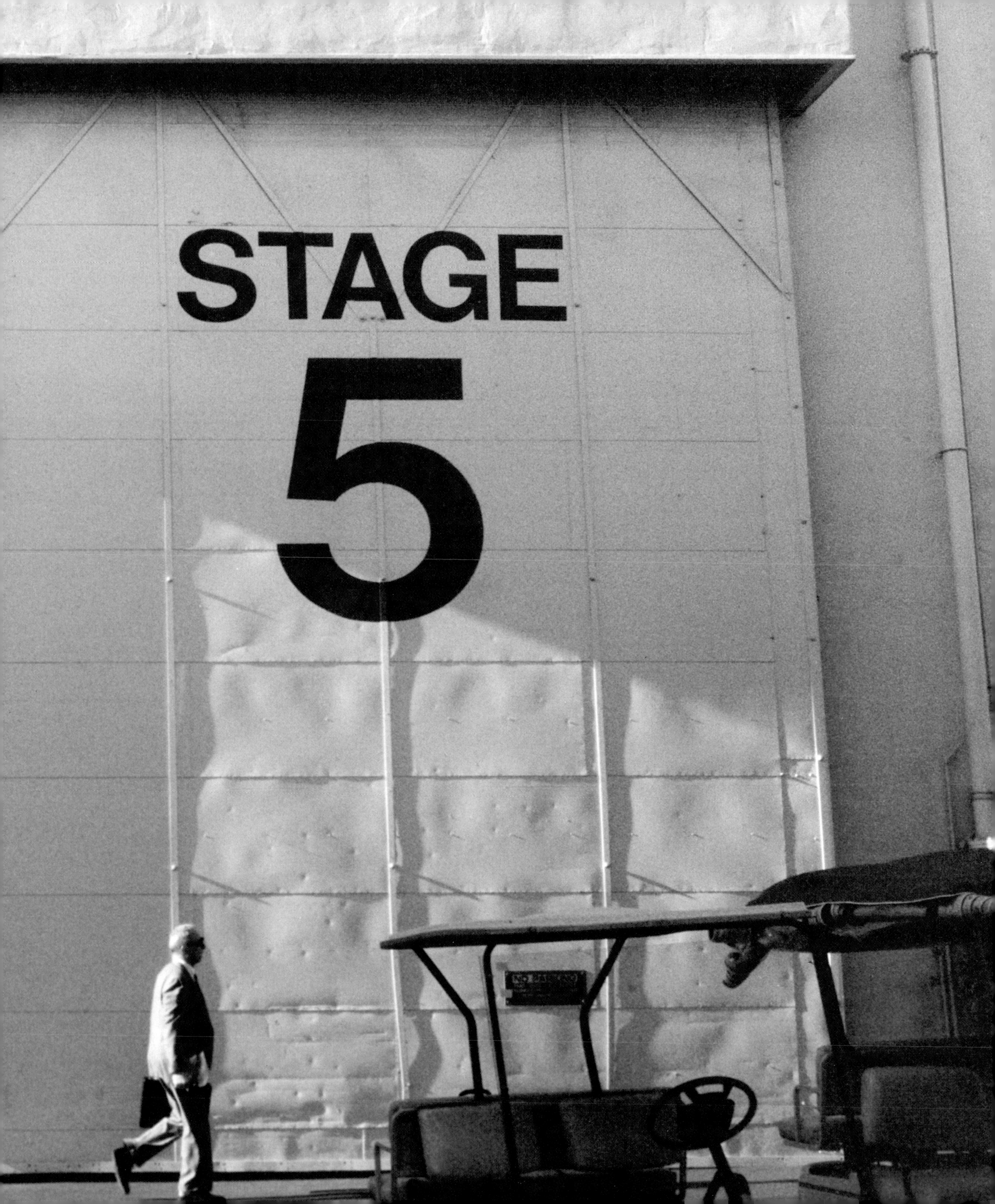
STAGE
5

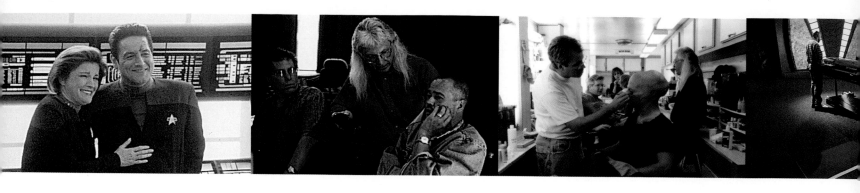

WHAT IT'S ALL ABOUT . . .
AN INTRODUCTION

THE INITIAL PREMISE OF THIS BOOK SOUNDED SIMPLE: TAKE 120 SECONDS OF THE AVERAGE *STAR TREK* TELEVISION EPISODE AND MOTION PICTURE, THEN BREAK IT DOWN INTO ITS COMPONENTS AND TELL THE READERS EVERY SINGLE THING THAT WENT INTO CREATING THOSE TWO MINUTES. Writing, acting, building sets, designing costumes, slathering on latex. Whatever it takes. Use one example from *Star Trek: Voyager*, one from *Star Trek: Deep Space Nine*, and one from the ninth *Star Trek* motion picture (*Star Trek: Insurrection*).

Piece of cake, seemingly. Except it wasn't.

For one thing, while 120 seconds sounded good in concept (and would have made a catchy book title), it meant absolutely nothing in the context of the assignment. Two random minutes of footage didn't necessarily include a coherent beginning and ending that would allow readers to make sense of the process. It made much more sense to cover a *scene*, which could run anywhere from a few seconds to a lot of minutes, or a short sequence of scenes (if you're cutting between the crew on the bridge and something happening in space outside the ship, that's actually a sequence of scenes, even though it looks like one scene to the viewer at home). It took a very short time for me to figure this out.

So the premise was modified, as was the title. I would dissect a scene or a sequence of scenes. The only criterion was that the scene should revolve around the captain of whichever incarnation of *Star Trek* I was covering. And that something interesting should be happening.

That, too, made things a little difficult. In some cases, a scene with the captain might not be the most interesting scene in the episode or movie. But it would make for thematic consistency throughout the book—so the captain it was.

The next step was to figure out which scene of the episode or film would be the best one to cover. This, I must admit, was something of a crapshoot. As I listened to the evolution of each episode at story breaks and production meetings, I could *guess* which scene might make for a memorable moment (or two or three), but I knew there was a chance that the scene would not turn out to be as awe-inspiring as it initially sounded. And I also knew that by the time that became apparent, it would be too late to turn around and start all over again with a different scene.

With all that in mind, and with some valuable input from the executive producers of *Star Trek: Voyager* and *Star Trek: Deep Space Nine*, here's what I ultimately chose:

From the *Voyager* episode titled "Hope and Fear," I chose the climactic fifth-act sequence where Captain Janeway and Seven of Nine manage to escape the clutches of Arturis. This sequence featured the captain in a prominent role, interesting new sets, a nifty new ship, and visual *and* special-effects wizardry.

From the *Deep Space Nine* episode called "Tears of the Prophets," I chose the sequence in which Sisko's closest friend, Jadzia, dies, and he addresses her remains. This sequence featured the captain in a prominent role, but contained very little in the way of fancy sets or technical wizardry. Instead, the focus was on the deep emotional resonance of the subject matter and the care that the writers and actors put into crafting the farewell sequence for a beloved *Star Trek* character.

For both of these episodes, I've provided information about the backdrop against which these scenes play out. I've taken you to the brainstorming sessions at the beginning of the writing process, touched upon the scenes that surround the chosen one, and talked about the postproduction period, from editing to the scoring session.

But I didn't do that for the movie.

From *Star Trek: Insurrection* I chose a sequence in which Picard and Worf try to contact Data, who doesn't seem to want to be contacted. Once again, the sequence featured the captain in a prominent role. It also featured ships, visual effects, and some exciting action. Because this motion picture will not have opened by the time you read this book, its sequence was a little more difficult to discuss, and if its section seems a bit shorter on detail than the other two sections of the book, there's a reason for it. I personally dislike the thought of people opening their Christmas presents early (and so do the people at the *Star Trek* office). However, I have nothing against someone giving the wrapped present a little shake (so long as the present isn't fragile). It won't tell you much about the contents, but it will pique your interest. Rick Berman is graciously allowing me to give you the literary equivalent of a little shake. So I haven't told you what came before the sequence, or after, or even given you the dialogue.

Cruel? Maybe. I can say no more.

STAR TREK
ACTION!

STAR TREK: VOYAGER
"HOPE AND FEAR"

92   CONTINUED: (2)   92

A final beat between them, then Janeway EXITS...

                                            CUT TO:

93   EXT. SPACE - QUANTUM SLIPSTREAM (OPTICAL)   93

The Dauntless speeding through the torrent. Suddenly,
we see a THRUSTER on the starboard hull FLARE OUT --
causing the ship to CAREEN out of control!

94   INT. DAUNTLESS - ALIEN BRIDGE   94

SHAKING HARD! Arturis hanging on for dear life! He
struggles to the helm, works it...

95   EXT. SPACE - QUANTUM SLIPSTREAM (OPTICAL)   95

The Dauntless out of control! The ship SPINNING and
SLAMMING against the sides of the slipstream, causing
powerful DISCHARGES of ENERGY! After a harrowing beat,
the ship begins to SLOW and its course evens out.

96   INT. DAUNTLESS - ALIEN BRIDGE   96

The shaking subsides. Arturis looks relieved. He
begins to work again, when suddenly:

                    JANEWAY'S VOICE
              Sorry about the bumpy ride.

He whirls to see Janeway, who's just stepped into the
room.

                    ARTURIS
              You can slow this ship down, but
              you can't stop it.
                    (beat)
              In four minutes, Captain Janeway
              will be gone... and a new Drone
              will be born.
                    JANEWAY
              Don't count on it.

The ship ROCKS again! Arturis works the helm
desperately... then the shaking subsides.

                                         (CONTINUED)

---

96   CONTINUED: 96

                    JANEWAY
              Seven of Nine has accessed your   *
              navigational systems. You taught
              us how to use this ship a little
              too well.

Arturis moves to another console, works it with intent.
Janeway tries to reach him on an emotional level.

                    JANEWAY
                    (compassionate)
              I can't begin to imagine your
              loss... but if you can try to see
              beyond your desire for revenge...   *

                    ARTURIS
              Revenge is all I have left!

                    JANEWAY
              No... as long you're alive...
              there's hope. Your people's
              knowledge, accomplishments,
              dignity... can survive... in you.
                    (quiet)
              End this.

He glances at her, and it looks like he might be
persuaded by her words... then he taps a final control.

97   INT. DAUNTLESS - ENGINEERING (OPTICAL)   97

Seven of Nine working a console... when an ENERGY
DISCHARGE CRACKLES around the entire console! A
section of the panel BLOWS OUT in a SHOWER OF SPARKS!
Seven of Nine recoils.

98   INT. DAUNTLESS - ALIEN BRIDGE   98

As before. Arturis turns to Janeway.

                    ARTURIS
              I've just destroyed the
              navigational controls. No one can
              stop this ship, now... not even
              me.

Janeway rushes to a panel. Arturis takes satisfaction
in her anxiety.

                                         (CONTINUED)

---

98   CONTINUED: 98

                    ARTURIS
              Two minutes to Borg space.

A long, terrible beat...

WHAM! The ship JOLTS. They both stumble! Arturis
looks shocked -- what now?

99   EXT. SPACE - QUANTUM SLIPSTREAM (OPTICAL)   99

The STARSHIP VOYAGER is CAREENING toward the Dauntless,
FIRING TORPEDOES, which SLAM into the enemy ship!

100   INT. VOYAGER - BRIDGE   100

Red Alert. Chakotay, Tuvok, Paris, Kim, N.D.s. Fast
action:

                    TUVOK
              Direct hit!
                    (reacts)
              The vessel's shields are down.
              Transporters standing by.

                    CHAKOTAY
              Get a lock on our people!

Kim works...

101   INT. DAUNTLESS - ALIEN BRIDGE (OPTICAL)   101

As before, SHAKING HARD. A couple of consoles EXPLODE,
SPARKING! Arturis is on his feet, rushing from station
to station, panicked, his world coming unraveled.

                    ARTURIS
                    (off console)
              Voyager.

Janeway reacts.

                    JANEWAY
              Come with me -- it's not too late!

Arturis grabs an alien HAND-WEAPON from out of a
station. He whirls on Janeway.

                    ARTURIS
              It is for you.

                                         (CONTINUED)

101   CONTINUED: 101

        Janeway DEMATERIALIZES. Arturis FIRES but the
        discharge goes right through her without effect!

        Another JOLT! Arturis is thrown to the floor!

102   INT. VOYAGER - BRIDGE   102

        As before.

                            KIM
                I've got them, Commander --
                Transporter Room Two!
                            CHAKOTAY
                Alter our slipstream -- hard
                starboard -- take us back the way
                we came!

103   EXT. SPACE - QUANTUM SLIPSTREAM (OPTICAL)   103

        Voyager BANKS hard! The SLIPSTREAM BANKS with the
        ship, BRANCHING OFF the original slipstream as Voyager
        flies offscreen!

104   THE DAUNTLESS (OPTICAL)   104

        keeps going in its own slipstream at top-speed! As it
        ZOOMS off into the distance...

105   EXT. SPACE (OPTICAL)   105

        A field of stars. In a blast of energy, the DAUNTLESS
        comes ROARING out of the slipstream and into normal
        space. It decelerates to a slow drift... and the
        CAMERA PANS to reveal --

106   FIVE BORG CUBES (OPTICAL)   106

        heading right toward us!

107   INT. DAUNTLESS - ALIEN BRIDGE   107

        Peaceful, now, no shaking. Arturis is on the floor.
        He sits up... dazed... but recovers in time to HEAR the
        voice of the COLLECTIVE:

                                                        (CONTINUED)

107   CONTINUED: 107
                            BORG
                We are the Borg. You will be
                assimilated. Resistance is
                futile.

        Off Arturis... bracing for the inevitable...

                                                        FADE TO BLACK.

        FADE IN:

108   EXT. SPACE - VOYAGER (STOCK - OPTICAL)   108

        at impulse.

                            JANEWAY (V.O.)
                Captain's Log, supplemental. We
                remained in the quantum slipstream
                for an hour before it finally
                collapsed. Our diagnostics have   *
                concluded that we can't risk using   *
                this technology again... but we
                did manage to get three hundred
                light years closer to home.

109   INT. HOLOGRID (OPTICAL)   109

        Janeway and Seven of Nine in their workout clothes,
        engaged in a game of "Velocity," as seen in the Teaser.
        Seven of Nine is FIRING her phaser at the glowing blue
        DISK, but misses, and the disk GLANCES off her arm and
        VANISHES.

                            COMPUTER VOICE
                Full impact. Final round to
                Janeway. Winner: Janeway.

        Seven looks frustrated. As the two of them cool
        down...

                            JANEWAY
                Nice play. You almost had me.

                            SEVEN OF NINE
                Almost.

                            JANEWAY
                Go again?

                            SEVEN OF NINE
                I must report to the Astrometrics   *
                Lab. There is work to be done.

As explained in the introduction, the following pages on Voyager feature a climactic sequence from the series's fourth season finale, "Hope and Fear." For all intents and purposes, that means Scenes 95 through 107 from the fifth act. However, as you'll see, in order to explain the actions or settings of the chosen section, it was sometimes necessary to include information regarding other scenes.

And, of course, as with any other investigation, it is always necessary to start at the very beginning....

A typical *Voyager* beat session in Jeri Taylor's office. *From left to right:* Bryan Fuller, Brannon Braga, Lisa Klink, Ken Biller, Intern-of-the-Moment Robert Doherty, Jeri Taylor. *Star Trek*'s interns are usually assigned to the show for a period of six or eight weeks. ROBBIE ROBINSON.

FEBRUARY 2, 1998

THE ENTRANCE OF THE HART BUILDING OPENS INTO A LONG, DIMLY LIT CORRIDOR. The second door on the right is open, spilling a warm glow into the hallway. This is Jeri Taylor's office, accessible and inviting, exactly how Taylor likes it.

Inside, Taylor waits at her desk. It's standard-issue wood-grained office furniture, not exactly what you'd expect for the executive producer of *Star Trek: Voyager*, but eminently practical. It's clearly the desk of a working writer, typically covered with notepads, completed scripts, scripts in progress, and unidentified bits of flotsam and jetsam. However, with the exception of the frowning gargoyle who guards Taylor's inbox, the rest of the room conveys the same amiable feeling as the open door, particularly the cushy old sofa and upholstered chairs that face her desk.

This morning, Taylor's warm smile betrays an unusual touch of sadness. She is about to convene the final story-break session in her tenure with *Star Trek*. But there's no time to reflect on that; the show, as they say, must go on.

By 9:25 A.M., *Voyager*'s other producers and writers—Brannon Braga, Joe Menosky, Ken Biller, Lisa Klink, and Bryan Fuller—have arrived and are casually settled into their seats. They're used to these biweekly gatherings, free forums where they discuss and contribute ideas to prosposed episodes, ultimately breaking them into beats or high points. Traditionally, the average break session runs a day or two, and when it's over, the writer assigned to the episode has a literary map of sorts, which will efficiently guide him or her from the teaser to the tag.

But this break session will prove to be very untraditional.

The casual atmosphere in the room belies a certain amount of pressure. Principal photography for the episode, listed as production number 194, is scheduled to begin on February 26, exactly twenty-four days away. All preproduction preparation, including casting, set design and construction, costume design and fittings, and so on, must be completed before the day they shoot. The first day of prep, when department heads will begin planning their work schedules for the episode, is only eight days away. And, of course, prior to any of that, a story must be conceived and fleshed out.

As the meeting commences at 9:30, Co-Executive Producer Brannon Braga hands out a four-page document to the room's occupants. At the top of the first page is written:

"UNTITLED FINAL EPISODE"
Preliminary Beat Sheet
Braga/Menosky
2/2/98

The preliminary beat sheet is the first version of the map mentioned above, and it is provided by the writer or writers who have been assigned to write the final teleplay—in this particular case, Brannon Braga and Joe Menosky. "We usually get the preliminary beat sheet on the day before or the day of the actual break session," explains Executive Story Editor Lisa Klink. "The assigned writer tries to sketch out at least the first couple of acts; he doesn't have to come up with a whole beat sheet independently. The preliminary is just something to get the meeting started, so that people have something to respond to."

For the next few minutes, the writers occupy themselves with reading the beat sheet. Then Gardner Goldsmith, an intern assigned to *Voyager*, writes the word "Teaser" (signifying the short scene that takes place before the opening credits) in the upper left corner of the shiny white "beat board" mounted on the wall. He waits to be told what to write next.

He will wait a long time. "We didn't have any clear vision of what we wanted to do," admits Taylor in retrospect. "It was a most unusual situation, something that had never really occurred."

For the next two hours and twenty minutes, there is a great deal of discussion in the room, further distillation of ideas that had been tossed around for a while. Prior to the meeting, says Klink, "we had talked about the story a *lot*! We had gone through lots and lots of different ideas and different feelings about what kind of note we wanted to end the season on. The preliminary beat sheet picked up one of those ideas and ran with it, while a number of entirely different storylines that we were considering didn't make it."

But that one idea on the beat sheet isn't quite gelling, possibly because the discarded ideas feel so established. One of them actually has been kicking around since the end of *Voyager*'s third season. It concerns the mimetic aliens that the writers would ultimately use in the episode "Demon." In the never-written story, the mimetic aliens somehow make it back to the Alpha Quadrant and arrive at Deep Space 9 to great fanfare, according to Taylor. "Everybody thinks that *Voyager* is home," she says, "and there are celebrations, and they see their loved ones, etcetera, etcetera. And it turns out to be an invasion or a dark plot of some kind."

The story had definite possibilities, which is why, after being shelved a year earlier, it cropped up a second time at the end of the fourth season. But, notes Taylor, "the more we discussed it, the more we thought that once they go home, even if it isn't really our characters, well, it undercuts whatever will happen when the *real* crew actually does get home. Which we *do* intend to have happen."

When the staff had initially decided against using that story at the end of the third season, Brannon Braga had come up with the idea for the two-part episode, "Scorpion," that introduced Seven of Nine. But this time around, finding an exciting alternative seems more difficult. "We were feeling the time crunch, and we were madly scrambling to come up with something else," says Taylor.

The "something else" that Braga and Menosky are offering in the preliminary beat sheet contains two important story germs. One concerns the conflict between the characters of Captain Janeway and Seven of Nine. The other concerns the encoded message that *Voyager* received from Starfleet Command earlier, in the fourth-season episode "Hunters." The beat sheet is not complete; it lists only a series of suggestions for the first two acts (of five). But at this point in the day, no one in Taylor's office is worried. "We trust the chemistry that occurs in the room," explains Jeri Taylor. "Many, many, many times, probably more times than not, we've had a germ of an idea, with no clear vision of how it's going to be amplified into a story, and we get together in the room and the magic begins to happen. It may take several days; it may take ten minutes. You never know which idea that someone tosses out will lead you to something that leads to something else, and you start getting lightning in a bottle. And so we trusted that it would happen again."

The discussion begins and the writers discuss what there is so far. In the teaser, Janeway and Seven play a highly competitive game on the holodeck; we sense the conflict between them. In Act One, Janeway obsesses over the mysterious message that *Voyager* received from Starfleet months earlier. They still can't decode it. Finally, Janeway's intuition gives her the key and the message plays at last, informing the crew about a radical new—but very risky—method of space travel called slipstreaming. Seven is aware of this method—and says that every Borg cube that ever attempted to use it was never heard from again. But Janeway decides to risk it anyway, thus increasing the tension between herself and Seven. In Act Two, the crew modifies *Voyager* according to Starfleet's specs and seeks out the nearest slipstream, only to find that it is "some kind of intergalactic highway" on which ships are zooming past so fast that being on *Voyager* feels like "driving a horse and buggy" on the freeway.

From this point, the beat sheet shifts into several long paragraphs of text under the heading:

POSSIBILITIES FROM HERE.

In the first possibility, Seven of Nine has a seizure, with "weird optical effects," that causes her implants to "fritz out." The Doctor reports that Seven can't survive in the slipstream. Seven is willing to forfeit her life to let the crew proceed, but Janeway says her mission is to save every member of her crew. Seven of Nine challenges her mentor and argues that *Voyager* should go on without her.

Playing devil's advocate, the beat sheet offers some commentary on this alternative:

The problem with this approach is that it feels a little like "One," where the crew can't survive in a particular part of space. So that leads us to possibility #2. . .

In this possibility, Seven does not suffer any adverse side effects from the slipstream. Instead:

. . . we are attacked by an indigenous alien ship. Turns out they don't like the fact that

we've entered their highway. And a brief SPACE BATTLE takes place at slipstream speeds. (This is a sequence we discussed doing in "Scorpion." Remember the firefight in Borg subspace tunnels?) We manage to disable the alien vessel, and the aliens on board abandon ship. But we end up with -- to use our highway analogy -- a *Porsche* in our possession. And this twist builds to our original notion: Voyager can't stay in the slipstream any longer, so Seven of Nine suggests that we take the gleaming new alien ship and proceed. The conflict between Janeway and Seven ignites. . . . Eventually Seven of Nine does take command of the alien vessel. But something goes awry in Act Five. Captain Janeway and "Captain" Seven find themselves face-to-face in a dangerous situation. Ultimately, Janeway is proven right. She beats Seven at their "game" once again.

The beat sheet ends with a statement—more of an understatement, actually:

There's a lot to figure out here!

The group begins discussing the information provided on the beat sheet, starting with suggestions about the type of holodeck game that Janeway and Seven can play in the opening shots. Then the talk shifts to deeper into the story and whether Seven would actually take over an alien ship. Ken Biller and Brannon Braga agree that Seven now would think of herself as a better captain than Janeway. Then Braga confesses that even though he's the one who put it on the beat sheet, he doesn't really like the idea of Seven breaking off on her own.

"If Seven were to take this other ship," Ken Biller queries, "would any of the others join her?" Biller starts to run through the list: Kim? Torres?

The topic shifts again, this time to the alien with the sleek ship. Who is this guy? Biller says, "What if this alien has a 'treasure map' of shortcuts through the galaxy that Janeway wants? What would he want in exchange? Information about *Voyager*?"

"No," Jeri Taylor speaks up abruptly. "Vengeance."

Everyone loves the idea.

"Up to that point, the ideas about this character's motivation were very intellectual," says Taylor. "They were in the head, and to me, that's dull. I think drama is built on emotion: You want to have characters who are feeling things, and you want them to allow the audience to feel something. Revenge is a visceral, emotional, *hot-blooded* kind of motivation that makes drama pop. That's what made Brannon and everyone else respond. So we began looking around for 'What was the revenge for?'"

They don't have an answer by 11:45, so the staff breaks for lunch. After two hours and twenty minutes, only one word has been written on the beat board—"Teaser."

Brannon Braga has disappeared.

Jeri Taylor lets the others know that the session won't reconvene until he returns. The recess stretches into two hours, then three, then four.

At 3:45 P.M., Sandra Sena, Taylor's assistant, calls each of the writers. Braga is back. The group returns to Taylor's office.

Braga has been to the mountain.

Only the Teaser would remain the same.

That is, he's been to see *Star Trek*'s executive producer, Rick Berman.

As Taylor says, the writing staff counts on the "chemistry" in the room to happen. It always has. But for some reason, on this particular occasion, it *isn't* happening, and Braga has realized it. "There wasn't a real strong direction in that room," he says. "It was kind of all over the place. So I met with Rick and he really helped put things into perspective. He's not working with the writing staff every day, so when he does get involved, he has a way of shaking things up and giving us a really objective viewpoint."

Braga has returned with some suggestions to move the story forward. "We should not decode the message at the beginning," he reports. Instead, the decoding should happen slowly throughout the episode. "And the alien should be extemely old, frail, and very intelligent. And he should be playing some sort of ruse on our crew."

"Well," says Jeri Taylor, "the only way to fill in the plot holes is to start writing it down." Gardner Goldsmith resumes his place at the beat board and writes, "Hologrid: Game as written on beat sheet," under "Teaser." Then he writes: "Act One."

"Is this message actually from Starfleet?" asks Lisa Klink.

"If it is," responds Braga, "then maybe this is really a Starfleet ship."

"If the alien built it, it isn't Starfleet," interjects Joe Menosky. "And if it is Starfleet, he didn't build it."

Ken Biller suggests they write a visual-effects "ship shot" in which the ship races past the camera at incredible speeds. Everyone agrees that such an exciting shot would be good for the episode. But Biller is worried. "If it isn't from Starfleet," he asks, "then how could this alien build such a great ship?"

Before they get around to that, they decide to re-explore the question of who the alien is. Where does he come from? Why does he want revenge? Is he after Seven? Maybe his race has been fighting the Borg. But if that's true, wouldn't Seven know?

"Maybe it was a long time ago and she can't remember it," Joe Menosky suggests. "Maybe they were assimilated as Species Number Four."

"That's too early," Brannon Braga says. "Make it Species Twenty-One. Or," he ponders, "maybe he's an El-Aurian, someone from Guinan's species."

"No." Jeri Taylor steps in. "We want him to have more interesting makeup than that."

Around this point, the staff begins to refer to the frail, old intelligent alien as "Yoda."

By 6:00 P.M., when Taylor calls an end to the

By turning the story around, the writers were able to use Captain Janeway's (Kate Mulgrew) reluctance to accept the *Dauntless* to mirror Seven's (Jeri Ryan) reluctance to leave the Delta Quadrant. RON TOM.

day's session, the highlights from eight possible first-act scenes fill the left column of the beat board, the majority of them identifying the potential locale for the scene:

- In the mess hall, Janeway sits working on the coded message;
- In space, a shuttle brings Neelix back from a supply mission;
- In the cargo bay, Neelix reveals that he's brought a "guest" back with him;

- In a corridor, Neelix says "Yoda" could help decrypt the message;
- In astrophysics, Seven recognizes "Yoda" as Species Twenty-One.
- Janeway, Paris, and "Yoda" decrypt the message, see that it has technical data as well as a set of coordinates;
- *Voyager* races past the camera;

And finally:

- Bridge: Everyone is there, including "Yoda." Huge exciting moment. They reach coordinates and see a "Silver Bullet" sitting in space. It's a Starfleet vessel!

"That ship probably sprang full grown from Brannon's head," says Jeri Taylor with a laugh. "He had, for a long time, talked about a sleek, new, spiffy-looking ship that he wanted to weave into a story in some way." As the writers groped for the building blocks that would provide the foundation for *Voyager*'s season closer, Braga's ship came in at last.

FEBRUARY 3

AT 9:30 A.M., A SMALLER GROUP REASSEMBLES IN TAYLOR'S OFFICE. Although these sessions are devoted to *Voyager*'s final episode of the year, there is still work to be done on the episodes that lead up to it. Joe Menosky is writing final pages for an earlier episode, "Living Witness," and Ken Biller is attending a Production Meeting for the season's penultimate episode, "One," which he will direct. The two men promise to join in the session after lunch.

The remaining writers immediately begin tackling the tough questions about the spiffy ship: Who sent it? Or who built it? If not "Yoda," where did he get it?

Suddenly the room becomes quiet. There are more questions being asked than answered. That's not good.

"I'm afraid this isn't dramatic enough for the finale," Braga moans. "Twenty-eight episodes and we get stumped now."

"The Janeway and Seven story will be fresh and cover it," Taylor says reassuringly.

"You're right," Braga says, but it is clear that he is still concerned.

Taylor sighs. "Sometimes this process is like pushing though mud. When it's meant to be revealed, it will be revealed."

Two words have been written on the beat board so far this morning: "Act Two." Now Braga dictates to the intern, who dutifully adds his comments to the board: "1. Hail ship. Scan ship. Mystery. 2. Space—Silver Bullet. 3. Bullet Bridge..."

Braga pauses. "I want the episode to stay alive!" he says suddenly, as if expressing some part of an interior dialogue. "I don't want to take time to explore the ship. The viewers will want to see how *Voyager*'s crew learns about the ship's functions, but I don't just want to show a boring instruction manual," he says.

"Perhaps Paris can tinker with the controls and inadvertently send it off," Jeri Taylor suggests.

The room is silent for several minutes, until Braga says, "Building an engine room warp core is too expensive."

"But we only have one guest star," Lisa Klink responds. "So we'll save there."

Another bout of silence. Then a discussion starts about bringing Seven into the story, about setting Seven and Janeway on an emotional collision course. No decision has been made about whether or not Seven goes with the away team to explore the ship. No decision has been made about whether the ship is alien or Starfleet.

"Maybe Seven should send the ship off, not Paris," Taylor says, audibly rethinking her earlier suggestion.

With more and more bouts of silence, the writers can hear their stomachs rumbling, and they break for lunch.

After lunch, Biller and Menosky add some additional voices to the mix, but eventually silence manages to overcome the writers yet again. Finally, Menosky speaks up. "I think the 'ruse' trick is the problem," he offers. "Why would he be trying to trick them? Let's just go for a straight story."

Biller agrees. "If we don't need to have a ruse, we can build on the conflict between Seven and Janeway. If Seven takes the other ship at the end of Act Three, maybe the crew can decide they have to save her in Act Four."

But would Seven be able to handle the ship without a crew? She does for a limited amount of time in "One," but, theoretically, this would be for much longer.

So maybe Seven shouldn't be alone. "If the bullet ship isn't big enough for the entire crew, they might draw lots to send a few home," Biller suggests.

Menosky agrees. He likes that idea better than the Seven versus Janeway one. "I just don't think the character conflict with Seven and Janeway works for this story," he says.

"I do!" Braga insists. Then, abruptly, he says, "Maybe we should just erase the whole board right now and throw it out."

"And do what instead?" Jeri Taylor asks.

It is 1:45 P.M. Beyond the glass windows of the office's south wall, *El Niño*–driven clouds cover the sun. Winter hasn't been this cold in California in over eight years. And no *Voyager* break session has been so devoid of ideas in the show's four years. The room is silent. The staff sits motionless, as if waiting for an epiphany.

Braga makes a sudden decision. "I want to take this back to my office and work out this story," he says. "I think it works and I think I can make it work. Gardner, type up what we've got there."

Goldsmith begins copying what he's written on the board. The second act has been broken into eleven scenes:

- Hail ship. Scan ship. Mystery;
- Space—Silver Bullet;
- Bullet bridge: Chakotay, Torres, Paris find it empty;
- Hear rumbling sounds in bullet corridor;
- Find engine room;
- Space, bullet submerges;
- *Voyager* sees bullet is gone;
- Bullet engine room trembling in some kind of slipstream;
- Bullet is ripping through space;
- C, T, P able to stop bullet engines, discover *Voyager* ten light-years away;
- In *Voyager* briefing room, Janeway understands. Starfleet sent experimental ship. Yoda agrees. They should abandon *Voyager* to get home. Gung-ho crew starts packing…

…and Braga takes the notes and heads for his office, determined to make the episode viable. Better than viable. A solid show.

"It was really the first time we'd hit a wall all season," he recalls. "We had some difficult episodes this year, but it was the first time we just totally short-circuited. It was the end of the season; everyone was tired. But we knew we had to do something special."

His talk with Berman the day before had helped, but Braga still felt that they were floundering at the break session. "And I realized that there were too many voices in the room," he explains. "I just needed to sort through what I thought the end of the season should be about."

The breakthrough would come in the middle of the night.

FEBRUARY 4

IN THE WEE HOURS OF THE MORNING, IN THE COMPANY OF HIS OWN THOUGHTS, BRAGA IS ABLE TO FOCUS ON WHAT HE WANTS: AN EPISODE THAT SERVES AS A PAYOFF TO THE THEMES OF THE ENTIRE FOURTH SEASON. "I wanted to do a story about Janeway and Seven that would somehow recap their relationship over the past year and take it a step further," he says. "A storyline that showed there were consequences to Janeway's making a deal with the Borg, and to bringing in Seven of Nine. I wanted it to be a bittersweet retrospective of Season Four, and yet a good action story."

Braga works out the structure and calls Joe Menosky, his collaborator on the episode. "We did the beats over the phone. Our breakthrough was when we decided that Janeway and Seven *shouldn't* be on different ships fighting each other. That's artificial. We were straining to do something that never would be believable. They should be working together. After that, we just came up with ideas right and left."

The two men quickly come to a decision about which ideas from the beat session will remain. Vengeance remains the alien's motive. The ruse concept is fleshed out, and a scene is constructed where the alien springs a trap. Janeway and Seven get thrown into the brig together. "They would have to get close," says Braga. "Janeway would have to tweak Seven's implants—to *touch* her." He smiles. "We liked that image."

In the long run, the story is not radically different from the one they labored over in the beat session. "We had the first couple acts down," says Braga. "But we couldn't figure out where to go from there. It was just figuring out how we would tell it. Most of the time you need all those people, but sometimes I just like to go off by myself and work."

FEBRUARY 5

A NEW BEAT SHEET IS DISTRIBUTED TO *VOYAGER'S* DEPARTMENT HEADS. AT THE TOP OF THE FIRST PAGE OF THE NINE-PAGE DOCUMENT IS WRITTEN:

SEASON 4 FINALE
by Rick Berman & Brannon Braga & Joe Menosky
2/5/98

"I thought he deserved story credit for his contribution," says Braga, explaining the addition of Rick Berman's name to the header. And indeed, the final story credit on the show will read precisely as it does on this beat sheet, with Braga and Menosky sharing the teleplay credit.

The beat sheet consists of fifty scenes that tell a story in five acts. The Teaser is very similar to the one on the preliminary beat sheet, but things begin to change after that. Act One now has eight beats, and Act Two has ten. Acts Three, Four, and Five are now present, with five, four and twenty-two scenes, respectively. The beats of the first four acts are written in a rather general way, occasionally resorting to phrases such as "Big scene as…" Act Five, on the other hand, is written very specifically, and its beats will be clearly recognizable in the actual script, soon to be titled "Hope and Fear."

But that script still awaits culmination. In the meantime, others who serve *Voyager* have no time to stand and wait.

FEBRUARY 9

THE CALENDAR IN JERI TAYLOR'S OFFICE NOTES THAT THIS IS THE FIRST DAY OF "PREP" FOR "HOPE AND FEAR." The majority of crew members on the series don't have the luxury of waiting for an actual script in order to begin working on an episode. Budgets must be prepared, production designs must be submitted for approval, construction materials must be purchased, and so forth. So the department heads rely on the information provided in the beat sheet and on uncounted conversations with the producers, both on the phone and in person, to start them off in the right direction.

"We start our work from the beat sheet," Production Designer Richard James explains, "and the producers keep feeding us their ideas while the script is being written."

For the season finale, James has spotted the part of the beat sheet that will be most crucial to his department. In deceptively simple terms, it reads:

> **"Thrilling moment as we reach coordinates . . . and discover a sleek, sparkling STARSHIP (which we'll call the "silver bullet") floating in space. Scans reveal -- it's a Starfleet vessel!"**

Fortunately, that's all James needs for his creative mind to begin figuring out what the interior of such a ship would be like. "We have to work in such a fast way," he notes. "It's not the best way, because without a script there are a lot of unanswered questions, like how many people we will be dealing with and what their entrances and exits will be. The many things that will happen within the space of the set dictate a lot of unknowns."

But James is used to working with unknowns. In fact, at one point he literally worked where no production designer had worked before. While still a college student, James took a summer job as a technical illustrator of engineering design. After graduation, he moved to California and got a position in the Environmental Control Engineering office for the Apollo Project. "The engineers were working with the concept of the cone interior," James says. "It was in the days before computers were in common use, so they were having a hard time 'seeing' the three-dimensionality of its shape." James was asked to provide illustrations to help the process, and soon he had worked out the problems with "placement and with storage areas." James laughs at the memory. "One day someone over there said to me, 'Richard, you're the first decorator in space!'"

These days, James's usual approach is to begin with a floorplan and to work upward, in "elevations." "We have a limited amount of space on a stage, so we work with what we call 'stage conditions.'" To ascertain what those stage conditions are, James does a "walk-through," measuring the areas of available floor space on the

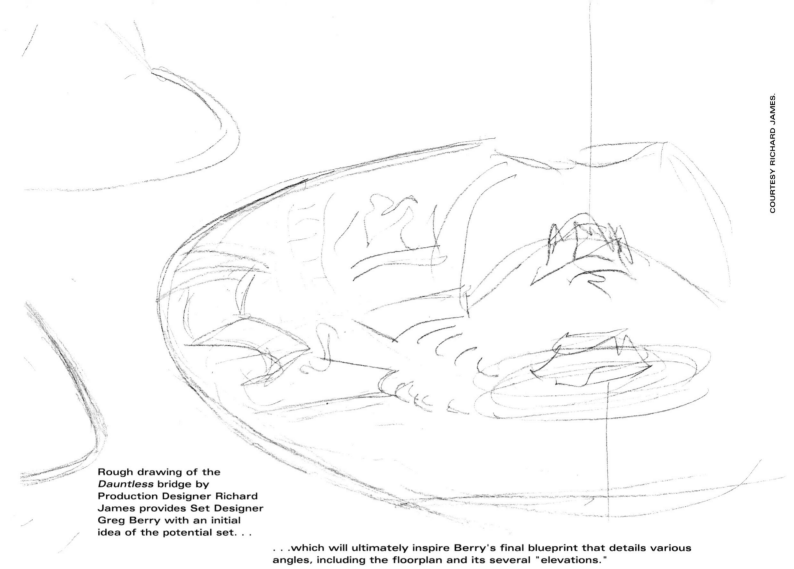

Rough drawing of the *Dauntless* bridge by Production Designer Richard James provides Set Designer Greg Berry with an initial idea of the potential set. . .

. . .which will ultimately inspire Berry's final blueprint that details various angles, including the floorplan and its several "elevations."

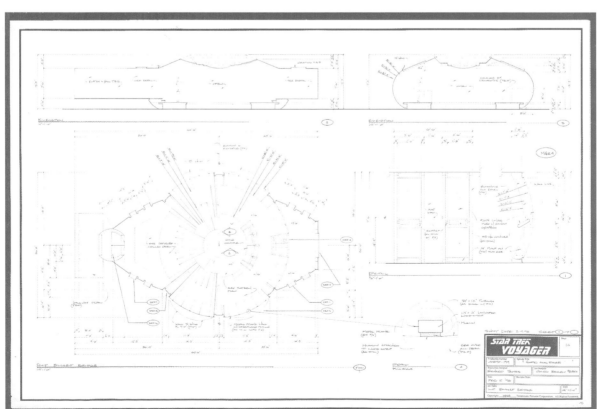

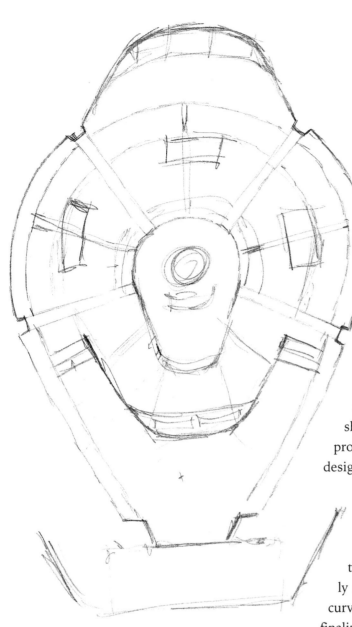

James's modified sketch of the _Dauntless_ bridge floorplan includes dimensions that will physically fit within the limited floorspace available for new construction on the crowded stage. COURTESY RICHARD JAMES.

three stages used by _Voyager_. Soon he discovers that the largest unused piece is located on Stage 16, sandwiched between the permanent cave set, the "museum set" (built for the episode "Living Witness," and later modified for use in _Star Trek: Insurrection_), and a set that is currently under construction for the _Voyager_ episode titled "One."

After returning to his office, James quickly makes some admittedly "rough" drawings. "Luckily, the designers working on _Voyager_ can understand rough things, and they can interpret these very crude sketches I give them," James says, smiling. He passes the sketches on to Set Designer Greg Berry.

James knows that for several of the "silver bullet's" interior sets, such as the corridors, he will simply "re-dress" corresponding _Voyager_ sets. But two new sets will need to be built from scratch: the bullet ship's bridge and its engineering room. And from what the producers have told him about two likely story points, the design and construction of those sets will be difficult. For one thing, the _faux_ Starfleet bridge will, at some point, be required to "instantaneously change," thus revealing its true alien nature. That's not an easy feat when you're trying to keep to a certain budget. And then there's the matter of geometry. The beat sheet's apparently simple description of a bullet-shaped vehicle suggests a curving exterior. Although that exterior shape hasn't yet been finalized, logic tells James that the interior sets will need to organically reflect those supposed exterior curves. Those interior curves will compound James's task—literally.

"The walls of the bridge will curve two ways, which is called a compound curve," James explains. "Of course, building such walls out of wood is too difficult for the cost and for the short amount of time we have." Instead, James decides to design the walls as a series of steel grids built in the proper arc and in the correct radius. The grids will then be covered with muslin.

"Muslin on gridwork takes the shape of a compound curve," observes Berry as he renders the detailed blueprints of James's design. "They can put lights behind the muslin in Federation-type colors, like red or blue. Then, when they do the changeover, they will switch it to an alien color. Hopefully it'll be a powerful enough change to make us believe that it has become a different ship." Thus, the grids will help to solve both of the problems that concerned James.

The bridge blueprints are still a work in progress, but as Berry completes specific aspects of them, he says, "The designs literally are being ripped off my table and taken to Special Effects."

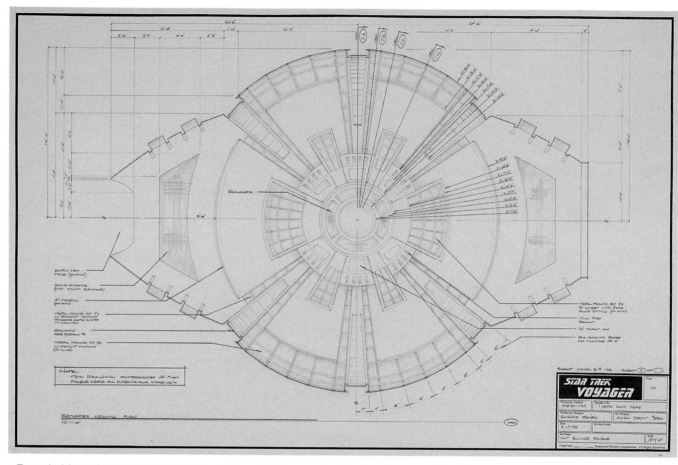

Berry's blueprint of the floorplan includes details needed by the Construction Department. COURTESY GREG BERRY.

FEBRUARY 16

PARAMOUNT'S SPECIAL EFFECTS DEPARTMENT IS SITUATED IN THE MILL, AN OPEN FLOOR WAREHOUSE-STYLE BUILDING THAT HOUSES THE CONSTRUCTION DEPARTMENT. It's where the majority of sets are built to the point of assembly. For "Hope and Fear," all of the wooden structures are the responsibility of Construction; metal work, such as the bullet ship's grids, is done by Special Effects. "The designer's drawings supply us with the different radius of each grid," says Special Effects Department Head Tom Mertz. "They're all at tapering radiuses, so it's pretty sophisticated. We draw full-size layouts on the floor of the Mill and then make forms out of wood." Mertz uses those wooden forms as a pattern to build the grids' ribs out of steel. "We have a programmable computerized metal roller," he explains. "We feed twenty-foot–long raw stock steel sticks into it, tell it what radius we want, and roll the steel right over the wooden frame."

After that, the resulting three-quarter inch by one and one-half inch rectangular tubes are welded together. "It's kind of like building a boat," Mertz notes. "We're going with rectangular-shaped tubing because the flat side gives us the width we need to attach the muslin." The special-effects crew will screw strips of wood onto the backside of each rib before delivering the steel-grid wall panels to Stage 16. And after the panels have been attached to the rest of the assembled set, the plan calls for members of the grip department to staple eight hundred square feet of muslin to the strips.

Drawing of *Dauntless* bridge elevation shows side-view construction details. COURTESY GREG BERRY.

Watching paint dry. Steel grids that will serve as walls on the *Dauntless* bridge set have been created with compound curves by Paramount's Special Effects Department. "They're shaped like bananas," jokes Department Head Tom Mertz. ROBBIE ROBINSON.

The wooden pillars that will support the grids are the first to go up. Construction is on Stage 16, also known as "Planet Hell." Note the craggy fiberglass planetary topography in the background, which has served as countless alien planetscapes. ROBBIE ROBINSON.

19

"This is the biggest show we've done for *Voyager* so far," observes Construction Coordinator Al Smutko as he stands among the wooden beams and plyboard sheets that will form the skeleton of the "silver bullet" bridge. "And even on *Star Trek: The Next Generation*, except for the pilot, we never did anything this big." Smutko, too, is basing his work on the beat sheet information, but with large shipments of wood being delivered and a staff of carpenters on hold, he has no margin for error. Communication is Smutko's best tool.

"I sat down with Richard James and tried to pick his brain," Smutko relates. "I needed to know what he thinks he'll put up here, because the drawings do not come out fast enough for me to turn in a true budget." Smutko then met with Co-Supervising Producer Merri Howard. "I asked Merri if I could start with something that I know we'll definitely need, like beams." After getting approval from Howard, Smutko had his crew begin assembling the platform that would become the floor of the bridge while he awaited additional blueprint information. "I work with the Art Department as closely as possible; they even ask me which part of the drawing I'll need first," Smutko says, raising his voice to be heard over a cacophony of construction sounds: the whine of electric saws; the rhythmic pounding of hammers hitting broad plyboard sheets; the rumble of a forklift transporting a stack of unusually curved iron grids. Above it all, the driving beat of a Chuck Berry song cuts through the din, just like ringin' a bell, as it pours from a portable radio tuned to an oldies station. The work schedule refers to this period as "preproduction," but to the men and women laboring on Stage 16 it looks, sounds, and feels like full production.

"Scheduling stage use is a little bit of a juggling act," admits Co-Supervising Producer Merri Howard. In fact, "One" is now shooting on several of the stages. With construction of the alien ship's bridge in full swing on Stage 16 and construction of its engineering room beginning on Stage 9, the competition for stage use is heated.

"The construction crew has been reporting in at times like 12:06 A.M. or 4:00 A.M., knowing that they'll have at least eight to ten hours before we come onto the set to start filming," Howard says.

Time's up. It's noon. The construction crew is going home after a long hard "day."

FEBRUARY 17

A PRODUCTION OFFICE ASSISTANT BICYCLES AROUND THE PARAMOUNT LOT DELIVERING FIRST DRAFTS OF THE SCRIPT, A SIXTY-EIGHT-PAGE TELEPLAY THAT HAS BEEN OFFICIALLY TITLED "HOPE AND FEAR." The alien ship, too, has received an official name: *Dauntless*. The name has its roots in a conversation that Braga had with Rick Berman more than a year earlier. As Braga recalls it, Berman said, "You know what a cool name for a ship would be? *Dauntless*." Braga liked the word, "so I just kept it in the back of my mind," he says.

With the arrival of the script, the department heads can now compare their advance work with this draft and see how close to the mark they have come. In the case of the fifth act, they are very close.

The beats of Act Five correspond directly to scenes in the script, with only a few of them displaced for dramatic purposes.

As you can see from the illustration on the following page:

- Beat 10 became Scene 95
- Beat 11 became Scene 96
- Beat 12 became Scene 99
- Beat 13 became Scene 100

9. **BULLET ENGINE ROOM**
    Janeway and Seven start initiating shutdown procedure,
    but it's not working. Arturis must be stopping them
    from the Bridge. They do manage to jam the engines and
    send the ship into a tailspin, slowing it down.

10. **SLIPSTREAM**
    Bullet ship out of control. It's course evens out.

11. **BULLET BRIDGE**
    Arturis working to stabilize course. He turns.
    Janeway is right behind him! She says, "It's over.
    Even now, Seven is accessing your primary systems. You
    taught us to use this ship a little too well." A TBD
    cat and mouse sequence unfolds, which culminates with
    the alien somehow getting the upper hand one last time.
    But then the ship rocks!

12. **SLIPSTREAM**
    Voyager has arrived and is attacking the bullet ship!

13. **VOYAGER BRIDGE**
    Fast action as we try to disable ship and get a lock on
    the crew.

14. **BULLET BRIDGE**
    Showdown. The alien's plan is falling apart. Two
    minutes to Borg space. Janeway tries to reach him.
    She's humane, willing to save his life if he can find a
    way to forgive her. But his quest for vengeance is too
    powerful, and he makes a final attack on Janeway.
    Looks like he might kill her -- when suddenly a series
    of rapid fire modular forcefields knock him back and
    unconscious.

15. **BULLET ENGINE ROOM**
    Seven working - she's just saved Janeway with
    forcefields. Calls Captain - Are you all right?
    Janeway says yes but she can't shut down the engines -
    One minute to Borg space!

16. **VOYAGER BRIDGE**
    We've got a lock! Chakotay: "Get them out of there and
    turn this ship around. We're going upstream!"

17. **BULLET BRIDGE**
    We see Janeway beam out. Arturis still dazed.

18. **SLIPSTREAM**
    Voyager turns upstream and escapes certain doom - but
    Bullet ship keeps going.

The final beat sheet correctly predicts the corresponding scenes in Act Five of "Hope and Fear."

- Beat 14 became Scene 98
- Beat 15 became Scene 97
- Beat 16 became Scene 102
- Beat 17 became Scene 101
- Beat 18 became Scenes 103 and 104
- Beat 19 became Scenes 105 and 106
- Beat 20 became Scene 107.

Life is good. Today, anyway.

FEBRUARY 19

Director Rick Kolbe shares his thoughts about the look of the sets. PETER IOVINO.

THE ENTIRE STAFF OF PRODUCERS, DEPARTMENT HEADS, AND OTHER "NEED TO KNOW" PERSONNEL GATHER FOR "HOPE AND FEAR"'S PREPRODUCTION MEETING. The meeting is the first half of a pair—a Production Meeting will follow in another week—so this is the first time the entire group sits down to discuss all aspects of production.

Everyone in the room has brought two items to the meeting: a script and a list of his or her department's needs. At this early point, the discussion centers mostly around budget. For instance, when looking at a shot that includes a viewscreen, Unit Production Mangager Brad Yacobian asks, "Is this a one-wall set?"

"I saw it as two walls," Production Designer Richard James answers.

"Okay," says Yacobian, seemingly agreeing. "Two walls that cost like one."

Starting on page one of the script, First Assistant Director Adele Simmons reads the exposition paragraphs, skipping over the dialogue. All the department heads, including this episode's director, Winrich "Rick" Kolbe, have questions or concerns.

"I've never shot in Astrometrics," Kolbe observes. Video Supervisor Denise Okuda describes the set to him. Kolbe will need more than a verbal description. "Can we walk though it this afternoon?" he asks. The set is one of several in which certain members of the company will need to attend walk-throughs in order to assess the complexity of their assignments. Astrometrics is an existing set, so it doesn't present much of a problem. Just go over and take a look at it. It's the nonexisting—or rather, the yet-to-be-constructed—sets that most concern the staff.

As an example, Kolbe feels that the *Dauntless* engineering room's warp core should look and sound dangerous. "I think the *Voyager* crew members should be able to stand on it and look down."

Brannon Braga likes that idea. "Kind of like the swinging pendulum area at the Griffith Park Observatory," he comments.

Production Designer Richard James shows them the engineering sketches and blueprints he has been working on. His plans are not as extravagant as Kolbe suggests, but that's fine with Visual Effects Supervisor Ronald B. Moore. If Kolbe wants to shoot from above the set and down into the core, Moore estimates, they will have to mount a bluescreen on the floor below it. Such a plan would greatly expand the number of required optical shots for the episode. It would also dictate that the floor of the set be built on a platform twenty feet above the bluescreen, which would also need to be raised above floor level in order to backlight it. And that would put the ceiling of the engineering set deep within the nonmovable rafters and permanent lighting fixtures at the top of the soundstage. Not a very realistic prospect, especially when you consider that you'd *also* have to put the camera and crew up there. Suddenly the physical height of Stage 9 becomes part of the discussion. There will be another walk-through.

FEBRUARY 20

THE SCRIPT CALLS FOR ONLY ONE GUEST STAR, AN ACTOR TO PLAY THE ALIEN ARTURIS. Not one of the actors that are being considered resembles the character type originally described as "Yoda."

"Arturis became much younger during the development process," notes Jeri Taylor. "There was never a decision to make him younger; he simply evolved that way. And then casting was the component that finalized the process. We wanted someone who could convey a large presence, and that need sometimes strips away people at either end of the age scale, and brings it more toward the center."

While Casting Director Ron Surma calls the agents of experienced or "known" actors, Taylor and Brannon Braga meet with "newer" people who have come to the office to "read," or audition, for the role. At this point, notes Braga, "We've read maybe fifty people. Some of them are very good, but we want someone special for the role. We'd like to cast someone with a 'name,' as they say, but," he shrugs, "we just can't get Tom Cruise."

"I always approach casting with a modicum of apprehension," observes Taylor. "Actors who would be very successful in a contemporary series may have a look or an articulation or a manner that is very twentieth-century, very 'now,' and that just doesn't translate into the twenty-fourth century. We need someone with classical training, but people who have well-established careers often will not read for episodic television, so we don't get to hear the words coming out of their mouths." That causes problems in the long run. "We've been burned on *Star Trek* many times this way," says Taylor. "We look at tapes of actors, they seem okay, and then they crash and burn when they're put to the test on the bridge of a starship."

Actor Ray Wise, who will ultimately be cast as Arturis, is a different story altogether. Although he does not audition for the role, the producers know he can be relied on for the task at hand. "Ray doesn't need to read for us," Braga says, "because he's been on the show before." Wise's previous *Star Trek* incarnation was as a "proto-Vulcan" named Liko, who appeared in *The Next Generation* episode "Who Watches the Watchers?"

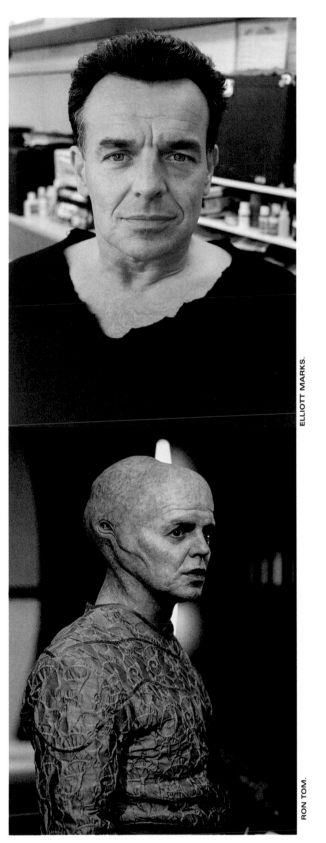

Actor Ray Wise as himself. . .and as Arturis.

Above: The foam-core model of the *Dauntless* bridge takes center stage at the Production Meeting as Jeri Taylor and Brannon Braga talk to the senior staff. *From left to right:* Josée Normand, Jim Mees, Louise Dorton, Richard James, Brad Yacobian, Merri Howard, Maril Davis, Joe Menosky, Brannon Braga, Jeri Taylor, Rick Kolbe, Adele Simmons, Dan Curry, Ronald B. Moore, Steve Welke, Al Smutko, and a farewell muffin basket. Not seen: Dick Brownfield, Rick Sternbach, Denise Okuda, Alan Sims, Kimberley Shull. HARRY LANG. *Left:* The calm before the storm. *From left to right:* As Adele Simmons reads, Dan Curry and Ronald B. Moore share a contemplative moment before launching into the contained chaos of production. HARRY LANG.

FEBRUARY 25

JERI TAYLOR IS ONE OF THE LAST TO ARRIVE AT THE 2:00 P.M. PRODUCTION MEETING. In front of her seat at the head of the table are two decorated bouquet baskets full of cookies and muffins, gifts from the staff for their exiting executive producer. Taylor immediately ad-libs a short speech, thanking the crew for the cookies, of course, but more importantly for the work they've done over the years. "It's been a wonderful joy working with this group," she says, tears filling her eyes. "This is my last Production Meeting. I'll miss these gatherings, and I'll think about you guys when you have your meetings next year."

After allowing a moment for the emotion to subside, Adele Simmons begins reading the exposition portions of the script. This time there is more to discuss than just the budget. There still are many unanswered

"Meanwhile, over on Stage 16..." the *Dauntless* bridge takes shape. Openings in the far wall will accommodate video monitors and backlit graphics. ROBBIE ROBINSON.

questions about sets under construction, visual effects that are being designed, character moves that are being choreographed. The meeting's agenda triggers a flurry of mental activity.

Every decision made about an early scene or set will affect the later scenes that take place on that same set, so everyone has to think ahead. For instance, beginning with Scene 23, when the *Voyager*'s away team first explores the bullet ship, a "trembling" is felt as the engines go on-line. This trembling is scripted to become extreme when the ship enters the slipstream.

"No trembling in slipstream," Director Rick Kolbe says unexpectedly, and without explanation. When the discussion reaches Scenes 38 and 39, where the ship actually goes into the slipstream, Kolbe repeats his directive.

"That was a good call on Rick's part," Brannon Braga says later. "Of course the ship shouldn't be shaking when they're in the slipstream; otherwise all the important dialogue in those sequences would be distorted by the shaking, and we wouldn't want that." Braga admits that they hadn't considered that fact when they wrote about the vibrations.

But there are more decisions to be made about the slipstream, some very basic, practical decisions. And as the discussion continues regarding Scene 38, Visual Effects Producer Dan Curry and Visual Effects Supervisor Ronald B. Moore become very involved. The script reads:

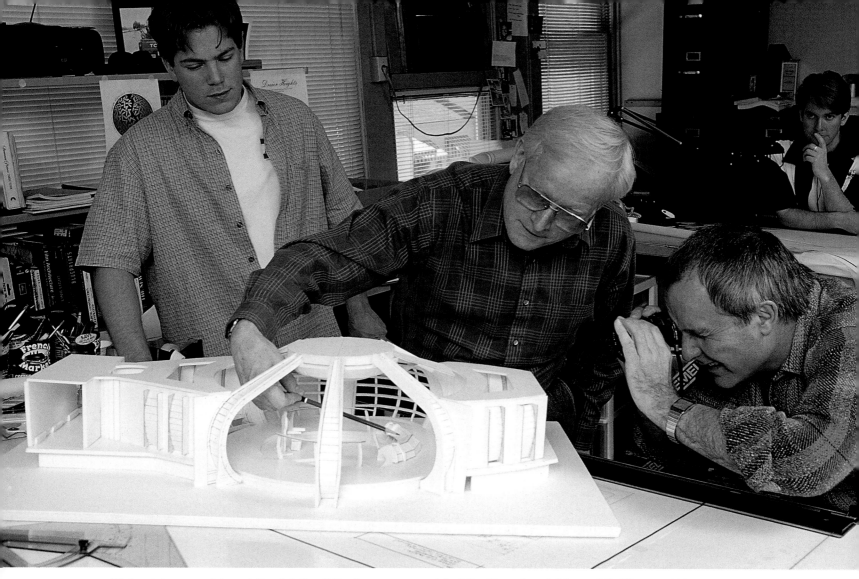

Richard James points out the details of the foam-core model of the *Dauntless* bridge, while Director Rick Kolbe peers through a viewfinder to plan camera angles. Greg Berry (left) and Greg Hooper (right rear) observe. ROBBIE ROBINSON.

38   EXT. SPACE - QUANTUM SLIPSTREAM (OPTICAL)

A TORRENT of ENERGY whipping past us at blinding velocities!

The Dauntless is RACING through the raging river of energy at breakneck speeds!

This is the first of eleven opticals—visual-effects shots—that depict the slipstream, the most difficult being Scene 103, in which *Voyager* will make a U-turn inside the torrent of energy. The question of the moment is, what does a slipstream look like? And how does it work? In fact, what does this bullet ship look like? And how will *Voyager* itself look when it is inside this river of energy?

These questions can't be answered immediately. Fortunately, the work will happen at the end of the schedule, during postproduction, which gives Curry and Moore time to arrange another meeting specifically devoted to their task.

Of more immediate concern is the design for the inside of the new ship. Actually, there are several designs for *Dauntless*, since the ship must first appear to be from Starfleet and then "transform" into an alien technology.

Production Designer Richard James has expanded upon the blueprints he'd shown a week ago. He has brought a foam-core model of the *Dauntless* bridge to the meeting, and although the model has been sitting on the table, the group's attention focuses on it for the first time. The open-grid construct of the bridge's wall will allow light to penetrate from all sides. A change in the lighting will change the mood and, hopefully, the entire "feel" of the set. This will eliminate the need for major optical work and reduce the physical special-effects work.

The color of the lighting will be extremely important. But what color would be most effective?

"Orange," Kolbe says spontaneously. The director notes that the change to orange will impart "an eerie feel."

Kolbe and James agree to meet in the Art Department the next morning so the director can look more closely at the model and begin to plan how he will place the camera and actors within the set.

The discussion eventually covers the entire script, with certain details noted: In Scene 96, Janeway cannot be wearing a combadge (because she took it apart in an earlier scene); in Scene 97, Special Effects Coordinator Dick Brownfield will ignite "practical"—real fireworks—sparks when Seven of Nine's console explodes; in Scene 98, the actors will stumble, but not fall down, so no stunt pads will be necessary. When they get to Scene 101, where the alien grabs a hand weapon, Rick Kolbe wonders aloud about placement of his actors. He asks, "Where has this weapon been hidden?"

"Anywhere," answers Jeri Taylor. "Because there's velcro everywhere."

"So it's *deus ex machina*," Kolbe comments, making a note about his freedom of choice on a lined pad.

After again touching on the extensive visual-effects scenes that build up toward the end of the episode, the meeting is called to a close.

"Listen up," Jeri Taylor insists, and everyone does. "We've got about two hundred fifty thousand calories sitting here," she says, referring to the bakery goods remaining in the baskets. Taylor makes it clear that she doesn't intend to consume all those calories herself.

Obedient to a fault—she's *still* the executive producer, after all—the staff descends upon the baskets.

And then there were none.

FEBRUARY 26

AT 9:00 A.M., DIRECTOR RICK KOLBE WALKS INTO THE *VOYAGER* ART DEPARTMENT OFFICE TO LOOK MORE CLOSELY AT THE THREE-FOOT-LONG MODEL OF THE *DAUNTLESS'S* BRIDGE. "Oh, I can place my camera right here," he says immediately, even as Richard James is setting the model down on the drawing table. Kolbe bends and places his face—and his thoughts—inside, his nose almost touching the two-inch-high representation of the main console. "And the light can come through from up here."

"That wall is one of the open grids covered with muslin," James interjects, "so you can position lights anywhere behind it and the light will just fill the bridge."

"Perfect," Kolbe says, "And over here…"

In a perfect world, the director could be planning his shots on the actual set. But this is the tightly calendared world of episodic television, and the *Dauntless* bridge set is still under construction. The best that can be hoped for is that it will be ready by the date suggested on the shooting schedule: March 4. In the meantime, the director will begin shooting the episode with scenes that take place on the more familiar *Voyager* sets. That will happen tomorrow, as soon as the crew wraps the previous episode, "One."

FEBRUARY 27

RICK KOLBE LOOKS AT HIS WATCH—9:00 A.M. "I HAVE TO BE ON THE SET AT 11:30," HE SAYS. The director flips through his notes one more time. He is ready to begin shooting the season finale, "Hope and Fear." Only "One" obstacle stands in his way—literally. "One" is still shooting. The production's crew members, all of the camera and lighting equipment, and five of the actors Kolbe will be using are working. While not officially on hold, "Hope and Fear" is on "wait."

Not that Kolbe has anticipated an early start. He knows that "One" shot until almost midnight the evening before. Following Guild regulations, each member of the crew, from the grips to the actors, is guaranteed eleven hours off following his or her "wrap" time. The day's shooting schedule—more commonly referred to as the call sheet—lists the crew call for "One" at noon. However, the first item listed at the top of the call sheet pertains to Kolbe's needs:

STAGE WALK--DAUNTLESS BRIDGE--1/2 hour before crew call--Epi. 194.

This will give the director twenty-five minutes to discuss the new set (still under construction, of course) with his key department heads. At precisely 11:55, after the walk-through on Stage 16, the cinematographer, key grip, and gaffer, who have taken a quick recess from "One," along with the unit production manager, rush back to Stage 8, where filming on "One" will continue. Kolbe and Adele Simmons return to the production office to consider their schedule. Unit Production Manager Brad Yacobian has made a "guess-timate" of Kolbe's start time: 3:30 P.M.

The call sheet from Day One of Episode #194. This daily document is regarded as "the bible" for the cast and crew. Note that those actors who were "badly burned" for the previous episode, "One," will need to make an additional visit to the makeup trailer before reporting back to the set for shooting on "Hope and Fear."

Everything seems funny after midnight. Regardless of the late hour, the cast and crew enjoy getting started on the final episode of the season. PETER IOVINO.

After a long day of shooting on the previous episode of *Voyager*, actors Robert McNeill and Robert Beltan rehearse a scene for "Hope and Fear." PETER IOVINO.

The exposed fluorescent bulb casts a warm glow on the actors' faces, highlighting McNeill's (Paris) and Beltran's (Chakotay) eyes. "You can't do a decent eye-light shot unless you remove the Plexiglas," says Bill Peets. In addition, Peets notes that such lighting "lends a kind of visual realism to the scene, as if the light were coming from the actual console." PETER IOVINO.

A production's call sheet is an intricate document. It lists a day's start times—the time individual cast and crew members are expected to arrive at their first destination of the day, whether the makeup trailer or the stage or the production office. It also lists any required props, film equipment, stunt people, etc., that aren't normally present. Most importantly, it lists the specific scene numbers that are scheduled for the day's work.

The second half of today's call sheet belongs to "Hope and Fear." The scenes listed are not in numerical order; they do not start at the beginning of the script and continue in the story order. Typically, the scenes are shot out of continuity, or out of sequence, to take advantage of an actor's availability or the use of a certain stage. There are fourteen scenes from "Hope and Fear" listed, drawn from six distinctly disconnected sections of the script. But there's a method to the madness. Beginning with Scenes 50, 12, and 13 allows actresses Jeri Ryan and Kate Mulgrew to be released early, which will make it possible to bring them in early the next morning when they're needed for different scenes. Other regular cast members will be kept later for their scenes tonight, and in turn, they will be brought in later tomorrow. The eleven scenes without Mulgrew and Ryan—72, 79, 83, 85, 87, 100, 102 from Act Five; 57 from Act Three; and 32, 33, and 37 from Act Two—have been grouped together because they all take place on *Voyager*'s bridge. Time dictates such groupings. Moving an entire film crew

Top: **Using a handheld viewfinder, Rick Kolbe kneels to get a better perspective of a shot, and to contemplate alternative angles.** PETER IOVINO.
Bottom: **A summit meeting. Chief Lighting Technician Bill Peets, Unit Production Manager Brad Yacobian, and Director of Photography Marvin Rush discuss their options for shooting on the** *Dauntless* **bridge.** PETER IOVINO.

off one set only to move it back to the same set later would be foolishly time-consuming.

It is Adele Simmons's job to help the production company avoid such foolishness. Generating each day's call sheet is one of the primary functions of the assistant directors. It's a critical job, one that can drive the average human mad with minute details.

But as they say, *somebody's* got to do it.

Even though they deal with a universe that runs out of synch with normal story continuity, the ADs provide continuity, giving structure to the chaos by keeping track of everything happening at any given moment. "Our focus is on maintaining everything going on with the actors, the set, any changes, and where we are with a scene," Simmons says.

Chief Lighting Technician Bill Peets, in white shirt, contemplates the effect created by removing the Plexiglas plate on the front of Paris's console to reveal hidden fluorescent lighting. PETER IOVINO.

The "changes" she refers to are variances from one apparently similar scene to the next, and tracking them can be very important when you shoot a number of scenes featuring the same characters on the same set out of sequence. Remember that missing combadge in Scene 96? Simmons does, and will make sure that its absence is noted on the call sheet for that scene. Similarly, she'll note whether a character's hair should be mussed, or a graphic altered on a bridge monitor.

The call sheet designates Scenes 100 and 102 as the tenth and eleventh scenes in the shoot. If the planned schedule holds, and "Hope and Fear" begins shooting at 3:30, Scenes 100 and 102 *should* be in front of the camera by 9:00 P.M.

But no one is ready to lay odds on it.

When the director has designed the shot, the grips will set up the dolly track that will allow the camera operator to emulate the moves Kolbe has dictated. PETER IOVINO.

FEBRUARY 28

BY THE CALENDAR, IT'S NOW SATURDAY MORNING, AND ROBERT DUNCAN MCNEILL (PARIS), KNOWN ON THE SET AS ROBBIE, AND ROBERT BELTRAN (CHAKOTAY), REFERRED TO AS ROBERT, ARE GIGGLING. They both have flubbed their lines during Take 5 of Scene 87, and the late hour isn't helping their concentration. Director Kolbe calls for Take 6. This time the performance is perfect.

"Rehearsal for Scenes one hundred and one-oh-two," Adele Simmons calls out. It is 12:42 A.M.

Obviously, the schedule is a little off.

"One" finally wrapped at 4:30 in the afternoon. After the filming equipment had been moved from Stage 8 to *Voyager*'s cargo bay set on Stage 9, the filmmakers took thirty minutes to devour an Italian dinner delivered to the set. Shooting started on "Hope and Fear" at 6:30. After completing the three scenes with Mulgrew and

Kolbe instructs Robert Beltran on a move that will make two people on camera appear to be four. PETER IOVINO.

Ryan, the company once again moved the filming equipment *back* to Stage 8—*Voyager*'s bridge set—for the remainder of the day's work.

The bridge is a comfortable set for the filmmakers; they know it well and they understand instinctively how to accomodate any last-minute decisions the director will make. A few hours earlier, as they started on Scene 87, Director Kolbe had knelt on the soundstage floor in front of Paris's navigational console and scrutinized the set through a viewfinder. Key Grip Randy Burgess watched Kolbe scan the set from right to left. Then Burgess turned and glanced toward his crew. Several grips began whispering into their walkie-talkies, and almost immediately additional grips had appeared from a side area of the stage, carrying something that appeared to be an oversize piece of toy train track. The grips carried the curved section of dolly track to where the director was kneeling, and Kolbe, without appearing to notice the men, moved slightly out of the way. The grips laid the track in place, then lifted the dolly with the mounted camera onto the track. In a matter of minutes, the camera was ready to pass smoothly from right to left, past the console, following the curve the director had drawn in the air with his viewfinder.

"Five-minute warning." Robert Duncan McNeill gets gussied up by Hairstylist Charlotte Gravenor and Makeup Artist Natalie Wood... PETER IOVINO.

... who then move on to Robert Beltran. PETER IOVINO.

Beltran steps "into frame" to deliver his line. PETER IOVINO.

All of that activity had taken place with very little verbal communication. But that had been several hours ago, when instincts were sharp. Now, judging by the increasing number of yawns on the set, the late hour is beginning to take its toll.

Scenes 100 and 102 would actually work as a single scene, if not for the fact that the script separates them with Scene 101, which takes place with different characters on a different set. Nevertheless, even though the scenes will be filmed as separate entities, Simmons refers to them as if they are a single scene. "Rehearsal for Scene one-hundred-one-oh-two," she calls again.

The actors are waiting at their characters' regular stations. This should not be an extensive rehearsal; the scene reads as a simple exchange of dialogue.

100   INT. VOYAGER - BRIDGE
       Red Alert. Chakotay, Tuvok, Paris, Kim, N.D.s. Fast action:

                    TUVOK
              Direct hit!
                   (reacts)
              The vessel's shield's are down.
              Transporters standing by.

                  CHAKOTAY
              Get a lock on our people!
              Kim works...

The 1st AD, cinematographer, camera operator, key grip, and gaffer all gather on the bridge near the director. "Rehearsal—Action!" Simmons calls. The actors dutifully go through their paces once and wait while Rick Kolbe mulls over his thoughts. "I want to show both Tuvok and Chakotay in the same shot," he says after a moment. Then he comes up with a way to imply that all four of the key characters are there while showing only two of them on camera. "Let's have Robbie sit in place so that Robert has to walk around him." This puts Paris out of the camera's sight line, but Chakotay's move around him indicates to the home audience that he's there. "And Robert should look toward Garrett's station when he says the line about getting a lock on our people." Again, Kim won't be seen, but the audience will feel that he's there. This eliminates the need for additional coverage, or insert shots, of the missing two individuals. The technique saves time and, of course, budget.

"Okay," Adele Simmons calls out. "The set belongs to Marvin." The actors step off of the bridge to relax for a few minutes, giving the set over to the cinematographer, Marvin Rush. Rush points at an area near the back of the ceiling and a member of the electrical crew climbs a ladder to add a bulb that will better backlight Tuvok. A stand-in assumes Tim Russ's position so that Rush can see how the lighting will throw his shadow across his console.

Meanwhile, several grips carry a sheet of plyboard onto the bridge and gently lay it down on the carpet just inside of Paris's station. Several others lift the dolly, with the mounted camera, off of the track, step up onto the platform with it, and carefully set it on the plyboard.

Off the bridge, Second Assistant Director Michael DeMeritt approaches Simmons. He already is think-

When a shot is ready to be photographed, Marvin Rush double-checks the framing and lighting through the camera's lens before turning the camera over to operator Douglas Knapp. During actual filming, Rush will observe the shot from the edge of the set or on a monitor, allowing him to see it as the audience will. PETER IOVINO.

ing far ahead in the shooting schedule. "I think that I should bring my crew in at 4:00 A.M. on Monday," he says, referring to the production assistants who must arrive before the makeup staff each day. Simmons takes the thought to Unit Production Manager Brad Yacobian. "It's too early to decide," he says. "We'll have to make phone calls over the weekend."

Simmons steps onto the bridge to consult with Marvin Rush. He's almost ready to shoot. "Five-minute warning," she calls. Members of the makeup staff approach the actors to touch up their faces, while wardrobe personnel tug at each uniform's sleeves and collar.

Off the set, a friendly conversation among several crew members elevates in volume to a disruptive level. "Shhhhhh!" The assistant directors simultaneously hush the talkers.

Brad Yacobian looks around the set. "Only one person should be talking," he says, in a tone reminiscent of an accusatory schoolteacher.

"Who's that?" calls a disembodied voice from somewhere in the building.

"Um," Yacobian pauses, thinking. "Rick."

Tim Russ and his stand-in, Lemuel Perry, enjoy Rick Kolbe's frequent jokes on the set. PETER IOVINO.

"Me? I should be talking?" responds the surprised director. "Well, okay. A man walks around the corner, looks at me and says, 'Are you from Pittsburgh?' I say, 'Do I look like I'm from Pittsburgh?'…"

The room falls silent, waiting for the punchline…

…which never comes. "Action!" calls the director.

Without a hitch, Tim Russ delivers his lines; then Beltran steps behind the unseen McNeill and delivers his own line while looking off camera, as directed, at Garrett Wang. Having Wang there guarantees that Beltran's eyeline—the trajectory of his gaze—is geometrically correct.

"Cut." The rehearsal seems to go well, but it is Simmons's job to confirm that all personnel from the various departments are happy. "Any objections to that rehearsal?" she calls out loudly.

"There are no objections," Yacobian mutters to himself while glancing at his watch. It is *his* job to be concerned about the fleeting time, but he doesn't make his concern evident—and won't unless it becomes a serious issue.

Now Kolbe gives a new direction to Robert Beltran. "Stand out of frame and step into it just before you start to deliver your line."

"We're doing a rack focus," adds Marvin Rush, informing the actors that the focus of the camera's lens will go from Russ, who speaks first, to Beltran, who speaks second.

"What lens are you using?" Kolbe asks as he sits down to watch on the two viewing monitors set up just off the bridge.

"One hundred millimeter," Rush answers, "at a T3 f-stop. The rack focus will go from thirty feet to seven feet and back again."

"Okay, let's shoot it," says Kolbe. Sound mixer Alan Bernard pushes a button on his cart, simultaneously setting off a bell inside the stage and flashing red lights outside the stage. Outside, the guards stop whatever traffic may be in the vicinity of the soundstage at this late hour.

It is 12:55 A.M. Take 1. Beltran doesn't look directly at Wang.

12:57 A.M. Take 2. Russ doesn't like the way he delivered his line.

12:58 A.M. Take 3. This time it's better. "Nice try," says the director.

12:59 A.M. Take 4. "Very good. Let's do one more."

12:59:30 A.M. Take 5. "Great!" says Kolbe. "Brilliant. Print that."

1:00 A.M. "Scene One-oh-two is up," says Simmons.

Scott Middleton steps in to mark the take. PETER IOVINO.

Yacobian approaches the monitor area. "Do you have Channel two on there?" he asks Camera Assistant Scott Middleton, who is running the last take for Kolbe.

Suddenly the image on one of the monitors flips from the *Voyager* scene to an image of Kate Mulgrew in twentieth-century dress. *The Late Late Show with Tom Snyder* is in midbroadcast of a show taped earlier that evening. Someone turns up the sound. Those members of the cast and crew who aren't busy gather around the monitor to watch. The actress and the interviewer talk about Snyder's adventures walking his dog.

On the *Voyager* bridge, electricians change a bulb in an overhead light and remove a standing lamp on the floor. The grips put the camera and dolly back on the track, still in place in front of Paris's navigation console. The move, this time, will go from left to right. Two grips carry ladders off the bridge.

On the monitor, Tom Snyder instructs his director to "go to the phones." The first caller asks Mulgrew how she got the job as the first female captain with her own TV series. Rick Kolbe watches both monitors closely. The bridge and the grips are on one. Mulgrew is on the other. "Thank you for *Voyager*," the caller says after Mulgrew responds to the question.

Mulgrew starts to tell a story. "At fourteen, I was a short-order cook…" she begins.

"How short were you?" Kolbe quips at the monitor. The crew chuckles.

On the bridge, Marvin Rush decides to change the camera's mount from the gear head they've been using to a fluid head, because it will give the camera "a bigger tilt and a smoother ride." That done, the set is once again ready.

1:24 A.M. Kate Mulgrew and Tom Snyder are discussing the movie *Stalag 17*. Robert Beltran, Tim Russ,

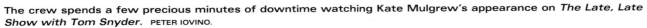

The crew spends a few precious minutes of downtime watching Kate Mulgrew's appearance on *The Late, Late Show with Tom Snyder*. PETER IOVINO.

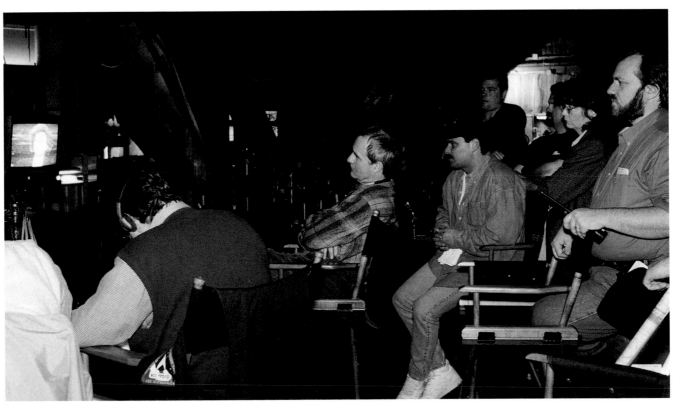

Robert Duncan McNeill, and Garrett Wang step onto the bridge for a rehearsal of Scene 102. Russ will not be seen in this shot, but he is "there for eyeline." The director waves to the video operator, and both screens suddenly show the same image of the bridge.

Mulgrew is gone.

```
102        INT. VOYAGER - BRIDGE
           Red Alert. Chakotay, Tuvok, Paris, Kim, N.D.s. Fast action.


                              KIM
                    Direct hit!
                              (reacts)
                    I've got them, Commander --
                    Transporter Room Two!


                           CHAKOTAY
                    Alter our slipstream -- hard
                    starboard -- take us back the way
                    we came!
```

The first rehearsal of the scene gives Kolbe an idea. He asks the actors to deliver their lines from Scene 100 and continue through 102. This, he feels, will put more emotion into the dialogue for the second scene. Before he begins the next rehearsal, Kolbe decides he doesn't like the angle of the lens at the end of the shot, when it pans and focuses on Paris. He asks camera operator Douglas Knapp to try several different angles and is finally happy when the top of Paris's console does not come into frame.

"It feels more natural now," Kolbe says and calls for a second rehearsal.

"That's better," the director says. He gets up from his chair among the monitors and goes to the set to suggest that Beltran stop his forward movement at a different position. A camera assistant immediately kneels to remove the taped "X" at Beltran's original "mark," and to place it at the new position.

"Would you like to shoot the next rehearsal?" Simmons asks.

"Yes!" calls out Yacobian.

1:32 A.M. Sound mixer Bernard sounds the bell. "One Hundred Apple," a camera assistant calls out. The new numbering system will indicate to the editor that even though this material includes Scene 100, it is different from the earlier footage, which did not carry a letter designation. In fact, "One Hundred Apple," is Scene 102 combined with the dialogue from 100. "Action."

The actors go through the scene. Kolbe calls "Cut," then comments, "Not too shabby."

1:34 A.M. Take 2. "This should be the martini shot," Simmons calls out, indicating the last shot of the night. Twenty-five seconds later, Kolbe calls, "Cut. Let's try another one."

1:36 A.M. Take 3. "Hold the roll please," Kolbe calls. "Robert, can you lean into the camera a little?

1:37 A.M. Take 4. "Good beginning, but..."

1:38 A.M. Take 5. "Cut. The camera did not follow."

1:39 A.M. The actors are now giggling. "Hold the roll."

1:43 A.M. Take 6. "Better. Once again for the camera."

1:44 A.M. Take 7. "Action." Twenty-one seconds pass. Everything goes smoothly. The actors are right on their marks and lines and the camera follows perfectly. The rack focus, this time from Chakotay to Kim to Paris, is exact.

"Cut," Kolbe says.

"And that's a wrap." Simmons says. It is 1:45 A.M. on Saturday morning. As the security guards wait to lock up, the weary crew begins packing away their tools; the actors head for trailers to remove their makeup and change clothes; the wardrobe staff prepares the costumes for cleaning; the props and camera equipment are properly stored away in their cases and loaded into the trucks for safekeeping; the ADs complete their production reports; and the rest of the world rolls over and pulls the covers up a little higher.

And yet the day's work has not been completed. Four scenes listed on the call sheet must be rescheduled. The producers had hoped that, with energy and luck, they would be able to catch up, but the production is still behind by approximately the same number of hours it was forced to delay its start.

"The energy was different because the crew has worked all week," Adele Simmons philosophizes, "and it's been a long day. The human factor is a big consideration. I mean, how much can you push and still have everyone working efficiently and safely? Everyone's spirit is willing, but the flesh gets pretty tired after those hours."

The missing four scenes will be worked into the schedule...somewhere.

MARCH 2

THE RAW FILM FOOTAGE FROM FRIDAY NIGHT/SATURDAY MORNING IS DELIVERED TO ONE OF LOS ANGELES'S PREMIER FILM PROCESSING COMPANIES, CFI (CONSOLIDATED FILM INDUSTRIES). The processed film then is delivered to Editel, a Los Angeles facility specializing in film transfer. There, the footage is color-corrected prior to being transferred into a state-of-the-art video format known as "D-2." "We correct the color every day," says Associate Producer Dawn Velazquez, "so that the producers can see the sets right away. That way if something is too dark or is incorrect, we can change it immediately."

With that D-2 tape now acting as the master, copies are made in three-quarter-inch video format and then delivered back to Paramount. Several copies go to the various producers who view the footage as dailies—the work from the day before—and a copy goes to one of the show's three rotating editors, who immediately prepares the footage for assembly.

"We get a three-quarter-inch copy around lunchtime," says "Hope and Fear" Editor Daryl Baskin. "The editing assistant inputs that into the Avid system, a computer program that works like a word processor, but with pictures instead of text. When it came in today, I cut it and put it in a bin (actually a computer file), and I won't look at it again until Rick Kolbe comes in and we assemble his cut."

The editor's job includes alerting members of the crew to any potential problems that he has discerned in the footage. While working with Scene 102, for example, Baskin hears a line of dialogue that concerns him. "Chakotay tells Tom to turn around in the slipstream," Baskin explains. "Well, a visual-effects shot showing them altering their position in the slipstream could be cost prohibitive." Baskin calls Dan Curry.

Across the lot, Curry, too, is concerned about the ramifications of that line of dialogue. In fact, he has been thinking about it since the Production Meeting and he has since discussed it with Brannon Braga and Ronald B. Moore. Chakotay's order leads into Scene 103, which is scripted as follows:

103   EXT. SPACE - QUANTUM SLIPSTREAM (OPTICAL)
VOYAGER SLOWS and BANKS in the opposite direction, FLYING back the way it came!

At this point, late as it seems, the producers *still* aren't sure what this slipstream will look like. "It's something created by the ship," Brannon Braga suggests. "It's not like a tunnel through space, because it's not something that physically exists. So it's not real clear in the script right now."

The idea for a ship-generated slipstream originated with "Scorpion" a year earlier. "We were going to have the Borg ships raising slipstreams and have big fights in those slipstreams," Braga recalls "But we had too many ideas for that episode and some just didn't make it. I knew the slipstream idea would come in handy someday."

Now the time to give the idea a "look" has arrived. "We want the slipstream to look very different from our warp effect and very different from the wormhole," notes Curry. "And that's the trick, because it should have a tunnel-like quality. Ron and I always spend a lot of time dealing with quasi-physics, so we're having some trouble with the concept of making a U-turn in there and breaking out of the wall."

The ongoing discussion will continue periodically until the visual-effects staff actually sits down in a computer graphics lab and begins drawing pictures. It will include such drastic suggestions as cutting out of Scene 102 before Chakotay says his line and then changing Scene 103 to a static shot of *Voyager* in space, backed by a log entry saying, "We turned around in the slipstream and…" But that seems more than a bit anti-climactic.

"The best approach would be a shot that shows *Voyager* making a U-turn while the other ship is still going straight," says Moore. "I believe that's a very difficult thing to do, and it's gonna take a lot of tries before we can please all of the people who have to approve it."

No matter what gets approved, the shot must be completely rendered in exactly thirty days.

The People's Choice: Senior Illustrator Rick Sternbach's submission to the producers is returned with one drawing—the one on the upper right—circled. This will be the exterior look of the *Dauntless*. Note the "scratch outs" over the protruding bridge, which the producers want Sternbach to eliminate. COURTESY RICK STERNBACH.

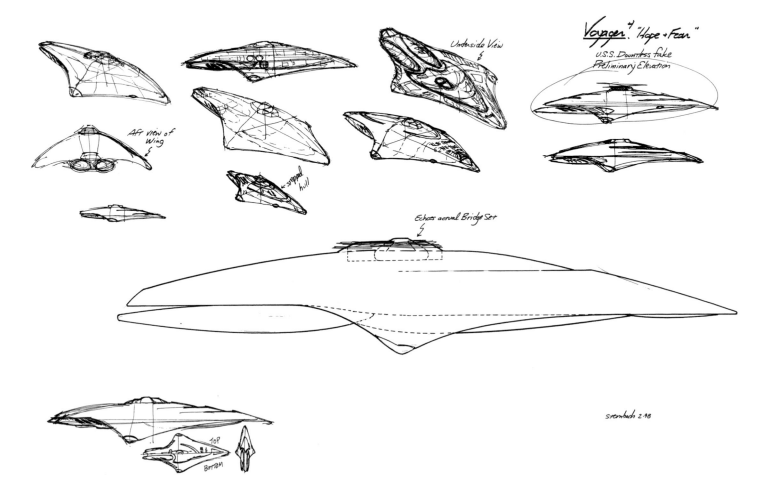

MARCH 4

RICK STERNBACH OPENS AN INTEROFFICE ENVELOPE AND REMOVES A FOLDED ELEVEN-BY-SEVEN-TEEN-INCH SHEET OF PAPER. Sternbach recognizes it immediately. As *Voyager*'s senior illustrator/technical consultant, he had been asked to submit "some ideas" for the exterior look of the *Dauntless*. Several days ago he had sent this same page of drawings to Supervising Producer Peter Lauritson. Now it is back. And one of the drawings is circled.

"This is a tentative approval for this design," Sternbach says as he snatches up a pencil and begins to draw. "As I look at this, I wonder what it is about this particular drawing that the producers liked enough to circle it. I know that they want the bridge module shaved off the top, so I'll smooth that over. But the first thing that I have to do is rough out a cross-sectional view for [Scenic Artist] Wendy Drapanas so she can create some backlit graphic designs." His pencil sweeps over the paper as he speaks. "I'll rough in some interesting hardware shapes and get this to Wendy in twenty minutes or less."

On Stage 16, the painters are putting the finishing touches on the *Dauntless* bridge while the advance electricial crew completes installing the hidden, built-in lighting. "Remember that this bridge actually is two

Grips and electricians assemble the *Dauntless* bridge's interior. The muslin-covered grids to the left and rear will also cover the front opening, leaving an unseen doorway to the far left as the only entrance. ROBBIE ROBINSON.

Recently painted Starfleet "plant-ons," sitting on sawhorses in Paramount's Mill, await being planted on the *Dauntless* bridge. They will later be removed when the bridge is "alienized." ROBBIE ROBINSON.

bridges," says Al Smutko. "It also has to turn alien." In order to accomodate that change, Smutko has had the bridge built first in the alien mode, with newly shaped consoles and chairs, while at the same time preparing a series of "plant-ons," or wooden Starfleet-style props that will fit snugly over those consoles and chairs. The schedule calls for the Starfleet look to shoot first—tomorrow morning. When the set shoots as an alien bridge five days later, the plant-ons will be removed. With the orange lighting shining through the muslin wall and a series of odd-looking video graphics and backlights, the same set should appear remarkably different.

Tonight, the painter's colors are all Starfleet.

"There are a lot of seams because of the curves," notes painter Dennis Ivanjack, who began his tenure on the lot as a Desilu employee and clearly remembers doing similar work on the original *Star Trek* sets. "We have to 'lose' those seams by filling them in. The carpenters use a lot of 'wiggle wood,' wood that bends easily and is very porous and rough. We have to fill it all up and make it smooth. We prime, we sand, we pack, we prime again." In fact, Ivanjack says, "We do so much sanding around here that the show is referred to as 'Sand Trek.'" Ironically, after all that smoothing effort, the painters' next task is to make the surface *less* smooth. "We apply our own bumpy surface over it, in a process called 'splatter,' by taking the head off of the spray gun," says Ivanjack. "That gives the wood a real metallic look that is enhanced when we put the final colors over it."

To accomplish all of this on schedule, "we have a day shift and a night shift," says Ivanjack, noting that the production uses four people on each shift for a full eight days—including Saturday and Sunday.

MARCH 5

SENIOR ILLUSTRATOR/TECHNICAL CONSULTANT RICK STERNBACH IS BACK AT HIS DESK. "I've been given orders to proceed with the top view, bottom view, side view, and fore and aft views of the *Dauntless*," he says. He looks at the tiny drawing that had been tentatively approved only the day before. "I notice that I stepped the bridge in a couple of places. And there's little thrusters and impulse vents, and some little chevron shapes on the nacelles. I'll reproduce all of the very vague details in a much cleaner form so it can be used by the computer graphics people."

True to his word, before the afternoon is over, Sternbach sends his drawings to Ronald B. Moore and Dan Curry. After discussing the drawings with Curry, Moore sends a copy to Computer Graphic Imaging Director Mojo at Foundation Imaging, an effects company in neighboring Santa Clarita Valley.

"The sketches really only show us one angle of the ship, so I told Mojo to generate a 3-D computer model with some sort of skin on it," Moore says. "I don't care what kind of skin, but I want to see what the ship looks

Rick Sternbach creates cross sections of the alien vessel the day after the producers chose his design.
ROBBIE ROBINSON.

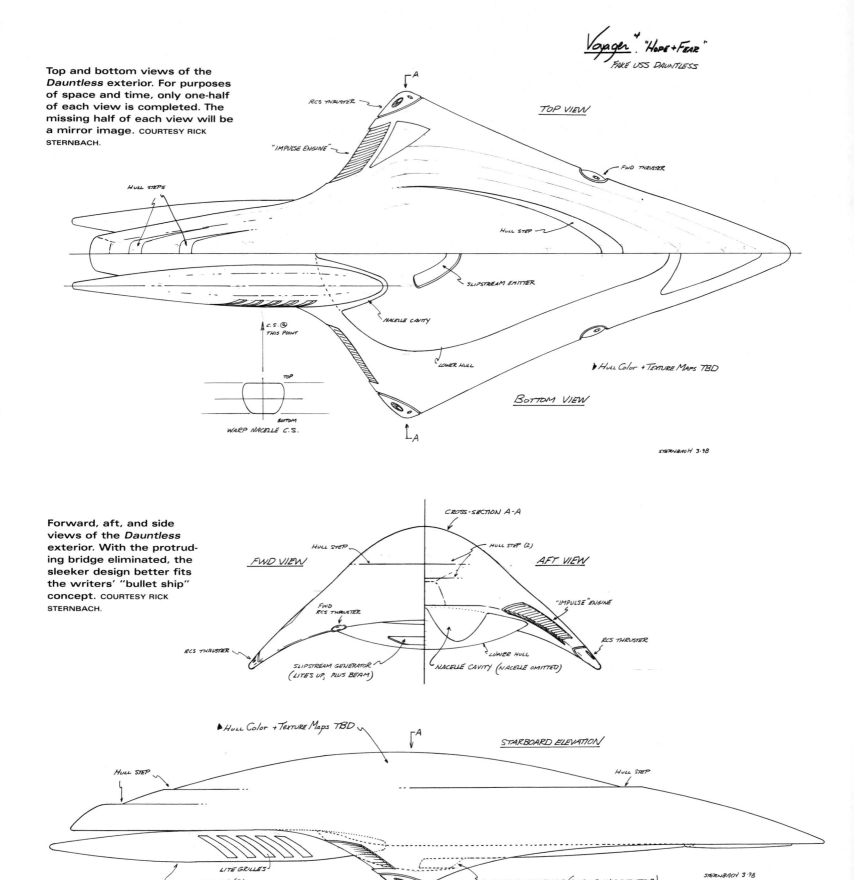

Top and bottom views of the *Dauntless* exterior. For purposes of space and time, only one-half of each view is completed. The missing half of each view will be a mirror image. COURTESY RICK STERNBACH.

Forward, aft, and side views of the *Dauntless* exterior. With the protruding bridge eliminated, the sleeker design better fits the writers' "bullet ship" concept. COURTESY RICK STERNBACH.

Voyager "HOPE + FEAR"
FAKE USS DAUNTLESS

RCS THRUSTER

TOP VIEW

"IMPULSE ENGINE"

FWD THRUSTER

HULL STEPS

HULL STEP

SLIPSTREAM EMITTER

NACELLE CAVITY

C.S. @ THIS POINT

LOWER HULL

► Hull Color + Texture Maps TBD

TOP

BOTTOM

BOTTOM VIEW

WARP NACELLE C.S.

STERNBACH 3·98

CROSS-SECTION A-A

HULL STEP

HULL STEP (2)

FWD VIEW

AFT VIEW

"IMPULSE" ENGINE

FWD RCS THRUSTER

RCS THRUSTER

RCS THRUSTER

SLIPSTREAM GENERATOR (LITES UP, PLUS BEAM)

LOWER HULL

NACELLE CAVITY (NACELLE OMITTED)

► Hull Color + Texture Maps TBD

STARBOARD ELEVATION

HULL STEP

HULL STEP

LITE GRILLES

WARP NACELLE (2)

RCS THRUSTER

SLIPSTREAM GENERATOR (LIKE OUR NAV DEFLECTOR)

STERNBACH 3·98

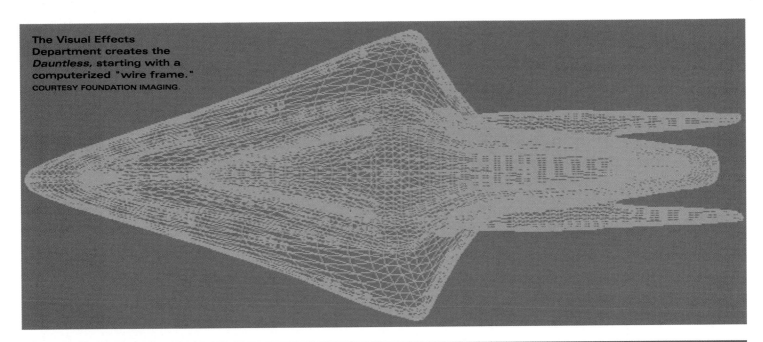

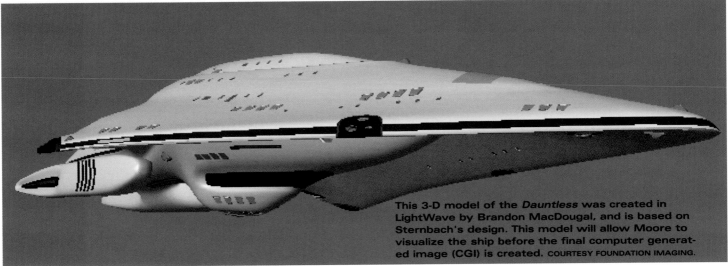

This 3-D model of the *Dauntless* was created in LightWave by Brandon MacDougal, and is based on Sternbach's design. This model will allow Moore to visualize the ship before the final computer generated image (CGI) is created. COURTESY FOUNDATION IMAGING.

like rotating around. And I hope I can see the model by the end of the week." Moore glances at his watch. It's Thursday evening.

"My first step is to create a rough outline of the ship," Mojo says as he watches his computer boot up. In rendering the *Dauntless*, he doesn't necessarily feel he has to start by generating a "wire frame." "Building a computer-generated model is the same as building a physical model kit. If you start with a big block of wood, you start shaving off pieces until you've got a shape you're happy with. I used a cube and basically modified the shape, shaving pieces off or stretching it out until I had the shape Ron was happy with. Of course, using the computer is better than assembling a physical kit, because I can use the 'undo' button." On screen, the form begins to resemble Sternbach's drawings. "It looks like a manta ray," Mojo comments. Then, a short time later he changes his mind. "Now it looks like a garden trowel."

Providing a 3-D image of the *Dauntless* is not the only task that the Foundation Imaging staff will be asked to perform. Now that they have been brought into the loop, they will be busy working on "Hope and Fear" for the next seven weeks!

MARCH 9

THIS IS THE SEVENTH DAY OF SHOOTING "HOPE AND FEAR." The entire day's work—seventeen scenes comprising eight and three-eighths pages of the script—will take place on the *Dauntless* 's engineering set. The lighting personnel begin at 6:00 A.M. for a "prelight."

Lighting this new set is a unique experience, because in addition to the traditionally lit design elements, like computer screens and backlit graphics, the warp core itself is composed of lighting components.

The design for engineering began when Richard James modified a *Dauntless* bridge sketch. "This is the first sketch of engineering that Richard gave to me," says Set Designer Greg Hooper, as he displays a faint pencil drawing rendered on a torn, folded, and wrinkled scrap of onionskin paper. Hooper translated the sketch into completed blueprints. "Richard told me about a concept that involved walking up some steps to a platform that circles the core like a catwalk," Hooper recalls. "The core doesn't go all the way to the ceiling the way *Voyager*'s does, and we can look down into it."

The final set doesn't exactly match Director Kolbe's extravagant idea from the Production Meeting. "That idea got nixed very quickly," Kolbe says with a laugh. "It would have required multiple optical shots, and there isn't enough time or money, so we're doing it all structurally." But the director is philosophical about the results. "It doesn't give us what we all originally wanted," he says, "but on the other hand it does give us something rather interesting, and the set certainly looks different from our usual engineering set up."

The call sheet for Day Seven. There's a lot to be done in the remaining two days of shooting. Note the large number of lighting cues mentioned; this will be a hectic day for the lighting technicians. Scene 97 is specified for "extremely low light" in order to accommodate the special-effects explosions.

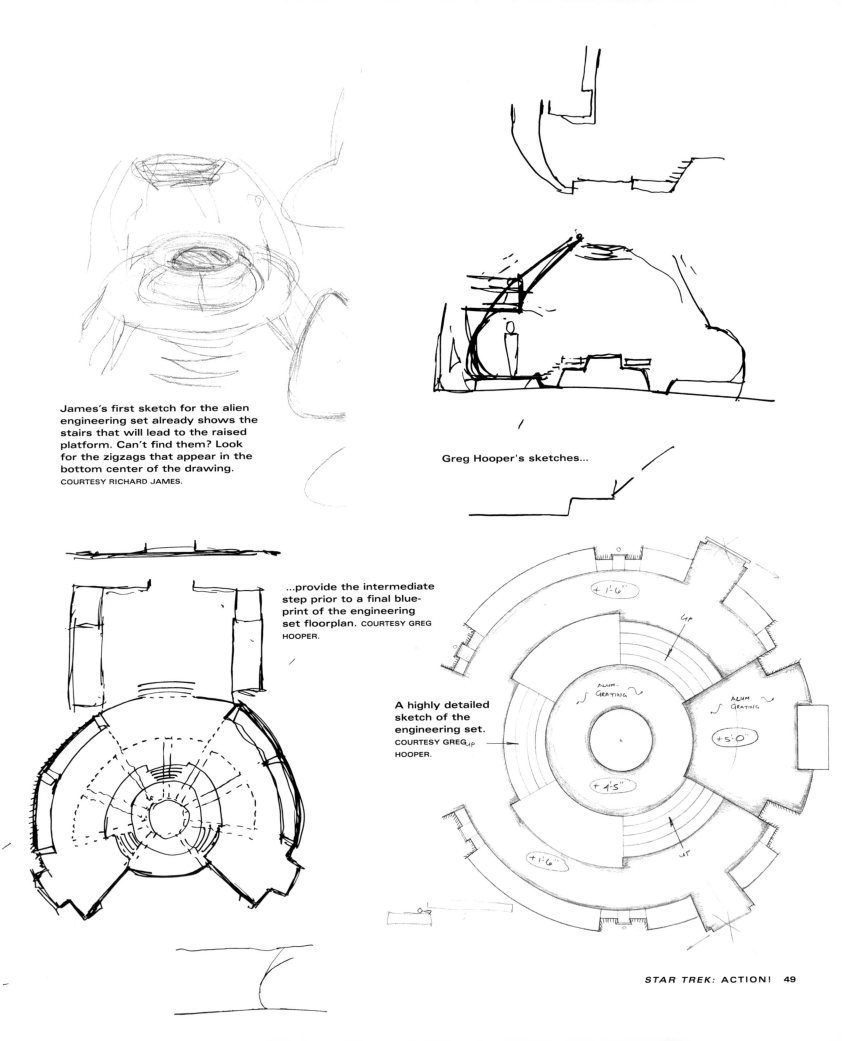

James's first sketch for the alien engineering set already shows the stairs that will lead to the raised platform. Can't find them? Look for the zigzags that appear in the bottom center of the drawing. COURTESY RICHARD JAMES.

Greg Hooper's sketches...

...provide the intermediate step prior to a final blueprint of the engineering set floorplan. COURTESY GREG HOOPER.

A highly detailed sketch of the engineering set. COURTESY GREG HOOPER.

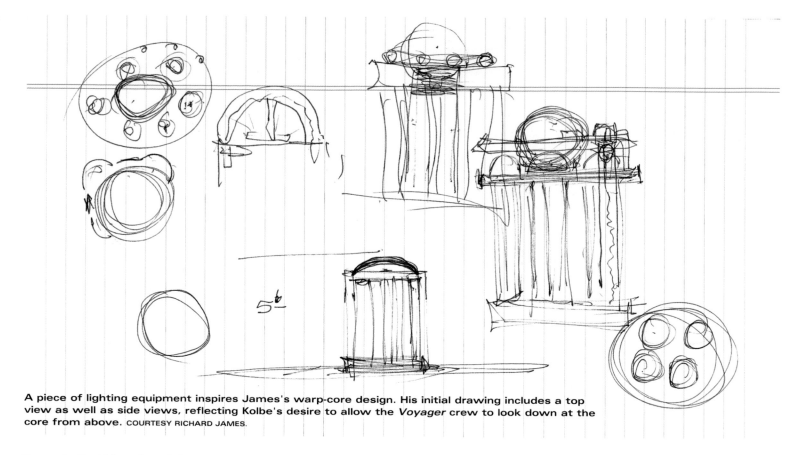

A piece of lighting equipment inspires James's warp-core design. His initial drawing includes a top view as well as side views, reflecting Kolbe's desire to allow the *Voyager* crew to look down at the core from above. COURTESY RICHARD JAMES.

Hooper's final blueprint of the warp core includes notes relating to its color and movements. COURTESY GREG HOOPER.

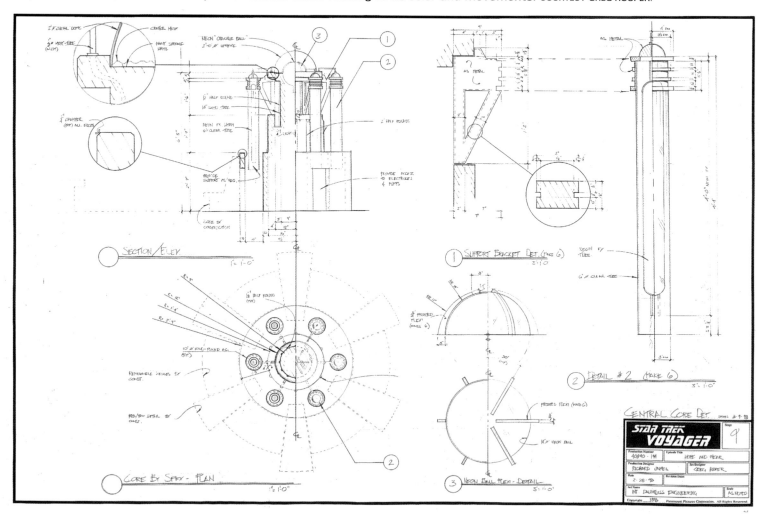

Richard James's second engineering sketch is of the core itself, and surprisingly, it is based on some commercial lighting equipment. "A fellow came in to show us some neon lighting equipment that he's manufacturing," recalls Greg Hooper. "We wound up creating this warp core incorporating a lot of his input."

The Art Department acquired six ten-inch–in–diameter glass tubes that incorporate a variety of elements. "Each tube is filled with water and there's a working neon tube in the center of each one," explains Special Effects Coordinator Dick Brownfield. A generator runs the neon. The bubbles that rise through the water enter the tubes via a manifold with needle valves. Brownfield controls the speed of the bubbles by increasing and decreasing the airflow, and the size by varying the openings in the needle valves. And what is Brownfield using for his pump? "I just hooked it into the stage's air-conditioning," he says with a smile. "It's house air."

In the center of the warp core, a glass ball crackles with electrical arcs. "It's just like the ones you've seen in gift shops," Al Smutko says. "Of course, it's the biggest one I've ever seen."

Actresses Kate Mulgrew and Jeri Ryan are the first cast members to arrive this morning. The rest of the cast has calls of 10:30 A.M. or later. But Mulgrew and Ryan, in street clothes, join the show's crew members for a 7:30 A.M. lighting rehearsal.

Construction on the *Dauntless* engineering set continues apace. The metal staircase, catwalk, and railings and the fiberglass ceiling were created from scratch by Paramount's Special Effects Department, the wooden floor and pillars by the Construction Department. ROBBIE ROBINSON.

"The pillars are similar to those on the *Dauntless* bridge," says Construction Coordinator Al Smutko, "but they're actually taller to accommodate the added height of the catwalk."
ROBBIE ROBINSON.

DO NOT HANG LOADS FROM
TRUSSES IN THIS STAGE
EXCEPT REGULAR SCAFFOLDS
FOR SET LIGHTING
LOADS TO BE APPLIED AT
PANEL POINTS ONLY.

Ever wonder what amazing substance is used to contain a matter/antimatter explosion? Wood. Pieces of the warp core are assembled inside Paramount's Mill by Assistant Special Effects Worker Willie Thoms. ROBBIE ROBINSON.

Mulgrew gingerly negotiates the steep staircase to the catwalk. ELLIOTT MARKS.

"The minute I heard my footsteps, I knew we were dead," says Mulgrew. The scene will have to be looped in postproduction. ELLIOTT MARKS.

The rehearsal begins with a safety meeting. "The staircase to the catwalk is very steep," points out Adele Simmons. "Please do not attempt to go down them facing forward. It's much safer if you all back down."

Scenes 92 and 97 are the first up this morning. Ninety-two is long, a full page and a half of dialogue between Janeway and Seven as they attempt to shut down the alien warp core. "This console is still supposed to be Starfleet, isn't it." Jeri Ryan says, not quite asking a question.

"Yes, that's right," Rick Kolbe confirms. He watches as she places her hands over the keyboard and is satisfied. Since nothing about the console is story specific, it is okay that Ryan wings it.

The lighting rehearsal confirms two anticipated problems, one pertaining to sound recording and one pertaining to shadows. "Can everyone outside of the muslin please stand still," calls out Marvin Rush.

"And can we turn off the Lawrence Welk Bubble Machine when it goes out of frame?" adds sound mixer Alan Bernard.

Eliminating the shadows being cast onto the muslin from off-set is relatively simple. The sound problem is somewhat harder to resolve. The noise from the bubbles and the neon generator intrude upon the actors' dialogue. In addition, the metal catwalk resonates with the sound of the actors' footsteps. The set is just plain loud.

Just as the *Dauntless* warp core reflects the genius of its alien designer, the realized set is a marvel of 20th-century filmmaking ingenuity. ELLIOTT MARKS.

Alan Bernard half-heartedly suggests that carpeting might take care of some of the problem, but the director nixes the idea.

"I want to be able to shoot through the holes in the floor," Kolbe insists.

"We obviously will be looping this whole scene," Kate Mulgrew says while walking gingerly up the steps. Later, she observes, "The minute I heard my footsteps, I knew we were dead. Looping is quite easy, but for me it's a bad transition. Much is lost in the translation, so I like to get it on the soundstage if possible." Mulgrew has obviously spent some time thinking about this aspect of filmmaking. "I feel that sound is often relegated to a secondary role," she explains. "If a take is good for camera, they like to print it and move on. So I've been asking for a certain discipline regarding sound all season."

Filming begins on Scene 92 at 9:05 A.M. By 9:44, the scene, a wide "master" shot and a close-up of each of the actresses, is complete. Mulgrew leaves the stage to participate in an interview with a waiting Canadian television crew.

Now Jeri Ryan is alone on the *Dauntless* engineering set for Scene 97.

97   INT. DAUNTLESS - ENGINEERING (OPTICAL)
Seven of Nine working a console . . . when a VIOLENT
ENERGY DISCHARGE CRACKLES around the entire console!
A section of the panel BLOWS OUT in a SHOWER OF SPARKS!
Seven of Nine recoils.

This short scene actually is composed of two shots. In the first shot, the console will light up; in the second, sparks will fly. For safety purposes, the second shot in the scene will be filmed first.

"This is an optical because the visual-effects people will enhance the sparks that I shoot over the console," notes Dick Brownfield. "I'm a pyrotechnician by trade, and I personally handle the sparks." Brownfield creates the sparks out of 3F black powder and titanium metal, along with a sparkling compound and some iron filings that he places into a mortar that he builds himself. "I ignite it with a little Z16 squib. The mortar is very directional. It puts the sparks right where I want them to go."

Rick Kolbe has the angle of his shots thoroughly planned as well. Now he is lying on his back on the floor under the catwalk with a viewfinder. Obviously, he wants the shot low. "If we stand topside, we will just see the core bubbling," the director says. "But I want to see the power system of the ship, and visually the most exciting part is actually underneath it."

At 10:07 A.M., the camera is in place, the lights are set, and the mortar charge is prepared. Jeri Ryan is called back to the set. When she arrives, Adele Simmons calls the crew to attention for another safety meeting. Then she talks to one of her production assistants. "Call the studio hospital and alert them we are about to have pyrotechnics on Stage Nine." This is standard procedure for all production. It's a "just in case" measure.

Marvin Rush has mounted the camera on a stationary dolly for stability. Since the sparks will be enhanced by visual effects, the camera must be "locked down." The slightest motion will render the later computer work worthless. "This is an optical," Simmons announces loudly. "Don't touch the dolly, the camera, the operator, or the lights."

Rick Kolbe huddles with Dick Brownfield and Jeri Ryan, giving each a cue. "Action, fritz, fritz," Kolbe says. For the filmmakers, the term fritz is a verbal representation of the electrical flashes they will create in just a few moments for this shot. Brownfield's cue to fire his mortar is the second fritz.

As the shot is set up, Ryan tries out some business. The robe is not Starfleet issue. ELLIOTT MARKS.

Because of the care taken before hand, Jeri Ryan ducks precisely on cue.

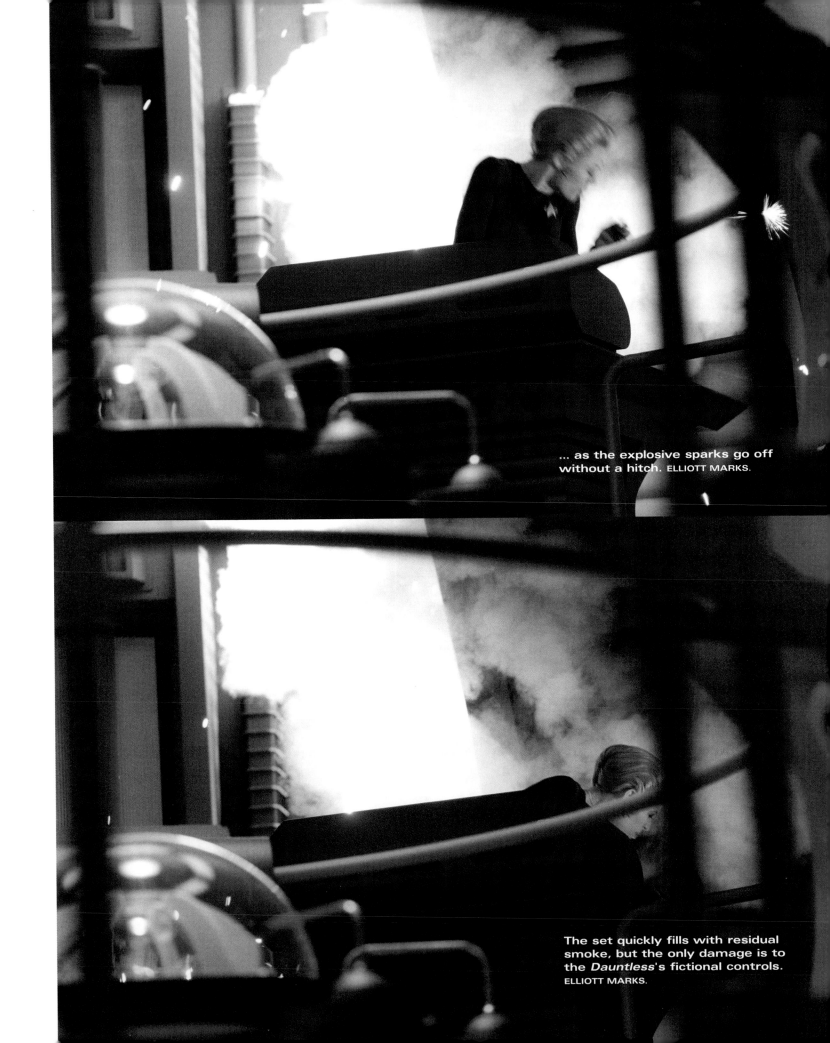

... as the explosive sparks go off without a hitch. ELLIOTT MARKS.

The set quickly fills with residual smoke, but the only damage is to the *Dauntless*'s fictional controls. ELLIOTT MARKS.

With the Starfleet facade dropped, the alien graphics
designed by Wendy Drapanas come to light. ELLIOTT MARKS

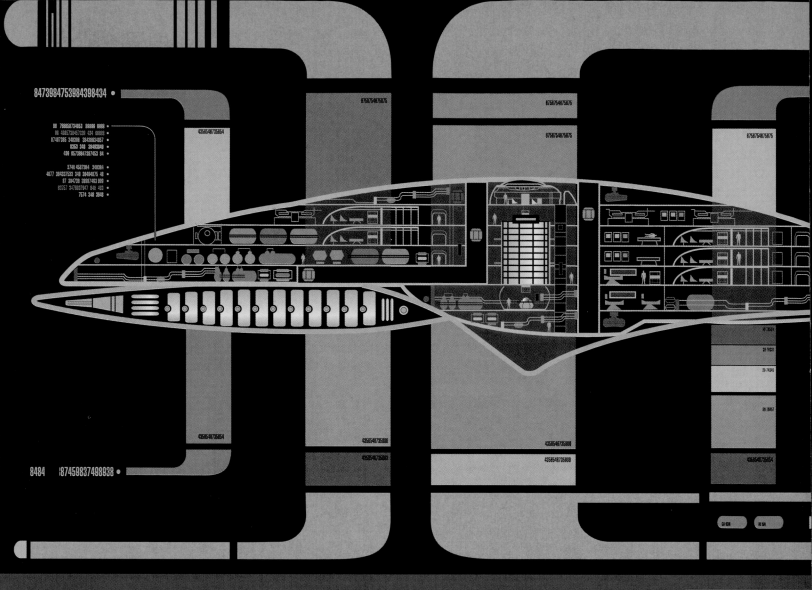

"It looks sort of metaphysical, don't you think?" says Drapanas of one of the alien graphics. "Like it's the brains behind the whole thing."
COURTESY WENDY DRAPANAS

Drapanas's rendering of Arturis's phony Starfleet-style cutaway of the *U.S.S. Dauntless* comes complete with little people, turbolifts, storage tanks, and crew quarters "to make it feel real," she says. "Then I added all the buttons and callouts." COURTESY WENDY DRAPANAS.

foot-by-four-foot gel. It's the gels that perform the magic. "The color of the gels is called 'Tangerine 135,'" notes Chief Lighting Technician Bill Peets. Peets points out a bank of overhead lights: a series of Super 4K's, which are three-foot-by-three-foot four thousand–watt lamps that throw off a very soft light with no shadows; a series of Baby 4K's, four thousand–watt lamps that cast their light in a smaller spread; and several Cyc lights, which are ten-inch halogen lamps that spread somewhat brighter light over a very large area despite their conveniently smaller size. The Cyc lights derive their name from their original purpose—they were designed to light backings known as "cycloramas." And all of these "overheads" shine through the colored gels placed in front of the lamps.

"The orange is what Rick wanted," Peets says, laughing, "but it was so overpowering that we've had to add some white with six three hundred–watt fluorescent boxes to cut the color."

This also is the first time the crew has seen the set with the Starfleet "plant-ons" removed to show the underlying alien console and chair shapes. And then there's the wall of backlit graphics, blinky lights, and video monitors. "We call it 'alien wallpaper,'" says Video Operator Ben Betts, from behind his video control board.

The graphics were created by Scenic Artist Wendy Drapanas, who found inspiration for the design on her desk. "I had a rubber band ball that just kept getting bigger, so I did a sketch of it," she laughs. "It looks sort of metaphysical, don't you think? I just started out with that shape and kept

Top to bottom: 7:46 A.M.—Using a cotton pad and alcohol, Makeup Artist Brad Look cleanses Actor Ray Wise's skin. The skin must be totally free of moisturizers, emollients, or anything of that nature to ensure that the prosthetics will adhere properly. After the cleansing, zinc oxide powder is applied to the nasal and labial folds.

After "seating" the main forehead/head appliance on Wise's head, Look begins gluing it down using medical-grade adhesive. Meanwhile, Makeup Artist Scott Wheeler double-checks the cheek appliances to make sure that their edges are good.

Look applies the right cheek appliance while Wheeler applies the left. The cheek pieces, as well as a forehead piece and two neck pieces, are made from a life cast of Wise's face.

Brad Look powders Wise's eyebrows, reducing the stickiness of the adhesive so that when they apply a secondary T-shaped forehead appliance it will not immediately adhere. Next they will attach a neck appliance that fills the area below the two cheek appliances. ELLIOTT MARKS.

building on it, and then Scenic Artist Jim Van Over added the video animation."

Tonight, the scenes to be shot include numbers 96, 98, 101, and 107, the dramatic ending to "Hope and Fear." While Rick Kolbe appears to be concentrating solely on making directorial choices such as camera angles, lighting, and safety, he's just as busy watching the crew. "Considering that this is the last shooting night of the season," Kolbe says seriously, "everybody is already on vacation or at least they're flying toward it. So my job is to make sure that they focus on the episode as well."

Actor Ray Wise appears in full makeup as the alien Arturis. "I gave him an extended skull," says Makeup Designer and Supervisor Michael Westmore. "Instead of a large skull typical of the aliens people think landed at Roswell, I kept it with skull-like proportions. If you look at him straight on, he looks like a bald man. Only his profile looks alien." The prosthetic skull extension that Wise is wearing, Westmore explains, "is thick foam rubber that's been vulcanized in an oven. If you push it in, it will bounce right out again."

The prosthetic head was not made exclusively for Ray Wise. Westmore cast it, "from the same plaster head that we used to make the Vorgons [from *TNG*'s "Captain's Holiday"]," he says. "All we had to do was get a cast of Ray's face and make some sidepieces to work as blenders over the edges of the piece."

Westmore has had this alien "look" in mind for some

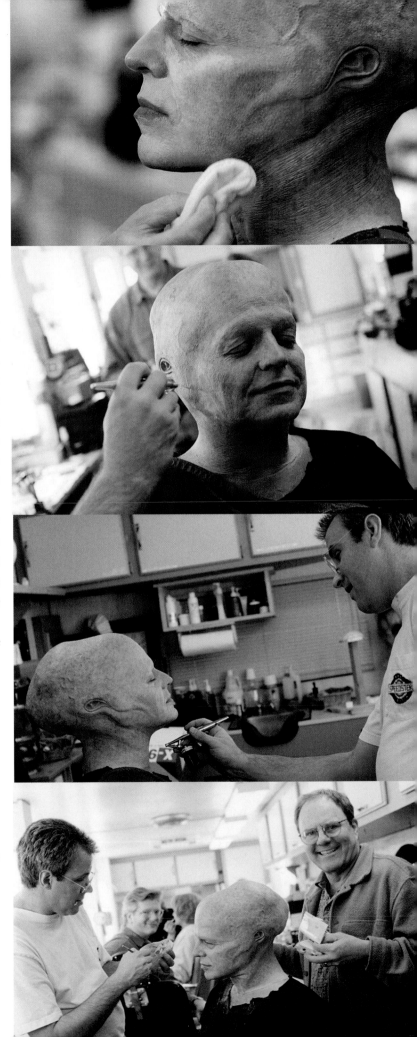

Top to bottom: After applying a thickened edge filler to prevent the appliances' edges from catching the light and the camera's attention, the artists use foam sponges and Q-Tips to apply acrylic colors to the areas of Wise's skin adjacent to the appliances. Then powder is applied to Wise's lips and cheeks and to the prosthetic appliances.

After using a small detail brush to paint age spots, Wheeler begins to airbrush color onto Wise, using a Paache-H Style single-action airbrush to meld the colors from the main appliance into the forehead appliance and the cheek appliances. He "speckles" the face with a pastel green, starting with the "veins."

Wheeler changes to using broad strokes and a maroon paint. He will switch colors again, to a greenish brown, just to break things up a bit.

9:23 A.M. As Scott Wheeler is completing the last step, applying rubber-mask greasepaint around the eyes and blending it with the adjacent acrylic paint, Michael Westmore steps into the trailer to see the results. He smiles. The only step left in Wise's transformation is a pair of contact lenses. ELLIOTT MARKS.

The master shot for Scene 96 begins with Mulgrew entering the scene from the rear of the set … ELLIOTT MARKS.

time. "I actually designed this makeup last year for a different show—not for *Star Trek*. But those producers did-n't use it. Now it's worked out great."

The cast and crew have been filming since 10:30 A.M. Now, at 8:12 P.M., the first camera rehearsal is called for Scene 96.

Kate Mulgrew, as Captain Janeway, walks around the set, and Ray Wise, as Arturis, sits at the front con-sole as he had a few nights earlier. Rick Kolbe feels that they should rehearse Scenes 96, 98, and 101 together. As before, the scenes are, essentially, part of one sequence, dramatically interupted only by a cut to the sequence in which Seven is showered with sparks in engineering, and by a number of exterior "ship shots." There is no reason to separate them for the rehearsal. Kolbe may even shoot them as one.

Kate Mulgrew has anticipated this possibility and has already prepared herself. "I broke the scenes down technically before I came in," she says, glancing at the margins of her script, which are filled with tiny notes, written in her hand. "I think about each scene a lot," she says. Her notes read, "This beat changes," and "Here's the transition." "Preparation has to take place alone, at home," the actress emphasizes. "Then once we set it up and rehearse it a couple of times, we can just shoot it."

Mulgrew's concern isn't only about the stage directions. She's equally interested in the character's actions and

... too far away for the boom mike, located above Wise's head, to pick up her initial dialogue. Her portion of the soundtrack will need to be looped. ELLIOTT MARKS.

Steadicam Operator Gavin Ames carefully tracks the shot. The Steadicam is not part of a production company's standard equipment; rather, such intricately balanced handheld cameras are owned and operated by specialists who are contracted for specific shots only. ELLIOTT MARKS.

"Arturis is diabolical," notes Costume Designer Robert Blackman, "but I didn't want to telegraph that. My job was to make him look interestingly curious but affable, so I just put him in a shirt and a pair of pants." RON TOM.

"We made two shirts for Arturis," notes Key Costumer Kimberley Shull, "because one of them [shirts] had to be a stunt double and get phaser burns on it." Actor Ray Wise actually wore a clean shirt to the set where Shull applied the burn. "I used Streaks and Tips, a spray-on hair color product," Shull says. "It will clean out somewhat."
ELLIOTT MARKS.

motivations. "The *Voyager* crew is under duress here," she points out. "If the captain shows any kind of hesitation under those circumstances, she could lose her support. So there's an action—the action is to 'get out,' right? To save myself. There's an obstacle—the obstacle is 'the guy'—and he's giving me the reasons that he's going to kill me. There's an objective—the objective is to 'make him understand that I did the only thing I could do when I sided with the Borg.'

"If I know those things, and I've technically broken down the scene," she continues, "then I just work within them until I finally can throw them away and just play it in the moment." Mulgrew pauses. "That's why I went to school for four years," she says, laughing.

On another part of the stage, Dick Brownfield fills a mortar with a metallic sparkling mixture. He is thinking ahead to Scene 101, as is the director. "We'll have to keep the actors away from the the console at that point," Kolbe notes. "The special effects will be right there." Kolbe and Wise choreograph Arturis's hand movements on the console to punch a specific area when he destroys the navigational controls. "Then you go stumbling back," Kolbe says, giving Wise his cue. Then, abruptly, Kolbe changes his mind. "Dick, can you put the sparks right in the center of the console? Say 'Yes,' Dick!"

Brownfield's answer is to simply walk away from the set and return a moment later with a ten-foot-long

Arturis levels his weapon at Janeway, but not in the way the weapon's creator had intended. ELLIOTT MARKS.

Property Master Alan Sims demonstrates the proper way to hold Arturis's weapon. "I planned for it to be held horizontally," Sims explains, "as opposed to twentieth-century weapons." Sims cast the weapon out of polyurethane resin, using a mold of a generic alien weapon first made for *The Next Generation*. He then cast a second barrel and connected the pieces with the original grip and an additional brace. SCOTT GIBSON.

Dick Brownfield and his special effects assistant, Wil Thoms, position a mortar filled with explosive compounds under the console. The charge is hard-wired to an electric switch so that Brownfield can explode it from a safe distance. ELLIOT MARKS.

wooden pole. Rather than mount his mortar on a solid surface, he will protect the console and the actors by personally holding the sparks at a safe distance from them. The solution is Brownfield's version of "Yes."

At 8:19 P.M., they rehearse again. Mulgrew circles the upper level of the bridge. When she stops, a camera assistant puts a strip of tape on the carpeting, indicating her "mark." Kolbe follows her trajectory, pretending he has a handheld camera, holding his fingers in a circle, looking through the circle as if it's a lens. PRO Steadicam Operator Gavin Ames has arrived on the set. While he slips into his leather camera harness, he watches the director's moves. "When the explosions happen, the ship will rock," Ames explains. The set, of course, cannot rock. So it's necessary to rock the camera instead. "And it's easier for me to rock the Steadicam ninety degrees than it is to do it with a Panavision camera with a stationary dolly head."

Kolbe decides to keep Arturis at the center of each shot, except for Janeway's close-ups. "Wham, jolt, they both stumble," Adele Simmons shouts when the action reaches that story point.

But Kolbe and Rush ultimately decide to shoot the three scenes separately. Rush is already worried that Scene 101's pyrotechnics may "white out" the shot.

Now Scene 96 itself will be composed of three shots, to be called 96, which goes all the way through, and close-ups 96 Apple and 96 Baker. While both actors will always be in the frame, Kolbe's plan is to focus on Arturis in the exteme foreground. That means Ray Wise will need to be illuminated separately from Mulgrew, who will be lit with ambient lighting only. The actors relax as the electrical crew swings into action. "Ten-minute warning," Simmons calls even before the electricians have started.

At 8:41 P.M., Kolbe calls "Action" on Take 1. It is perfect.

8:42 P.M. Take 2. Perfect again. "Number two is best," says Kolbe. "Print it."

For the next shot, 96 Apple, Arturis will follow Janeway around with his eyes. At 8:43 they do a camera rehearsal. The geometry is difficult, so Rush suggests they do a rack focus from Mulgrew to Wise. "Let's try it," says Kolbe. In the end they decide that cutting between a series of close-ups will work better. The shot is shortened, and close-ups are added to the "shot list." The actors step away while the electrical crew hangs one more fluorescent box over Arturis's position. Mulgrew will be closer to camera than she was in the previous shot; she joins Hair Designer Josée Normand at the nearby makeup table for a touch-up. Close by, Merri Howard, who is taking her turn tonight as clock-watcher, scrutinizes the "postproduction" schedule. This may be the final night of shooting, but for many, the episode is far from finished.

9:12 P.M. Everyone is on their marks. "96 Apple—Take 1," calls Simmons. Mulgrew's motion and the camera's moves don't quite match.

9:14 P.M. Take 2. Better.

9:14 P.M. Take 3 is called, then—"Cut," calls the Steadicam operator. "Camera reload."

9:19 P.M. Take 3. "Cut. Print," calls Kolbe.

9:22 P.M. Take 4. "Cut. Even better. Print that too." Then Kolbe calls to Script Supervisor Cosmo Genovese, "Wait. Print number four only."

Now the camera team sets the Panavision camera onto the dolly. Scene 96 Baker is a close-up of Janeway. Marvin Rush decides to shoot it with the Panavision camera and a hundred-millimeter zoom lens at a T3 f-stop. "A tight close-up is much easier to hold stable on the dolly than it is on the Steadicam," Gavin Ames says as he hangs the Steadicam on its upright stand. "And with the hundred-millimeter lens, it's going to be very tight."

Because the light on Mulgrew's face is very low, the camera's aperture is set at a T3 f-stop—wide-open—allowing the most light possible to strike the film.

9:34 P.M. 96 Baker. Take 1. "Let's do another for safety," says the director.

9:36 P.M. Take 2. "Cut. Print."

"Move on to Scene one-oh-one," Simmons calls, sounding happy that they are moving so quickly. Of course, everyone has been concerned about Scene 101, which will be composed of five separate shots. And in the first, the script says, "A couple of consoles EXPLODE, SPARKING!"

While Dick Brownfield installs his "sparks" (there will be two mortars working simultaneously, one mounted on the pole, one on the floor), two grips cover the set around him with protective fireproof blankets. A few feet away, the director talks to Ray Wise about the physics of picking up Arturis's weapon. "I'm about two minutes away," Brownfield says just as Paramount's fire marshal arrives at the set.

"We'll get a rehearsal and then have a safety meeting," Simmons responds.

Dick Brownfield stands on a ladder and holds the ten-foot pole, the mortar mounted on the end hanging only six feet from the actors.

9:52 P.M. Rehearsal. "Boom! Boom!" Kolbe shouts; then he and Brownfield discuss where the sparks will be.

9:53 P.M. Rehearsal. When Wise picks up the "gun," Mulgrew wiggles her fingers and whispers "sh-sh-sh-sh," feigning a "beam-out."

9:54 P.M. Simmons requests the entire crew's attention for a safety meeting, explaining exactly where the sparks will fly. "Is everybody comfortable?" Pause. "Picture!"

9:56 P.M. "Action!" The actors jump back as two bright clusters of sparks flash across the *Dauntless*'s console. "Let's get the smoke out of here," Simmons calls immediately.

"No," Rick Kolbe stops her. "Let's leave it in here. It looks good."

The filmmakers gather to discuss the shot. They don't like it. "Rather than keep it as one shot, let's break it into two," the director says. Now Scene 101 has *six* shots in it. "Shoot Kate's first."

As Brownfield reloads the mortar on the pole, Simmons says to the crew, "This will be a single of Kate. With sparks." Ray Wise moves away from the set, because he won't be needed. Marvin Rush positions himself behind the console, planning ahead to the second part of the shot, the one with Arturis. Simmons watches Brownfield closely. "We'll have sparks on a stick in a minute," she says.

10:02 P.M. "Scene one-oh-one Apple. Take One." As the sparks fly, Mulgrew jumps backward. "That looked great! Print it!" Kolbe shouts through the smoke.

Now Brownfield rigs the second mortar, the one that sits on the ground. The wires must be hidden under a piece of carpet, not because they might be visible, but so that the moving Steadicam operator, who will follow actor Wise to the back panel, doesn't trip over them. Brownfield also rigs a flashbulb tree under the console. His preparations take nine minutes.

"When Adele says, 'Jolt,'" Kolbe tells the Steadicam operator, "please delay your move for one beat. That's the only adjustment from the last shot."

Meanwhile, the Panavision camera is being prepared for the last shot in the sequence. It must be "locked down" for Janeway's optical beam-out.

10:14 P.M. Ray Wise is in place. 101 Baker. Three takes and exactly ten minutes later, the director says, "That's pretty good. Print it."

10:24 P.M. "Let's shoot Kate's dematerialization," Simmons says. "Oh, and happy birthday to Dick Brownfield." A grip tapes a translucent plastic sheet onto one of the built-in overhead bulbs to dim the light directly under it, while Marvin Rush sits down on the dolly to operate the camera.

10:33 P.M. 101 Chicago. Take 1. At the end of her dialogue, Mulgrew stands perfectly still. "One...two... three!" Rick Kolbe counts. Mulgrew quickly steps out of the camera's frame. "One...two...three..." Pause. "Cut. Good. Print. Let's do one more for safety."

For economy of time, Kolbe and Simmons decide to shoot Scene 107 now, since all of the elements are perfect for Arturis's encounter with the Borg. Marvin Rush asks that the floor be wiped down, since it shows footprints and will be in the shot—and that one overhead fluorescent light be removed.

10:44 P.M. Rehearsal. Simmons reads the Borg transmission speech while the Steadicam circles Wise. Rush asks Gavin Ames to change to a thirty-five-millimeter lens and for more of the "railing" to be in frame. The operator quickly makes the adjustments and they rehearse one more time for the camera.

10:48 P.M. Scene 107. Take 1. The Steadicam is to start moving when Arturis sits down in the chair. "Action." Wise sits, and the camera moves. "Cut. Perfect. Print it," Kolbe calls out.

"Back to one-oh-one," Simmons responds.

It takes exactly one hour to complete the remaining close-ups.

"Move to Stage Nine," Simmons calls out, and the stage is a rush of activity. Only three corridor scenes are yet to be photographed for "Hope and Fear." And at 12:50 A.M., Simmons gives her last order of the season to the crew. "That's a wrap. See you in June."

MARCH 11

AN INORDINATELY LONG STAIRCASE LEADS TO PARAMOUNT'S EDITING ROOMS ON THE HAGGAR BUILDING'S SECOND FLOOR. When the puffing messenger arrives from Editel, an editing assistant loads the daily tape into the Avid system. "The main formula for editing *Voyager* is very specific," says Daryl Baskin. "We open every scene with the master shot so the audience can see where we are and who's in the room. Then we go in tighter. Then, depending on the scene, you kind of open back up to the master and let it play. There may or may not be some close-ups mixed in there. And that's the formula."

Baskin demonstrates on his Avid monitor. "On Scene ninety-six, the master goes all the way through," Baskin explains. "Rick Kolbe shot it twice, but he printed only the second one. That makes my job easy, but if I should find something wrong in the print, I can call to have any part of the other one printed. We call that unprinted film 'B-Negative.'" Baskin finds no problems in assembling the scene from that master, the two angles on Arturis and the one on Janeway. Most of the other scenes prove to be relatively standard as well—until he comes to the last part of Scene 101, when Arturis grabs his gun and Janeway dematerializes.

"The timing of the scene is funny because we *see* Arturis grab the gun," says Baskin. He explains that every Starfleet beam-out is timed at four seconds long. Since the visual-effects "sparkles" will not be added until later, the editor generally adds a four-second temporary sound effect so that the producers will understand what's happening when they screen the footage. This time, however, that four seconds isn't long enough to allow for all the action. "I don't want to show Janeway beaming out before Arturis grabs his weapon," Baskin explains, "but in the time allotted, she has to. If she doesn't, she really would get hurt."

Baskin cuts several variations of the material, looking for one that makes sense in the allotted four seconds. He tries pre-lapping the sound, starting it while Arturis is on screen grabbing the weapon and Janeway isn't on screen. Again the timing doesn't work. Finally, Baskin head-trims the shot, cutting off the beginning of the action and not showing the alien pick up the weapon at all. "Now when we see him, he already has it in his hand," the editor says, satisfied with his compromise. "So when Janeway says, 'Come with me; it's not too late,' we hang on her for a beat and the beam-out starts. When Arturis turns around and the audience sees Janeway again, it's the last half second. She's already gone, and it'll just be sparkles. It's the only way to make the timing work."

At this point the only elements needed to complete the show are visual-effects shots, and music, and sound effects, and dialogue replacement and... The list goes on. The show has entered the period refered to as postproduction. It goes like this—

MARCH 18

DARYL BASKIN AND SUPERVISING EDITOR J. P. FARRELL ASSEMBLE THE FIRST ROUGH CUT, OR OFF-LINE CUT, OF THE EPISODE—THE ENTIRE FORTY-THREE MINUTES' WORTH OF SCENES. Where they encounter missing visual-effects shots, they insert holes, and write a chyron message on each such as

"EXTERIOR. NORMAL SPACE. VOYAGER COMES OUT OF SLIPSTREAM AND BANKS TO STAR-BOARD."

The chyron provides only an approximation of the visual that will be inserted in the hole, but the length of the hole—the number of frames at twenty-four frames per second—matches the length the visual will be.

Farrell then transfers the compiled information—the time-codes of the first and last frames of each edit—onto a computer zip disk. This off-line cut has numerous bumps in the edits, as well as odd sounds in the audio. Those imperfections will be corrected, or on-lined, after the director, the producers, and the postproduction staff all have screened it. Hopefully, they won't ask for too many changes along the way.

MARCH 23

RONALD B. MOORE LOOKS APPROVINGLY AT MOJO'S MONITOR. The model of the *Dauntless* rotating on the screen looks good. Moore is not concerned about the model's nondescript pinkish-beige color; the image is a test ship, after all. "We don't know the texture yet," he says, refering to the missing surface detail such as deck plates and phasers. "And we probably won't have an approved color until sometime in May."

Choosing a color, and getting it approved, is a difficult task. "We've narrowed our choices down to five," Moore says, "copper dark, copper gloss, copper light, gray gloss, and gray. The gray gloss is the most traditional, but I feel that the ship should be a bit more radical. After all, it may *look* like a very, very modern Starfleet vessel, but it's actually alien technology." Moore expects to render five versions of the ship, one in each color, to the producers. "Copper light is the one I like," he says.

Mojo and the Foundation staff have also been busy working on an image of the slipstream. "What does something that's real esoteric like a 'slipstream' look like?" Moore asks rhetorically. "The concept is very difficult."

"The concept of the slipstream is speed!" Mojo interjects. "Right from the beginning I knew the direction I wanted to take. The environment the ship is in would make it look as if it's moving really, really fast." Mojo first

Ronald B. Moore (*Left*) points out a detail on the unapproved *Dauntless* model to CGI Director Mojo at Foundation Imaging. ELLIOTT MARKS.

After developing the *Dauntless* model in a nondescript white, the visual-effects team made several color choices—their favorites being in the copper family. COURTESY FOUNDATION IMAGING.

U.S.S DAUNTLESS COPPER

The *Dauntless* model in a standard gray. COURTESY FOUNDATION IMAGING.

U.S.S DAUNTLESS GRAY

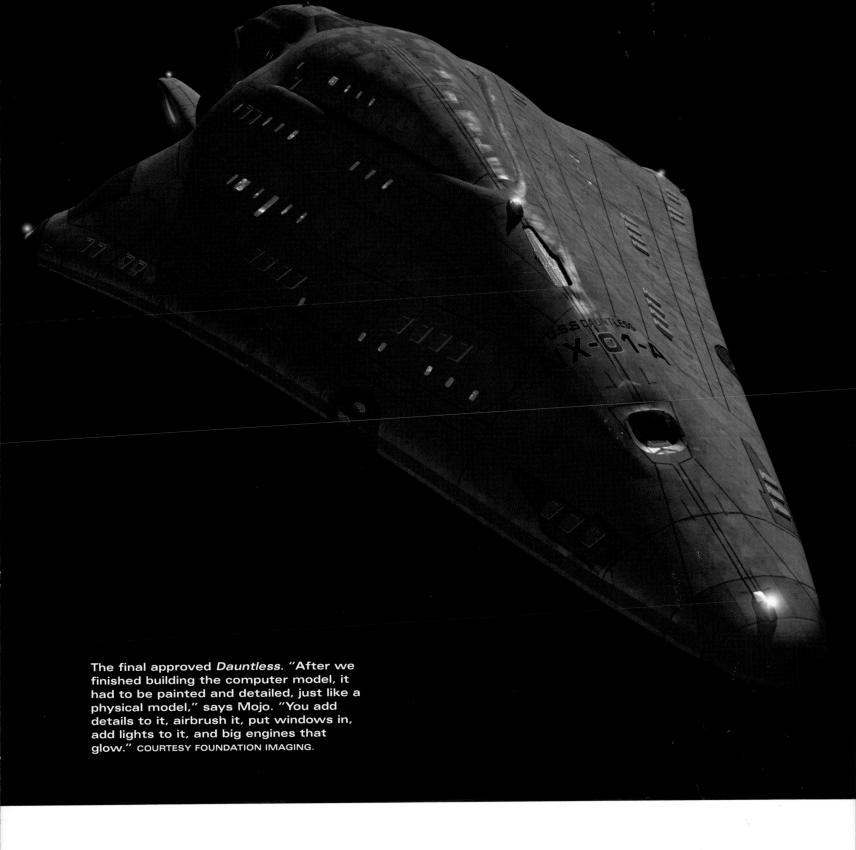

The final approved *Dauntless*. "After we finished building the computer model, it had to be painted and detailed, just like a physical model," says Mojo. "You add details to it, airbrush it, put windows in, add lights to it, and big engines that glow." COURTESY FOUNDATION IMAGING.

Why use CGI? "There wasn't time to build a physical model," explains Ronald B. Moore. "Also, the *Dauntless* needs to distort when it goes into the slipstream, and that's really hard to do with a model." COURTESY FOUNDATION IMAGING.

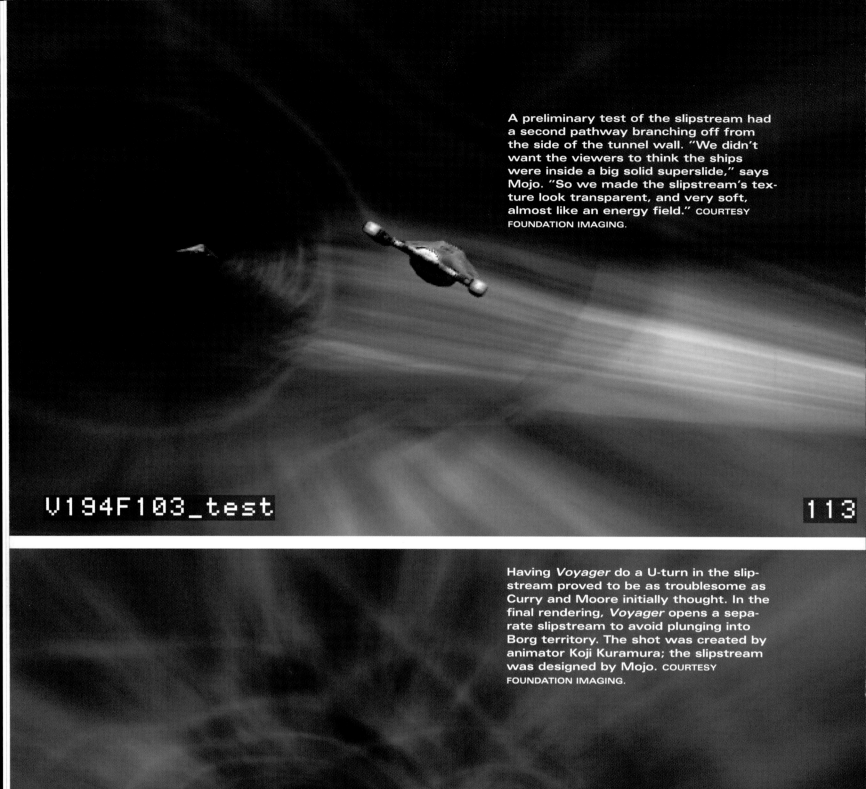

A preliminary test of the slipstream had a second pathway branching off from the side of the tunnel wall. "We didn't want the viewers to think the ships were inside a big solid superslide," says Mojo. "So we made the slipstream's texture look transparent, and very soft, almost like an energy field." COURTESY FOUNDATION IMAGING.

V194F103_test

113

Having *Voyager* do a U-turn in the slipstream proved to be as troublesome as Curry and Moore initially thought. In the final rendering, *Voyager* opens a separate slipstream to avoid plunging into Borg territory. The shot was created by animator Koji Kuramura; the slipstream was designed by Mojo. COURTESY FOUNDATION IMAGING.

The *Dauntless* pops out of the slipstream and enters Borg space. The background nebula is a modified, high-resolution image captured by the Hubble Space Telescope. The slipstream entrance/exit effect was created by animator John Teska. COURTESY FOUNDATION IMAGING.

A Borg cube comes down to block the audience's view of the *Dauntless*. The new cubes, created specifically for *Voyager*, are a hybrid of the models seen in *The Next Generation* and *Star Trek: First Contact*. "The shot was not in the script or in my notes," says Ronald B. Moore. "When I got the first test of the shot from Foundation, they had just put it in, and it worked great." 3-D modeling for the shot was done by Emile Smith and Koji Kuramura. COURTESY FOUNDATION IMAGING.

though an image from "One" is on his screen, he's discussing "Hope and Fear" on the phone with Dan Curry, who is at the Paramount lot directing second unit photography for an episode of *Deep Space Nine*.

Moore sets down the phone and picks up the manuscript. "Liz makes me this 'prayer book,'" he says. On the pages, short scene descriptions are listed next to scene numbers, frame numbers, and time-codes. "What I look for is blank spaces. Like, here…" Moore reads from the bottom of a page, "'Scene Ninety-five. Exterior. *Dauntless* out of control, slams against the slipstream.' See? It's all blanks. We still need it."

The pages tell Moore exactly which shots he has or hasn't completed. "For Scene Ninety-seven, we enhanced some energy discharges on Seven of Nine by digitally compositing squibs (stock footage of small explosions that Curry and Moore photographed years earlier) onto the practical sparks (the ones shot on the stage). There are two shots in the scene, so I used the squibs to bridge the cut. It ties the two together."

The next visual-effects shot is Scene 99. "We have a six-second shot with *Voyager* careening toward *Dauntless*," Moore explains. "We're doing two shots here. But Mojo can't finish them yet because he didn't find out what the ship looks like until last Friday." Which means the color of the *Dauntless* has been approved. Sort of. "Peter Lauritson liked copper gloss, and Dan and I liked copper light. I split the difference," Moore says, with a chuckle. "I figure if I go right in the middle, I'm safe. Of course, that means we have to do all of the shots involving the *Dauntless* by the day after tomorrow. And of course, we have to add the torpedoes before Paul Hill moves it on to our final composition." Down the hall, in another bay, artist Greg Rainoff is animating the phaser fire for Scene 101, but he already has the torpedo element for Scene 99 prepared.

"We have Janeway doing a beam-out in Scene One-oh-one," Moore says, continuing down his shot list. "The transporter element was developed by Dan Curry back with the pilot. We do a fade and add the element on top of it. It's pretty standard, but this one is a little different because we cut to do an animated shot of Arturis's phaser fire." Of course, because his weapon is alien, Moore opted to animate his phaser fire in a non-Starfleet color. "We picked up the orange motif of the *Dauntless*," he explains. "I like to do things like that when I can, because it just adds to the flavor of the show."

Moore turns the page on his prayer book. "Now, Scene One-oh-three," he says. "Whooee. There was a whole lot of talk about that one. The script says that *Voyager* does a U-turn in the slipstream. I never thought it was going to look good, and Dan and I didn't want to do that, and instead we wanted to have the ship break out into normal space. But Rick Berman sent a note saying he wanted it to turn around in the slipstream." He pauses. "Paul, can you put one-oh-three up on my monitor?" Moore asks the compositor. The scene appears. In it, *Voyager* is chasing a bland-colored "temp" of the *Dauntless*. But the slipstream looks wonderful. "Finally, I figured out what the effect needed to look like. I explained to Foundation that I wanted them to essentially lay two dimes on top of each other and then move the top one to the right and see what happens." The dime analogy turned out to be a good idea. "Now there's a double exposure of the slipstream, then one veers to the right and *Voyager* takes this hard, knife-edged right turn into it. Well, we're almost finished with it, and it looks a heck of a lot better than if we'd followed our initial instinct.

"We're still working on Scenes One-oh-four and One-oh-five," Moore says with a shrug. "I've seen temps, but we haven't done the final yet."

"The average *Voyager* show has about forty optical shots," Elizabeth Castro says, as Moore ponders the far-too-many blank spaces on the sheets in his hand. "And one show only had twelve. 'Hope and Fear' has seventy. And that's not counting the stock shots."

APRIL 30

PETER LAURITSON SUPERVISES WHILE THE EDITORS CUT THE VISUAL EFFECTS INTO THE SHOW, IN WHAT IS CALLED THE OPTICAL ON-LINE SESSION. When they finish, the show is "locked."

Except for the audio tracks.

MAY 5

AT 6:00 A.M., IN PARAMOUNT'S MUSIC BUILDING (NAMED, APPROPRIATELY, THE CROSBY—AS IN BING—BUILDING), SUPERVISING COPYIST ROBERT BORNSTEIN AND HIS STAFF LABOR OVER SHEETS OF MUSIC STAFF PAPER, COPYING—BY HAND—MUSICAL PARTS FOR FORTY-FOUR MUSICIANS. For Bornstein and the other copyists, the early work hour is not unusual or unexpected. This afternoon, after all, a scoring session is scheduled.

By 1:30 P.M., people carrying musical instrument cases can be seen entering several of the entrances to the studio. Dennis McCarthy arrives at Scoring Stage M at 1:45. The scoring session for "Hope and Fear" is scheduled to start at 2:00. Music Editor Gerry Sackman joins the sound mixer and the recordist behind the mixing board in the window-lined booth. Inside the quiet booth, conversations are easily heard. But the other side of the glass is an entirely different world. There's only one word to describe it—*loud.*

The high pitch of twelve violinists tuning their instruments slices through the nearby discordant pitches of tuning violas, cellos, and basses. Across the room, the tones change to brass and reed sounds, but they are still tuning sounds, with no musical form intended. Not even the two percussionists near the back wall can add rhythm to the cacophony; they too are tuning. An electric guitar adds to the volume; a synthesizer chimes in, creating another whole orchestra all its own. Then, suddenly all of the instruments come together, and for five seconds, a single chord fills the room, in tune, in pitch, in unison. Tuning time is over. The musicians turn toward the conductor's podium. But Dennis McCarthy is not there. He's off in the corner getting a soft drink, and, as usual, laughing.

Before each musician is a music stand, and on each is the individual's "part" of the musical score, the ink, almost, as they say, still wet. Oddly, most of the parts are not fully notated. On some of the parts, the rhythmic bars are indicated, along with the key signatures and the key or chordal modulations, but knowing the correct *individual* notes to play is left to the musicians themselves. Throughout the next four hours, as McCarthy is conducting, he will often call out—"Those of you who have notes…"

"They're all my buddies," McCarthy says. "We've been recording together for years. They know what I want and I know what they can play."

Occasionally, McCarthy suggests changes in the timing or the chordal structure of a cue right there from the podium. It's a moment that McCarthy terms, "Pencils up!" And he doesn't find the method at all unorthodox, or unusual. "I can see the score in my head," he says. "The violin players are all playing pretty much the same thing, so when I dictate to one of them, I'm dictating to them all. Sure, the brass and woodwinds are all playing different stuff, but…" He pauses. "I just start with an idea, like 'E-minor over this or that,' and just start barking notes at the guys. I just yell, 'Everybody got a pencil? Well, roll tape.'"

Also helping the musicians is the fact that the cues are all very chordal and nonrhythmic. And that's standard practice on *Star Trek*. "Right after 'Encounter at Farpoint,' Rick Berman told me that he didn't want themes,

Composer Dennis McCarthy puts on his conductor hat—or headphones—for the scoring session. The orchestra of forty-four musicians are all friends; the majority of them have been recording together since the first *TNG* episode. ROBBIE ROBINSON.

During the scoring session, Music Editor Gerry Sackman takes notes from inside the control booth. The notes will be important when dialogue, music, special-effects sound, and Foley are "married" at the final dubbing session. ROBBIE ROBINSON.

Sometimes he even amazes himself. Musicians gather behind McCarthy as he listens to the playback in the control booth. Not bad, considering he wrote several portions of the score the night before. "I write real fast," he says. "And I don't sketch. I just start on the left edge of the paper and go to the right edge." Seated on McCarthy's left is Dawn Velazquez, to his right is Recordist Paul Wertheimer. ROBBIE ROBINSON.

that the music should just state where it's going and that's all," McCarthy notes. "Occasionally I can sneak a theme in, but I think the last time I wrote a melodic piece was in 'Year of Hell.'"

In front of the podium, a monitor plays the segments of "Hope and Fear" that correspond to McCarthy's cues, and he conducts the orchestra according to the mathematical timing on the monitor. But he doesn't conduct the segments in story order, or even in the order they are listed on the cue sheet Sackman has provided him.

The cue sheet breaks down the cues by time and instruments. The list confirms that the cue for the final action scene has been broken into two parts, one timing out at two minutes and one second, the other at two minutes and twenty-five seconds. The second cue, coincidentally, begins with Scene 96 and runs through Scene 108, when we see *Voyager* in normal space.

The sheet also stands testament to McCarthy's and Sackman's sense of humor: each cue has been given a name, and not necessarily one that sounds like it belongs on *Voyager*. McCarthy has dubbed the sequence where Seven of Nine is attempting to access the *Dauntless*'s primary systems, while Arturis destroys the controls, "The War of the Buttons." He calls the second half of the sequence, "The Rescue." And the final scene is named "Ode to Summer," because, McCarthy says, "It's the last cue that will play on *Voyager* this season."

Now, only one hour and thirty-four minutes into the session (which is expected to last from four to six hours), McCarthy says, "Let's do the last action sequence. I'm in the mood." That means "The Rescue" is up.

VOYAGER 40840-194 (04)

Studio: "M"
Date: 5/6/98 (WED.)
Time: 2:00 P.M.

"HOPE AND FEAR"

Composer: **DENNIS McCARTHY**

Total Time: 21:20

M-	Cue Title	Reel	Part	Timing	Violins	Violas	Cellos	Basses	Woodwind 1	Woodwind 2	Woodwind 3	Woodwind 4		Horns	Trumpets	Trombones	Tuba	Keyboard	Synth.	Harp	Guitar	Fender Bass	Percussion	Drums	Total	Pages
11	POOR SPORT			:05	12	4	4	4	1	1	1	1		6	3	3			1		1		2		44	1
15	THE DAUNTLESS			:09	12	4	4	4	1	1	1	1		6	3	3			1		1		2		44	7.5
21	THE GIFT			1:12	12	4	4	4	1	1	1	1		6	3	3			1		1		2		44	4
22	MR. TOAD'S WILD RIDE			3:21	12	4	4	4	1	1	1	1		6	3	3			1		1		2		44	18.5
31	MONTAGOSITY			1:41	12	4	4	4	1	1	1	1		6	3	3			1		1		2		44	8
32	SOMETHING FISHY			:58	12	4	4	4	1	1	1	1		6	3	3			1		1		2		44	4
33	DASHED HOPES			2:03	12	4	4	4	1	1	1	1		6	3	3			1		1		2		44	11
41	CLOSE CALL			:20	12	4	4	4	1	1	1	1		6	3	3			1		1		2		44	1.5
42	KIDNAPPED			2:50	12	4	4	4	1	1	1	1		6	3	3			1		1		2		44	22
43	REVENGE			:43	12	4	4	4	1	1	1	1		6	3	3			1		1		2		44	3.5
51	PURSUIT			1:06	12	4	4	4	1	1	1	1		6	3	3			1		1		2		44	12
52	WAR OF THE BUTTONS			2:01	12	4	4	4	1	1	1	1		6	3	3			1		1		2		44	17
53	THE RESCUE			2:25	12	4	4	4	1	1	1	1		6	3	3			1		1		2		44	14
54	ODE TO SUMMER			:21	12	4	4	4	1	1	1	1		6	3	3			1		1		2		44	2.5
23	PARANOID			:03	12	4	4	4						6	1	3			1		1		2		38	1
12	UNKNOWN MESSAGE			:23	12	4	4	4	1	1	1	1		6		3			1		1		2		41	2
13	RESTING			:07	12	4	4	4						6		3			1		1		1		36	1
14	DEEP THOUGHTS			:19	12	4	4	4	1	1	1	1		6		3			1		1		2		41	2
15A	ALTERNOSITY			1:13	12	4	4	4											1		1				26	1

McCarthy's and Sackman's "cue sheet." The sheet lists the length of time for each cue, and a breakdown of the instruments that will be required. For this particular session, except for the woodwinds and trumpets, it's all of the musicians, all of the time. COURTESY GERRY SACKMAN.

McCarthy rehearses two bars of the music twice, listening for the balance of the percussion each time. Then, "Let's roll it." Just as he points his baton into the air in the classic conductor pose, he turns to look down at something on his hip. "Why do I even have a beeper?" he asks rhetorically. "Everyone I know is here." The entire orchestra laughs.

"Okay. And…," he pauses, "…one, two, three, four, five," and the room fills with music. Two minutes and twenty seconds later the piece is on tape, and McCarthy walks to the booth to listen. Everyone in the booth likes the take, but McCarthy feels that several bars in the beginning need to be fuller. Back at the podium, he reverts from conductor to composer and calls out a series of changes.

To the percussionist: "Don't come in at beat seventeen, wait until twenty-one."

And to the brass: "Guys, I need you to crescendo from the fourth beat of bar forty-two up to the 'and' of beat three in bar forty-three. [These bars correspond to Scene 103, where *Voyager* curves off in its "U-turn."] Then keep that level happening, and still crescendo. We need to have the YO! thing happening there. But save something for bar forty-eight when we go into the tempo change."

To the drummer: "On the suspended cymbal, keep on truckin' through forty-four, forty-five, and forty-six."

Then to all: "It's just a matter of filling in on those dynamics. Everything else is going great, and I have nothing else intelligent to say, so…" McCarthy again raises his arms and his baton. "…Roll it."

After the take, McCarthy again enters the control booth to listen. The take is perfect. "You know, I didn't write that until last night," he suddenly admits. "I'd finished about thirty percent of it and just said, 'This ain't happenin'!' It went straight into the shredder and I started again." Which explains why the copyists were busy so early in the morning.

McCarthy has one other little secret. "I used Jerry Goldsmith's *Voyager* theme twice there," he reveals. "Obviously I used it full-bore when we cut to see the ship in normal space at the very end. But I also used a few seconds of it earlier when we see *Voyager* firing at the *Dauntless*." He's talking, of course, about Scene 99. "That's in-your-face *Voyager* theme."

MAY 11 AND 12

AT 9:00 A.M. DAWN VELAZQUEZ SUPERVISES THE LAST POSTPRODUCTION SESSION: DUBBING. "We're laying in all the dialogue, the music, the sound effects, the background sounds, and the Foley track," she explains. With the episode playing on a full-size movie screen, Velazquez and three sound mixers sit at the board, working in tandem. One mixer concentrates on dialogue and some of the background, the second mixer works with the music and the Foley, and the third handles the sound effects and the rest of the background. Starting at the beginning of the episode, the group will view the show three times, or, as they say, "make three passes." The show may be forty-three minutes long, but for many reasons, the three passes will take two full days to complete.

"We begin with a write pass," Velazquez says as the mixers begin to write in all of their computer moves, at the same time locking the dialogue into the new master they are creating.

"Then we do the record pass." Velazquez stops the mixers from time to time to make changes. "Can that be a little louder, please?" she says. Then, "Can we fade that into the music?" and "Make the background a little heavier."

The third pass is the playback pass. "We'll play it through and just listen," the associate producer says when the credits start. "Of course, we'll go back and forth and forward and backward, over and over and over and over."

MAY 13

EARLY IN THE MORNING, PARAMOUNT TELEVISION'S OPERATIONS DEPARTMENT BEAMS THE SHOW UP TO A PASSING SATELLITE, THEREBY DELIVERING IT TO THE BROADCASTERS.

MAY 20, 1998

AIRDATE!

Over fifteen weeks have passed since the writers first sat down to break a story for the final episode. Now that episode is on the air. The result of that first meeting and all of the hard work performed by hundreds of people is being broadcast. All of that effort, and it's over in an hour.

After a welcome but short hiatus/vacation, those writers have returned to their desks and already are working on Season Five—all, that is, except Jeri Taylor.

"I will miss Jeri," Kate Mulgrew says. "She created Captain Janeway, and I will very much miss that voice." Mulgrew ponders for a moment. "I think that Jeri's great desire was to endow all of these characters with a humanity. And she did that. Now they have to take wing—and that's what Brannon's going to do for them very well.

84   CONTINUED: 84

Bashir can see that Sisko isn't himself.

                    BASHIR (cont'd)
          Are you alright, Captain?

                    SISKO
          I've been better...

85   INT. SURGERY   85

Sisko ENTERS to see Worf standing by a bio-bed where
Jadzia clings to life.

85A   CLOSE ON WORF AND DAX   85A

sharing this final moment.

                    DAX
          I'm sorry...

                    WORF
          Save your strength.

But Dax is determined to say something to him.

                    DAX
          Our baby... would've been so
          beautiful.

And with that, Dax exhales her last breath and dies.
Worf immediately lets out a bloodcurdling SCREAM of
pain and rage.

STAR TREK: DEEP SPACE NINE
"TEARS OF THE PROPHETS"

83   INT. PROMENADE   83

Worf and O'Brien grimly emerge from the airlock and
make a beeline for the Infirmary. Moments later,
they're followed by Sisko, Kira and Jake. Sisko
looks drawn, strained, as if a great burden weighs
heavily on his shoulders. The Promenade is filled
with solemn-looking Bajorans, most of whom are
gathered around the shrine. Upon seeing Sisko,
Sahgi, the Bajoran girl we saw earlier, rushes up to
him. Sisko, Jake and Kira stop, while Worf and
O'Brien continue into the Infirmary.

                    SAHGI
          Emissary! My mother says all
          the orbs are dark -- that the
          Prophets have abandoned us.
               (not waiting for a
                response)
          You have to find them, Emissary.
          You have to ask them to come
          back.

Sisko doesn't know how to answer her.

                    SISKO
          I'll try.

Satisfied, Sahgi runs back to her mother. Kira
manages to smile at the Emissary, though she is
clearly shaken by the loss of the Prophets. Sisko,
Jake and Kira head off toward the Infirmary --

84   INT. INFIRMARY   84

Sisko and Kira ENTER to find O'Brien with Odo and
Quark, waiting silently for word of Dax's condition.

Looks are exchanged, but nothing's said. Nothing
needs to be said. After a beat, Bashir emerges from
surgery. One look tells us all we need to know.

                    BASHIR
               (to Sisko)
          I was able to save the Dax
          symbiont, but we need to get it
          back to Trill as soon as
          possible.
               (a beat)
          There was nothing I could do for
          Jadzia.

                                            (CONTINUED)

85   INT. SURGERY   85

Sisko ENTERS to see Worf standing by a bio-bed where
Jadzia clings to life.

85A   CLOSE ON WORF AND DAX   85A

sharing this final moment.

                    DAX
          I'm sorry...

                    WORF
          Save your strength.

But Dax is determined to say something to him.

                    DAX
          Our baby... would've been so
          beautiful.

And with that, Dax exhales her last breath and dies.
Worf immediately lets out a bloodcurdling SCREAM of
pain and rage.

87   INT. CARGO BAY   87

A long, sleek, jet-black coffin containing Jadzia's
body sits in the middle of the otherwise-empty Cargo
Bay. One of the Cargo Bay doors OPENS and Sisko
ENTERS. It's the next day and Sisko's grief is not
as raw anymore. He walks over to the casket and
stares down at it for a moment. When he speaks,
it's with gentle affection that covers a deep and
profound regret.

                    SISKO
          The funeral service is due to
          begin in a few minutes,
          Jadzia... but I need to talk to
          you one last time.

87   CONTINUED: 87

Sisko pauses to collect his thoughts.

                    SISKO
        When I first met you, you said
        that my relationship with Jadzia
        Dax wouldn't be any different
        than the one I had with Curzon
        Dax. But that's not the way
        things worked out. I had a
        helluva lot of fun with both of
        you. But Curzon was my mentor.
        You... you were my friend. And
        I'm going to miss you.
                    (a beat)
        I should've listened to the Prophets
        and not gone to Cardassia... maybe
        then you'd still be alive.
                    (a sudden flash of anger)
        Why aren't you here, Jadzia? I
        need you to help me sort things
        out. Something's happened to
        the Prophets... something that's
        made them turn their backs on
        Bajor, and I'm responsible. But
        I don't know what to do about
        it. How to make it right.
                    (a beat)
        I've failed as the Emissary and,
        for the first time in my life,
        I've failed in my duty as a
        Starfleet Officer.
                    (a beat)
        I need time to think... clear my
        head. And I can't do it here.
        Not on the station. Not now. I
        have to get away... so I can
        figure out a way to make things
        right again.
                    (a beat)
        I have to make things right,
        Jadzia. I have to.

And off this anguished moment --

                                        CUT TO:

88   INT. OPS   88

Kira, Odo, O'Brien, Bashir and Jake are gathered by
the stairs. The door to the Captain's Office OPENS
allowing Sisko, carrying a shoulder bag, to come
down the steps.

                                    (CONTINUED)

---

88   CONTINUED: 88

                    SISKO
        The station's all yours, Major.

                    KIRA
        She'll be here when you get
        back.

                    BASHIR
        Sir, this leave of absence
        you're taking... how long do you
        think you'll be gone?

                    SISKO
        I can't say exactly.

                    ODO
        We'll be waiting.

                    O'BRIEN
        Best of luck, sir.

                    SISKO
        Thank you, Chief. My thanks to
        all of you.

Sisko walks over to Jake.

                    SISKO
        Let's go home, Jake.

89   NEW ANGLE   89

as Sisko and Jake ENTER the Turbolift.

                    SISKO
        Landing Pad "C".

And with that, the Turbolift descends. HOLD ON the
faces of the group as they watch Sisko and Jake
disappear out of sight.

90   ANGLE ON KIRA   90

as she turns and walks to the Captain's Office.
Curious, Odo follows after her.

91   INT. CAPTAIN'S OFFICE   91

Kira and Odo ENTER and step over to the desk.

                                    (CONTINUED)

The following pages cover the climactic sequence from Deep Space Nine's sixth-season finale, "Tears of the Prophets," the series's 150th episode. Scenes 83 through 87 deal with the death of Jadzia Dax, and its impact on her close friend, Captain Benjamin Sisko. As with Voyager's "Hope and Fear," the evolutionary process for the script begins with the writers' break sessions—but with a significant differ-ence. DS9's producers had already come up with a story premise for the finale, one that they would have to change in order to accomodate a human factor that was outside of their control....

"It was the end of my contract and I thought about the two sides of doing just one more year," says Terry Farrell. "But I really wanted to move on with my career and do something different. I knew that was what was going to make me happy." JERRY FITZGERALD.

THE TAIL THAT WAGGED THE DOG

TERRY FARRELL WAS LEAVING.

Months of discussions were over and the actress had made up her mind. She wouldn't be returning to *Deep Space Nine* for its seventh, and final, season. The word had not yet spread to the general public, although the gossip on any number of science-fiction websites was that Farrell's departure from the series was a strong possibility. But in the third- and fourth-floor offices of the Hart Building, home to *DS9*'s producers and writers, that word had become cold, hard reality. And the scenario for the season's final episode, which the writers had discussed for months, was about to change in order to reflect that word.

Jadzia was going to die.

It wasn't an act of petty vengeance. It was an act of dramatic necessity. But it really wasn't anyone's favorite choice.

"I didn't want to kill Jadzia," says *Deep Space Nine*'s Executive Producer Ira Steven Behr. "To me that has very little to do with good storytelling." It's not, he explains, a matter as clear-cut as giving a character like Hamlet a good death in his one play. "It's like Hamlet's been in *one hundred fifty* plays," says Behr. "This is the final play. And you have all this baggage that you don't need to have. It can't be 'What's good for the character.' It's 'What's good for the character in terms of the character's position on the show, her position with the fans, what the fans want to see.' None of that has to do with what makes a good episode."

If he'd had his choice, Behr says, "I'd have been very happy to end the season with Jadzia alive and do the last episode of Season Six as we originally had conceived it, with the perceived death of the Prophets." That "perceived death" had been on Behr's mind for quite some time. "I had talked about it with [Executive Producer] Rick Berman a couple of years ago," he recalls. "We have certain ideas about how we want the seventh season to end," Behr adds cryptically. The decision to keep the Prophets out of the series for a while would facilitate those ideas. And during that period, "I thought it would be nice to send Sisko back to Earth, believing the Prophets had been killed," he says.

According to Story Editor Bradley Thompson, Behr had broken the news to his writing staff about the intended sixth season finale in typical no-nonsense style, gathering the group together in one spot and announcing: "'Okay, don't tell anybody about this, but at the end of the season we're gonna send Sisko to Earth and all the gods [Prophets] will be dead!'"

To which Behr's team had responded: "'Okay, Chief—we'll follow you!'"

Like a snowball rolling down a powdery slope, the story germ had started taking on girth. "We began discussing the final episode of the season pretty early, back in September [1997], I think," says Co-Supervising Producer René Echevarria. "We basically knew that we wanted to give Sisko a big setback, and have the Dominion attack the Prophets in some way, shape, or form."

Because the writers were busy with other episodes, the idea stayed on the back burner for several months, although the writers were conscious of the fact that they were "building the box that we needed to get us there," according to Echevarria.

"These things work out in strange ways," adds Supervising Producer Hans Beimler. "When we started working on 'The Reckoning,' we kind of knew, in a general sense, where we were going to go in the finale. Not in the specifics, but in the kind of show that we wanted to do. And we knew that we'd have to set up the theme of the finale in an earlier episode."

It quickly became clear to everyone that "The Reckoning"—a story in which a Prophet and a Pah-wraith inhabit corporeal bodies to fulfill an ancient prophecy by "duking it out" on the Promenade—could be that episode. "Ira kept saying that it would be great if the events of 'The Reckoning' would somehow help us to set up a weakness for the Prophets," says Echevarria. "And in a sense, they do, because by the end of the episode, time is sort of out of joint and things are not as they were destined to be."

"We loved the idea of the prophecy being unfulfilled and that this would somehow play into a later episode," says Story Editor David Weddle, who co-wrote the teleplay for "The Reckoning" with Bradley Thompson. Weddle and Thompson's original thought was to have Sisko be the one to defy the prophecy because he can't help intervening on his son's behalf. But the writing staff ultimately decided that Sisko's burden of guilt was, by this point in the season, heavy enough, and that it would be a more interesting irony if it were Bajor's religious leader who threw everything into disarray. This worked just as well for everyone, says Weddle. "The Pah-wraiths weren't defeated and that enabled Dukat to call upon one."

In fact, that episode worked *so* well as a setup for the finale, that it created some minor problems later on. "'The Reckoning' was a much more sophisticated, complete show than we had originally anticipated. We wound up using ideas that we *thought* were going to come in the last show," says Beimler. The themes of "good versus evil," for example, played very effectively in "The Reckoning," so the writers didn't bother to save them for the finale, as they had once intended. "It's kind of like robbing Peter to pay Paul," he says, laughing. But by doing that, they forced themselves to create something even more sophisticated for the finale. "It allowed characters like Sisko to go further, in a way that would make sense to the audience, so that it didn't seem like he was taking a left turn out of nowhere at the end of the season."

In a way, the announcement of Terry Farrell's departure would do much the same thing, forcing the writers to come up with additional twists and turns that they had not foreseen.

BROKE, BUT NOT BEATEN

ONE OF THE FIRST THINGS AN OBSERVER MIGHT NOTICE AT A *DEEP SPACE NINE* STORY-BREAK SESSION IS THAT THERE IS NO PRELIMINARY BEAT SHEET.

"We used them for the first couple of years," Behr says. "But we've pretty much dispensed with them. We don't have time. And basically, at this point, it's such a group activity. *We'll find it in the room,*" he recites like a mantra. "*We'll find it in the room.* Sometimes that bites you on the ass and sometimes it doesn't, but sometimes having the beat sheet will *still* bite you on the ass."

On the afternoon of March 18, l998, Behr's assistant, Robbin Slocum, places a series of short phone calls to the various members of the *Deep Space Nine* writing staff. Just as she drops the telephone handset into its cradle, her boss walks out of his office to pick up a stack of messages from the corner of her desk.

"They're on their way," Slocum says. Behr smiles and steps into the outer hallway to greet his compatriots. One by one, the members of his writing staff arrive: Hans Beimler from the office next door on the Hart Building's third floor, René Echevarria and Co-Executive Producer Ronald D. Moore from the floor directly above. Weddle and Thompson, who are "chained" to their computers writing, are unable to attend.

The group stands in the hallway for a few minutes talking about "Profit and Lace," the *DS9* episode that will finish shooting that evening. Then the conversation segues to the inevitable topic of the impending end of the season.

"We've got one episode shooting," Behr notes, "and one about to start shooting. There's one ready to prep, and there's the one we're about to break. And that's it." He looks at his staff. "So let's do it."

Julie Gesin, an intern assigned to the series for a six-week period, joins them as the writers are settling into their favorite seats in Behr's office, which, for all intents and purposes, is very similar to the office of Jeri Taylor, his *Voyager* counterpart, down on the first floor. Sofa, chairs, and a beat board.

Gesin stations herself in front of the board, ready to write. The board is not blank. Several beats defining the Teaser had been written there during a short meeting the day before. And in the lower right corner, a series of disconnected thoughts and ideas wait to be inserted where needed.

In a way, the notes on the board take the place of the absent beat sheet. "The creative process is sometimes erratic, so we put those little notes off to one side," Hans Beimler explains. "They're bases that we might want to touch, scenes or snippets of scenes, or insights that people have. But since we don't know the story's infrastructure yet, we don't have them in the right order."

In a nutshell, here's the very rough storyline the writers think they're about to "beat" into submission: Sisko and some of his crew are off-station in the *Defiant*, fighting the Dominion near a "biogenic plant" (its properties and importance never really explained) that is protected by a defensive grid. Dukat steals a shuttle or a ship and then steals an Orb, either from Bajor or from the station. He takes that Orb into the wormhole and somehow uses it or a chroniton bomb to blow up the wormhole aliens, also known as the Prophets. Upon discovering Dukat's plan, Jadiza follows him, getting killed somehow in the process. How Dukat would escape is also unresolved.

The session begins. The writers have been discussing this storyline for so long, at lunches and myriad meetings for earlier stories, that it seems almost as if they are pulling thoughts from one another's minds. To the visitor graciously permitted to attend (sans camera, of course; that would have been too intrusive), the conversation sounds oddly disjointed, full of half-spoken thoughts that everyone except the visitor seems to understand.

And like the notes in the corner of the beat board, those thoughts are not in any particular order. In fact, although it was one of the last elements to enter the storyline and it won't happen until the end of the episode, the death of Jadzia is first and foremost in everybody's minds.

"Write Dax's name at the beginning of Act One," Behr says. Throughout, the writers will continue to refer to the character as Dax, even though Dax—but not Jadzia—will survive the events of the episode. Behr opts to introduce a key story element at random, knowing that he'll figure out a place for it later on. "Dukat steals an Orb. The audience will invest in it. They know Dukat. They don't have to see it."

The discussion immediately shifts to a different point in time. Dukat somehow kills Dax in the wormhole. Ron Moore considers this, and then speaks up. "Perhaps Dax stays on the station," he says. "That sounds like the most uninteresting thing, but then we can cut back and have her killed in a firefight there."

Ira Steven Behr and Hans Beimler, the writers of "Tears of the Prophets," take in the ambience of one of their favorite sets. In the background, Louis Race listens to P.J. Earnest, an additional assistant director brought in to help handle all the extras used in the episode. ROBBIE ROBINSON.

"Her death will be meaningless unless she's helping to save someone's life," suggests René Echevarria. "We've already seen the pointless death of Tasha Yar (in *TNG*'s "Skin of Evil"), the ironic death of James Kirk (in *Star Trek Generations*) . . ." His point made, his voice trails off and he allows the thought to lie fallow.

"Where is Bashir?" Behr asks abruptly. Obviously, if he were in the same location as Jadiza, the doctor would attempt to save her life. Before the writers go to script, decisions will need to be made that place every character in an appropriate and strategic location during key scenes.

Now Behr returns to Echevarria's earlier comment. "If she saves Worf, it will feel 'written'," he points out. "It will feel like a writer's convention."

"But she's got to save *somebody*," Echevarria insists.

"In what way does her death have to resonate?" Behr queries, looking at each of the writers. "With a scene where Sisko and Worf find her? Or with us [the audience] seeing her die saving someone?"

"Have her save someone," Beimler responds. "Or save some*thing*. The station."

"Have her save something that is part of the plot," Echevarria joins in. "Like a puppy," he jokes. "Or the Orb."

"I want us to *see* her die, not just hear about her death in dialogue," Behr asserts. Moore agrees.

Character motivation is always a big part of beat session discussions, but there were never any doubts that Dukat was capable of murdering Jadzia. Despite episodes where the writers seemed to "humanize" the character by adding sympathetic facets to his personality, "Dukat was *always* a Nazi and was *always* evil," according to Hans Beimler. ROBBIE ROBINSON.

The room grows quiet, and after a moment Behr breaks the silence. "Let this be a lesson to all of us," he intones gravely. "Remember when we were thinking we'd kill O'Brien because we thought that Colm [Meaney] wasn't coming back?"

Rumors are always circulating in Hollywood that this actor or that actor may not return to a series, and *Star Trek* is no exception. In Meaney's case, the actor's burgeoning motion-picture career, in both the U.S.A.

and his native Ireland, have led to the frequent hypothetical discussions along the lines of "What would we do if...?" during his tenure on *Deep Space Nine*.

"It is not easy to kill a character!" Behr says, concluding his brief lecture.

Later, Behr would wax more philosophical on the subject. "We had many discussions about what constitutes a heroic death and stuff like that," he says. "There were a lot of clichés to try to avoid. And some clichés that were necessary; clichés become clichés because they do speak the truth. So it was a minefield we had to go through. It's much easier talking about a scene with special effects—you know, why we would choose this battle scene or why we would choose to shoot the battle with these ships rather than those ships. Then you get a rinky-dink discussion that's filled with specifics. But we're in deep waters here. We're talking about the death of a lead character on a television show and how and why this way and not that way."

Back in the room, the writers are still pondering the end of Jadzia. The process is a little like fishing, with one writer throwing out an idea and hoping the others will respond to the bait. "Does Dukat blow up Jadzia's shuttle when she's chasing him?" Behr asks.

"What if he just **kills** her?" Moore says. It's more of a statement than a question. Trust Moore, the man who killed K'Ehleyr (in *TNG*'s "Reunion"), James T. Kirk (in *Generations*), and Vedek Bareil (in *DS9*'s "Life Support"), to cut right to the chase.

No one responds. There is a brief moment of quiet. Very brief.

"Coffee!" Echevarria shouts abruptly, glancing at his watch. He stands, switches on a window-mounted air-conditioning unit, and leaves the room to attend a scheduled meeting with Co-Supervising Producer Steve Oster.

Behr isn't happy. "If we take the Dax equation out of it, we have the perfect story," he states. "We kill the wormhole aliens."

"We've got to kill *her*," Moore reminds him. "She must die nobly. She must be killed by our big villain. And he must succeed in his plan."

"Or," Beimler wonders aloud, "does he just **kill** her?"

Behr recalls an idea that Beimler had previously suggested. "What if we just go to the station, and Dax is already a prisoner, firing is going on, Dukat takes her to the temple, and then he kills her."

Suddenly Ron Moore is animated. "We'd need to see her get captured," he says emphatically.

Behr ponders. "That adds a whole other layer of failure."

"The two things that you need are for her to be smart and for her to do some kick-ass action," Beimler observes.

"What if she's wounded?" Behr asks. "And Dukat says, 'How're you doing?' She says, 'I'll live.' He says, 'No you won't.'"

The other writers like it.

"That'll work."

"Great."

"Okay," Behr says.

They move on to other issues. The biggest problems are in deciding which set to use for each scene, and how to get all of the characters into the story. "We've got to have Jake in this episode," Behr says, sounding worried. "It's the final episode of the season. But there's no way to get Rom into it. I feel bad for Max [Grodénchik]."

"Maybe we can have him there when Dax dies," Moore suggests.

"Have we done anything with Kira or Garak?" Behr asks.

Moore says they haven't.

"Then take Dax out of the first act and put Kira in there instead," Behr says. "That'll be cool."

There is another segue in the conversation, and Behr reflects on the current status of Starfleet and the Federation, which have reached a point to which no other incarnation of *Star Trek* has ever aspired. Not even the Borg painted our heroes into such a tight corner—at least not for an effort that threatened to go on as long as the Vietnam war. "We have committed ourselves to a costly and lengthy struggle," Behr notes.

"Victory or death," states Moore.

"That's it! Victory or death!" Behr repeats, happier. "Now it's starting to sound like an end-of-season story!"

The breaking process commences, and the notes that were listed on the lower right side of the board are integrated into the story columns, divided by acts, one by one. For the fourth beat of Act Two, Behr decides, "This is the place to have Dax say she's not leaving the station." He dictates a scene that has Dax and Kira walking to an airlock to meet Garak. For now, the war will go on without her.

As they go over the second beat of Act Three, Ron Moore gets nostalgic. "This is going to be our last Sisko/Dax, 'Old Man, what'll I do?' scene." However, the evolution of the script will prove him wrong. There *will* be one additional "Old Man, what'll I do?" scene, although the conversation will be poignantly one-sided.

By 5:20 P.M., three acts are laid out on the board and it seems like a good point to stop. The meeting is called to a close and the writers go back to their other duties.

STORMING THE BEACH

AT 4:00 P.M. THE NEXT DAY, BEHR AND BEIMIER START AGAIN. ALTHOUGH THEIR STORY IS SET DUR-ING THE TWENTY-FOURTH CENTURY, THEIR THOUGHTS ARE FOCUSED ON WORLD WAR II. "Missing in action" are Weddle and Thompson, who are apparently casualties of war, as is Moore. Echevarria will join the assault later. For now, it's just the two veterans, which is somehow fitting since they're the ones who will actually be writing the script.

"How do we get into Act Four?" Behr asks. He and Beimler launch into a discussion about D Day, the historic date in 1944 when the allied forces began the invasion of France, and the conversations that took place at the French city of Calais prior to the Battle of Normandy. After a while, however, it becomes apparent that some of the discussion focuses not on the actual historical battle, but on Hollywood's Oscar®-winning re-creation of the events in *The Longest Day*.

No great surprise. Behr is an avid classic-film buff, with a particular fondness for *The Wild Bunch* and *The Magnificent Seven*, as astute viewers of *Deep Space Nine* may have already guessed. Over the years, the show's writ-ers have played with riffs that provide homage to everything from *Brigadoon* to *The Godfather*. Actual historical events, too, have frequently inspired the writers.

"It's not that we use them as blueprints," explains Beimler. "It's more like, if you don't learn the lessons from history, you're condemned to repeat them. So you have to take details from history and use them as a starting point. If you understand the dynamics of those details, then you can move on to your own dynamics. We're not trying to duplicate D Day, or *The Longest Day* or anything like that. But that doesn't mean that we don't think about *The Longest Day* while we're writing, and thinking about why the events in there played out in a certain way."

Back in the war room, Behr begins rethinking the earlier acts. "Do we have the scenes in the Teaser in the right order?" he wonders. "Maybe we should have the Rommel scene at the top."

Another World War II reference. Rommel was a famous German field marshal, particularly well known for his military strategies in northern Africa's Sahara Desert.

Behr hops over to a different detail. "I don't think we need the defensive grid. We need a border. We need to find the weakest point in the border."

Seconds later, he changes his mind. "No, let me take that back. We don't need the biogenic plant. We'll keep the defensive grid."

The clock is ticking, and they're wasting too much time on the nitty-gritty. Realizing this, Behr gets a wicked gleam in his eye. "Sisko should say, 'We've got to move before cancellation!'"

Then it's immediately back to business. "Julie," he says to the intern writing at the board, "go back and take out any mention of the biogenic plant."

He returns to an earlier question. "So how do we start Act Four? We'll have a lot of cleaning up to do in Act Five, so we've got to think of Act Four as the usual Act Five."

"But is it too soon?" Beimler wonders. "I'm afraid we may lose the tension."

Behr considers. "One problem is that the defensive grid may be too much like the minefields. And another problem is that we're not worried about a defensive grid around a planet, we're talking about a defensive grid in space! How do you *not* get around a defensive grid in space?" He thinks for a few seconds. "This sounds like a job for Andre Bormanis," he says, referring to the science advisor for both *Deep Space Nine* and *Voyager*.

At that moment, reinforcements arrive. Or, rather, reinforcement. René Echevarria sits down and immediately enters into a discussion about the undefined defensive grid. Does it fence off one planet? Three planets? Does it matter? What if Weyoun takes his fleet away before the grid goes up?

And then, an epiphany! Forget about a defensive grid—make it a defensive *platform*! In fact, *lots* of defensive platforms. Suddenly Behr gets excited about the potential for optical shots of these defensive platforms.

The excitement is contagious. "Can they spin?" Echevarria asks enthusiastically.

And how about the platforms *shooting out rays…*?

The line of conversation doesn't really advance the story, but it serves to inspire the writers, stirring up their collective imagination, which is as important as anything else. "Okay, we can move forward now," Behr says. It's 5:05 P.M.

"We've got to show the battle," Beimler says emphatically.

Behr follows Beimler's line of thought. "Some of our ships get through the lines of defense. Then the platforms come on-line."

It's writing time. Julie Gesin gets up to return to the board, marker in hand.

"Okay," Behr dictates. "Beat One. Dominion briefing room." And Gesin starts writing:

ACT 4 -

1) Int. Dominion Briefing Room

      Weyoun and Damar. "Federation's attacking, what do we do?"

      "Put the defensive grid up."

2) Ext. Space.

3) Int. Defiant.

      Sisko on the bridge. 1st ships entering defense grid, going though very little resistance.

      Suddenly the defensive grid comes on-line.

4) Ext. Space.

      The Battle of Hans 666.

      Intercut with:

```
         Int. Defiant Bridge.
         The battle raging.
5) Ext. Space, Runabout.
6) Int. Runabout.
         Kira & Garak spot Dukat's ship and give chase.
         Intercut with:
         Ext. Space.
         Runabout firing at Dukat's ship, disabling it.
7) Int. Runabout.
         We bash up Dukat's ship. Beam him over, he won't surrender.
```

"What do we do now?" Behr asks. "This is a big act."

"Cutting away from the battle for a long time would be bad," Beimler warns.

"What's the objective here now?" Echevarria asks. "To get us to Deep Space 9?"

There has to be some communication with the station now, they decide. But should the crew call the station, or should the station call them?

"Kira calls the station to say, 'We've been snookered!'" Behr suggests. "And the station responds, 'No kidding!'"

Or something to that effect. Behr's phrasing for the station's response is actually a bit more colorful, but definitely wouldn't make it past the censors.

Echevarria is satisfied with Behr's suggestion, but Beimler is not. "When Hawaii was being attacked by the Japanese, it was Hawaii that made the call to Washington," he points out. "That's the historical reality."

Echevarria smiles. "This is a very small point that you two should work at incessantly while you're writing the script."

"Yes," Behr agrees, "but watching you guys argue is fun. It's just like old times." He moves on. "Okay. It's not Dukat that they've been chasing. They call the station. There's no answer."

Behr starts dictating again:

```
8) Int. DS9.
```

Behr stops. "Where would this be?" he asks. "The cargo bay?"

"Ops," Echevarria answers.

```
         We see a flashing panel as a body falls over it. Dax is there as
         they shoot down Jem'Hadar attackers. Dax talks on comline to
         Odo, who is down in the docking ring corridor.
9) Int. Docking Ring Corridor.
         Odo tells Dax they have the Jem'Hadar contained. Neither of
         them can figure out a reason for this attack. What is the
         objective?
```

"What happens?" Echevarria interupts. "Is this where she's gonna get killed?"

Absolutely the last "Old Man, what'll I do?" scene in *Deep Space Nine* . . . or is it? If a relationship can extend over two lifetimes, why not three? "We're already talking about the seventh season, and there's plenty of juice we're going to get from a new Dax," says Behr. ROBBIE ROBINSON.

Behr nods. "Yes. And the audience is gonna buy it. Beat Ten."

"Wait." Beimler stops Behr. "I think we should see Dax go down a corridor with a gun first."

"Is she down in the docking ring?" Echevarria asks.

"Okay," Behr agrees. "We'll change Beat Nine. Dax says, 'I'll send out a search team.' Now we won't need the scene with Odo. Julie, erase everything from the middle of Scene Eight."

And once again the conversation turns to the subject of Dax's death. Do we see her die? Should she get to say good-bye? Should the crew just find the cadaver?

"There's more to play if she and Sisko *don't* have a final scene," Beimler comments.

"But I think that cheats the audience," Behr answers. For the next ten minutes they discuss the dramatic potential of each choice. Finally, Echevarria sides with Beimler, although he will recant that decision later on.

Back to Beat Eight:

> Dax realizes they've turned off the internal sensors. They figure out that the attackers
> had another purpose.
> 9) Int. Promenade.
> Dax, weapon in hand, moves down empty Promenade.

10) <u>Int. Temple.</u>

            She finds Dukat taking Orb.

"Oy veh! This is big!" Behr likes what is being created. "I think we should have ninety minutes for the final episode!"

Jem'Hadar get the jump on her. Dukat stabs Dax.

And that ends Act Four.

"Does the audience know yet why Dukat is stealing an Orb?" Echevarria asks. The writers discuss it. It must be made clear.

    ACT 5 -

"So where are we going?" Behr asks. "To the battle?"

"Yes," Echevarria and Beimler respond in unison.

1) <u>Ext. Space - Defiant.</u>

            The battle continues. We gain the upper hand. Sisko hears
            that Starfleet troops have landed on Cardassian planet. Bring
            in more ships.

Behr stops to make a mental note. "We've got to call Andre Bormanis in the morning and tell him we're going to use these defensive platforms and have him find a weakness that we can exploit in the battle."

            We've got to establish a beachhead.

2) <u>Int. Dominion Briefing Room.</u>

            Damar and Weyoun react to this major defeat.

3) <u>Ext. Space. Wormhole.</u>

            Dukat's ship flies into the wormhole.

4) <u>Int. Dukat's ship (whatever that ship is).</u>

            Dukat opens Orb box.

5) <u>Int. Orb experience.</u>

            a. Dominion briefing room.
            b. Temple.
            c. Ops/Captain's office.
            Dukat meets with wormhole aliens. They expected him. He
            takes out a chroniton bomb.

    The writers pause to discuss how the Prophets would appear to Dukat. Another reinforcement arrives as Ron Moore enters the room, but Hans Beimler has to go.

6) <u>Int. Dukat's ship.</u>

As Dukat comes out of the wormhole --

The Orb is destroyed in the box.

The wormhole destabilizing.

7) Ext. Wormhole.

Dukat comes zipping out.

Cut to:

Something occurs to Behr. He instructs Gesin, "At the end of Beat One of Act Five, put this in: 'Sisko gets a call from DS9.'"

They go back to where they left off.

8) Int. Promenade.

Sisko and Worf grimly come to Infirmary. Met by Kira, who

says, "She's still in surgery. Captain, there's something I want

you to see."

9) Int. Temple.

The Orbs have melted. The wormhole is gone. The monks are

crying. The gods are dead. The Prophets are no more.

"Can we go to Worf screaming, 'NOOOO!'" Behr asks. "Can we get away with that?"

"Yes," answers Ron Moore. "We need the Promenade to be burning, Worf screaming, the whole nine yards."

A shattered Sisko exits to:

10) The Promenade.

Sisko comes out into the smoky room, rushes to the Infirmary.

11) Infirmary.

Sisko rushes in, finds Worf over Dax's dead body.

Behr pauses and the three writers discuss how to end the last scene. They decide to put Sisko into civilian clothing.

12) Int. Promenade.

We hear Sisko at beginning of his last Captain's Log. He has

resigned from Starfleet.

13) Ops.

Sisko in civies, carrying his stuff out of Captain's Office. Says

good-bye to troops. Refuses to change his mind. Turns the station over to

Major Kira.

14) Ext. Deep Space Nine.

We see a small shuttle leaving the station.

The time is 6:45 P.M. Not counting all the conversations that have taken place since September, the two break sessions ran a total of five hours and five minutes. The story is complicated. And big. And filled with phenomenal visual-effects opticals that will undoubtedly be very costly and very time-consuming.

The people responsible for making sure that everything on the show comes in on time and under budget will be pushed to the limit in the next few weeks, particularly with some key members of the staff, like Supervising Producer Peter Lauritson, devoting a great deal of their time to *Star Trek: Insurrection*. Taking a last glance at the beat board as the writers drift out of his office, Behr can only shake his head. "Wow," he says. "Steve Oster is going to be a very nervous man."

BEHIND THE LINES

TWO DAYS LATER, BEHR AND BEIMLER ARE HARD AT WORK ON THE TELEPLAY, WHICH IS MOVING FARTHER AND FARTHER AFIELD FROM THE NOTES ON THE BEAT BOARD. "Everything is becoming very, very different," comments Behr.

Is that unusual?

Not really, according to Beimler. "You think that once you put it on the board you have it, but every story changes once you get into it," he says. "It happens when you're writing the dialogue, or when you really start to think about the structure."

"You sit down and you look at it," concurs Behr, "and you say, wait a second, wait a second. This isn't right. This is too much. Or it's not concise and clear enough. Or it's not audience-friendly enough. Or it's not truthful enough. Or it doesn't go down a narrative path that takes the audience where we want them to go. A person can go in with a broken beat sheet that supposedly gives him license to sit down and dash out sixty pages, and look at it and say, 'Hell, no! This works, and this, and this kind of works, but I'm gonna change *this*.' That's the key to the well-developed television writer. Your instincts have to take over when you're alone with the script. Your *true* instincts."

Scriptwriting, concludes Beimler, is "a continuing process. An evolving process."

And that process will move into yet another phase once he and Behr deliver the first draft of the script to the rest of the writing staff and receive their comments.

GROUP THERAPY

FOR A WRITER WHO PERCEIVED EVERY WORD THAT HE HAD PAINSTAKINGLY COMMITTED TO PAPER AS PERFECTION, THE "NOTES" PERIOD AT *DEEP SPACE NINE* WOULD BE AKIN TO SPENDING TIME ON THE LOWEST LEVELS OF HELL.

Fortunately, the *prima donna* quotient within the writing staff seems to be relatively low. Notes are a way of life. Everybody gives 'em. Everybody gets 'em. And everybody appreciates them.

Notes are exactly what they sound like: comments and suggestions penned or penciled into the margins of the distributed scripts. "What the writer is primarily interested in," says Weddle, "is what *isn't* working for us, and whether we have any suggestions."

Notes may consist of dialogue changes, ways to streamline the plot, or solutions to gnarly technical problems. The primary emphasis is on constructive criticism; good penmanship ranks a lot lower. "Sometimes you can't even read the handwriting," Beimler says and laughs. "But you know that person wrote a note so he must have something to say. Then you have to go down to the person's office and say, 'Hey . . .'"

Notes may be given verbally as well. "Usually, we have a meeting of the whole gang after we get a first draft," says Beimler. "And if Ira doesn't feel the second draft is close enough, we'll have another meeting. Once it starts getting close, though, the individual writers just have impromptu one-on-one meetings."

After a week of writing, March 30, Behr and Beimler distribute their first draft of a teleplay with the temporary title, "Tears of the Gods," to Echevarria, Moore, Weddle, Thompson, and Creative Consultant Michael Piller. Aside from the fact that Jadiza dies, there is little that will not go through major changes.

In this early draft, Dukat has an Orb that he has stolen from Deep Space 9 and a chroniton generator (as opposed to the chroniton bomb mentioned on the beat board). After flying

"We liked the idea of these two people talking about a future, to show that this relationship was solid," says Ira Behr. ROBBIE ROBINSON.

into the wormhole, he opens the Orb and confronts the Prophets. Then he activates the generator, which begins to kill the Prophets in much the same way as the Keiko/Pah-wraith intended in a previous episode, "The Assignment."

In the meantime, Dax finds that Dukat has stolen the Orb and follows him into the wormhole, leading to a scene that Echevarria recalls clearly. "Dax beams into Dukat's ship and sees the open Orb case," he recounts. "Then we return to Dukat's point of view, from within this disorienting Orb experience, in which he's being approached by the various Prophets in human form. The Sisko/Prophet approaches Dukat and says, 'What are you doing? You're killing us,' and Dax approaches to say something Prophet-like. Then she punches him and you realize that it's not a Prophet at all," he says, laughing at the thought of the unproduced scene. "It was a neat gag. She punches him and *sets him down*. So basically, Dax manages to stop Dukat from killing the Prophets completely, but she gets killed in the process. That was the first draft. The story changed a lot in the second."

There were other aspects of the draft, however, that the writers didn't like, key among them the manner in which Dax died. Michael Piller, the former executive producer of *Deep Space Nine*, pointed out in no uncertain terms that the two writers had not given Jadzia—a character he had helped to create—"a worthy death and a worthy send-off." As Piller recalls, "While they're in 'Prophetland,' Dukat kills Dax with a phaser blast, or a disrupter blast, and I felt that they had missed an opportunity for drama and for the emotional impact of her death. It felt rushed, and you really lost the chance for the good-bye scene that would leave the audience choked up."

Piller's comments might have struck a bell with Ron Moore, who, along with writing partner Brannon Braga, had received similar criticism about the original way that they dispatched Captain Kirk in *Star Trek Generations*. A scene in which Kirk was shot in the back by his nemesis was deemed too "unheroic" for *Star Trek*'s legions of loyal fans, so the scene was rewritten and reshot prior to the release of the film. But at least this time the change would be made *before* the death was committed to film.

Behr was philosophical about the response. "We were throwing it out there, as we often do, to the voices, to hear what the feedback is," he says. "It's always a dicey thing. There are times when I trust my instincts completely in terms of what makes a good tale, and in those instances, I will forever believe that my choices were right, whether they get the response I want or not, and whether they're executed well on stage or not. But the death of a leading character is less about instinct than about market research, in a manner of speaking. So it's not only about what's right to Ira Behr, it's about what's going to please the people. So we threw it at the group and we had no big jones about holding on to it or not."

So the manner of Jadzia's death began to evolve and would not complete that evolution for some time. In the meantime, there were other details to deal with. "The story that we'd come up with in the break session was kind of clunky and complicated," admits Echevarria. "It had so many plot threads going on. Dukat had to get a shuttle, a chroniton generator, an Orb—all of those things that he needed. And I recall that Ron Moore finally said, 'Couldn't this have to do with the Pah-wraiths? Wouldn't it be much simpler if all Dukat has to do is help the Pah-wraiths get into the wormhole?'"

That really pared the story down, notes Echevarria. After that, it was simply a matter of asking the right questions. Such as, "What if Dukat goes to Cardassia to say, 'I need a Bajoran artifact,' and then he lets a Pah-wraith into his body, transports it to where the Orb is on the station, and *boom!*"

"It was much simpler," says Echevarria. "And it tracked better with what we'd seen in both 'The Assignment' and in 'The Reckoning.' It has a more mythic feel than a tech thing would."

Beimler agrees. "It never felt right, even at the break session. Ira was never content with the notion. It was all too mechanical, all comings and goings in spacecraft. It didn't have the kind of mythic proportions that we were looking for. So it really ended up being a bookmark until we found something we liked a lot better."

Once again Behr and Beimler locked themselves in Behr's office, this time to simplify the script. "Finding the story during the break session, with all those voices in the room, has ups and downs, but the ups far outweigh the downs," Behr relates. "Still, there's a certain amount of *quiet* when you're away from that room. And when I work with someone, be it Hans or whomever, that quiet is still there, because it's two minds on the same wavelength. They used to say that Laurel and Hardy were two minds without a single thought. Well, Hans and I are two minds with only *a* single thought. So we're one up on Laurel and Hardy, but just one."

The notes session had a productive effect. "We just said, 'Okay. Screw it. Forget about the stealing of the

Orb and all that stuff. Who cares how he steals the Orb?' We realized that with the Pah-wraiths we didn't even need an Orb to get where we wanted to go. And there was something nice about having Gul Dukat, the butcher, be the guy who's suddenly into the Bajoran religion and who learns which little statuette to crack open to get a Pah-wraith to fly up his nose. Once we went with that, that part of the story just fell together."

THE PRODUCTION MEETING

ON APRIL 8, AT 3:30 P.M., THE PRODUCTION MEETING FOR *DS9*'S SEASON FINALE IS ABOUT TO BEGIN. As producers and department heads enter the spacious room, they look around curiously. The setting is unfamiliar to some. Their usual meeting place is a conference room in the Cooper Building, located on the west end of the lot. But that room is booked, so the Production Meeting has been relocated to an available conference room of appropriate size.

This is the boardroom for the Marathon Office Building (MOB), the newest building on the lot, and it is usually filled with executives from the Motion Picture Marketing Department, which is based in the building. Unlike some of the conference rooms in the older buildings allocated for production use, the boardroom of MOB has no thumbtack holes in the walls, no metal folding chairs, and no noisy window air conditioners.

No one seems to miss those accoutrements, however. As far as conference rooms go, this one has its charms. The most noteworthy feature of the room is a huge conference table in the shape of an open-ended rectangle, a solid wood tabletop inlaid with mahogany strips. Dozens of black leather chairs on casters line both the outer and inner perimeter of the U. At one end of the room is a wall full of state-of-the-art audio-visual equipment; at the other end, a kitchenette is tucked inconspicuously behind a swinging door.

The conference table can easily accommodate sixty people. For once there'll be elbow room and chairs for everyone at the Production Meeting.

Several of the attendees straggle in a few minutes late. MOB is located on the far east side of the lot, nearly a half mile away from the *Star Trek* offices. But no one is complaining about the walk. In fact, many appreciate spending the extra minutes outdoors. Today the sun is shining and the sky is bright blue. It's a perfect spring day in Southern California and for the moment, all thoughts of the season's unrelenting *El Niño*–driven storms have been forgotten.

In front of each attendee lies a copy of the season closer's final draft, which is dated April 8, 1998. Above the date is the episode's new title: "Tears of the Prophets." The title was Beimler's idea, and he came up with it "the usual way," he laughs. Which is to say that he sought inspiration in poetry books, *Bartlett's Book of Quotations*, and so forth. After coming up with approximately a dozen candidates, he walked into Behr's office and read him the list. The winner was "Tears of the Prophets," a title that readily harkens back to an ominous prophecy in "The Reckoning" that predicted "the Prophets will weep."

Coordinating Producer Robert della Santina kicks off the meeting with a short speech. "Thank you for the season," he says, reminding everyone that this is the last time they'll meet together until after their summer hiatus.

Ira Behr immediately picks up the sentiment. "We really appreciate the job you all do," he says, scanning the faces of his staff. "You amaze me sometimes. Even when some of the group goes away to work on the movie (*Star Trek: Insurrection*, of course, but everyone knows what he means), the rest of you just step right in and we go on. Thank you. And I can't wait until next season."

The Production Meeting, where ways to create an exciting episode are balanced against keeping the budget under the gross national product of a small country. With the spectacular space-battle sequences planned for "Tears," an effort is made to use stock (previously filmed) visual-effects shots for simpler scenes. Thus, for the Siskos' departure from DS9 in Scene 93, the effects team decides to reuse a shot of the station from the series's title treatment and combine it with an image of a shuttlecraft. *From left to right:* Steve Oster, Hans Beimler, Ira Behr, Allan Kroeker, Louis Race, and Dan Curry. ROBBIE ROBINSON.

As with a number of positions on the series (such as the composers, visual-effects teams, and scenic artists) the job of first assistant director typically alternates with odd and even-numbered shows. Louis Race serves in that capacity for production #550, aka "Tears of the Prophets." His counterpart, B.C. Cameron, is hard at work on #549, "The Sound of Her Voice." Race begins reading the script's descriptive exposition paragraphs aloud, prepared to pause whenever anyone has questions or suggestions. Some of the suggestions will be applied to the final product; some won't. In fact, although this is designated the "final draft," some of the scenes that Race reads will be quite different by the time the show airs.

As it turns out, the first suggestion is Race's own. And it's on the very first line.

FADE IN:

1. <u>INT. BAJORAN SHRINE</u>

CLOSE ON a happy, eight year-old Bajoran girl, as she runs up
to Kira.

Scenic Artist Denise Okuda (second from left) asks what will be on the wall monitor in the Dominion briefing room. Ira Behr observes that Damar's line, "I believe you owe me an apology," demands an intriguing visual. The Art Department will design an animated schematic of Federation forces getting creamed by the newly activated weapon platforms. *Left to right:* Laura Richarz, Okuda, Joe Longo, and Gary Monak. ROBBIE ROBINSON.

"I think we should have more children," Race says.

Steve Oster, who is present, in part, to make decisions regarding the production's budget, nods his approval. It's not as simple a decision as it seems, and Oster doesn't make it lightly. Adding more children to the scene will have an impact on more than one shooting day, so the decision is an expensive one.

"I try to be efficient and group together elements that cost money," Race explains later. "When we have scenes with a lot of extras, I try to schedule them so that they'll all shoot the same day." But working with children, whose employment by film and television productions is strictly controlled by California labor laws, is a different matter, he points out. "They can only work a certain amount of time, so I try to schedule no more than one scene with them on any given day." Scene 1 takes place in the Bajoran Temple, while Scene 83, an additional scene featuring Sahgi, the "happy Bajoran girl," takes place on the Promenade. A "company move"—which involves rolling all the equipment to a new location—can take anywhere from ten minutes to five or six hours. "Shooting the Temple and then moving to the location in the Promenade on the same day would have been very difficult," says Race, "so it was actually more efficient to pay the money and bring them back." And obviously, bringing back one child would be cheaper than bringing back several, but the quality of the scene comes first. Sahgi will be given her costly playmates.

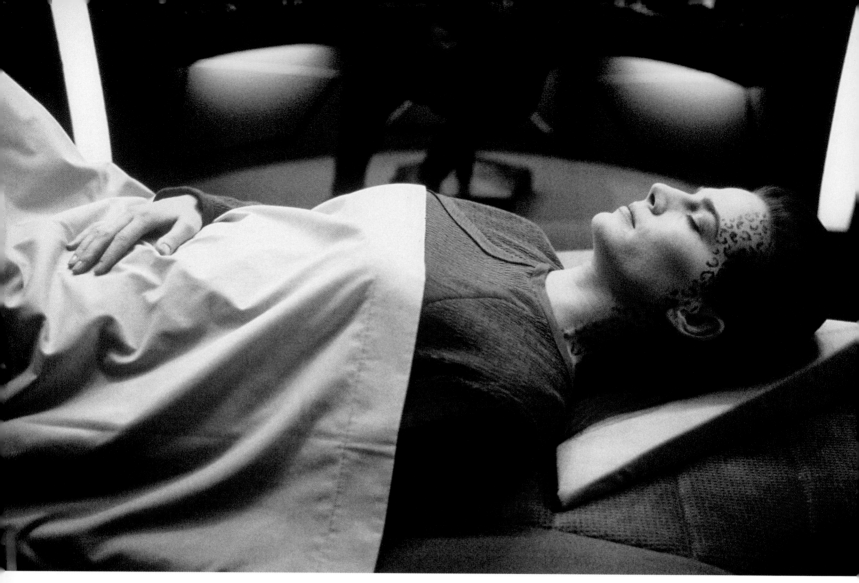

Jadzia will get a few more minutes of life to say "one poignant line" to Worf. Behr and Beimler opt to pull a story thread from the subplot regarding Jadzia's desire to have a child with her husband. ROBBIE ROBINSON.

Race continues reading, with members of the staff periodically asking questions. What wardrobe should the celebrating Bajorans be wearing? (Fancy festival garb.) Will the first scene be backlit? (Yes.) What does the medal that Ross awards to Sisko look like? (It's supposed to look like Christopher Pike, but whether or not it will look like Jeffrey Hunter is undecided; in any event, it will never end up on camera.)

In the middle of Scene 8, Visual Effects Producer Dan Curry notes a line of dialogue in which O'Brien tells Sisko that he "notices something strange" about the warp signatures of the Dominion's bigger ships, the cruisers and the destroyers. "There are no established Dominion destroyers yet," Curry points out.

Behr considers this for a moment. Finally he says, simply, "Okay." There will be a later discussion regarding this detail, but the scene will ultimately be dropped from the episode for other reasons.

A moment later, Behr himself brings up a detail that he doesn't want anyone to miss. During this early scene in the Captain's office, Sisko's baseball must be in plain sight. "It is very important here," he stresses, and notes are taken by the appropriate members of the staff.

The process continues, script line by line. When they reach Scene 20, where the Starfleet and Klingon

"TEARS OF THE PROPHETS" DAY O/O DAYS CAST													Report created Wed, Apr 8, 1998					Page 1
April — Day of Month:	13	14	15	16	17	18	19	20	21	22		Rehearse	Travel	Work	Hold	Holiday	Loop	Start	Finish	TOTAL
Day Of Week:	M	Tu	W	Th	F	Sa	Su	M	Tu	W										
Shooting Days:	1	2	3	4	5			6	7	8										
0. ...																				
1. SISKO	SW	W	W	W	W			W	WF					7				4/13	4/21	7
2. KIRA			SW	W	W			W	WF					5				4/15	4/21	5
3. O'BRIEN	SW	W	W	W	W			WF						6				4/13	4/20	6
4. BASHIR		SW	H	W	W			WF						4	1			4/14	4/20	5
5. DAX		SW	H	W	W			H	WF					4	2			4/14	4/21	6
6. ODO					SW			W	WF					3				4/17	4/21	3
7. QUARK				SW	WF									2				4/16	4/17	2
8. WORF	SW	W	W	W	WF									5				4/13	4/17	5
9. JAKE		SW	W	W	H			WF						4	1			4/14	4/20	5
10. GARAK	SW	H	WF											2	1			4/13	4/15	3
11. DUKAT									SW	WF				2				4/21	4/22	2
12. WEYOUN										SWF				1				4/22	4/22	1
13. DAMAR										SWF				1				4/22	4/22	1
14. VIC				SWF										1				4/16	4/16	1
15. NOG			SWF											1				4/15	4/15	1
16. MARTOK	SW	W	H	WF										3	1			4/13	4/16	4
17. ROSS	SW	W	H	WF										3	1			4/13	4/16	4
23k. SAGHI (k)					SW			H	WF					2	1			4/17	4/21	3
24. LETANT	SW	W	H	WF										3	1			4/13	4/16	4
25. GLINN										SWF				1				4/22	4/22	1

TENTATIVE

A preliminary "Day Out of Days" schedule is put together for the cast on April 8. This will give the actors a loose idea of the day they will start work (abbreviated as SW) and finish (WF). Some characters, like Weyoun, Damar, and Vic Fontaine, will film all of their scenes in one day (noted as SWF, for start-work-finish). Days off: H for On Hold.

brass meet with a Romulan delegation, Race produces a stack of Polaroids, shots of extras. "How many people are in the room?" he asks.

"Twelve," Behr decides.

"So I'll bring in fifteen to look at," Race says, as Behr glances through the photos.

"The Romulans should be told how to act Romulan," Behr mentions. "No chuckling. They are clearly arrogant."

Director Allan Kroeker, seated next to Behr, listens intently, but doesn't speak up until they reach Scene 22, which is set in the holosuite's Las Vegas Lounge program. "It's going to be a challenge not to have the whole set there," Allan Kroeker says, disappointment in his voice.

While the set is not described in the script, Kroeker is astute enough to realize that the single scene does not warrant decorating the back walls and filling the bar with patrons. The disappointment is personal. Although Kroeker has directed a number of *DS9* episodes, his avowed favorite is "His Way," in which both the lounge and its star performer, Vic Fontaine, were introduced.

The call sheet for the fourth day of filming. A makeup and hair note indicates that Worf should let his hair down in Scene 85—as was described in the April 8 version of the script—but the practical considerations of having him unbraid his wig on-camera after Jadzia dies proved too great. A wardrobe note mentioning that Bashir should be in tuxedo for the scene at Vic's Las Vegas Lounge would not be realized either.

"We can fly her easily," comments Special Effects Coordinator Gary Monak. "The ceiling to the Temple set opens up. And the wires are already installed on the top of the stage."

At this point, Stunt Coordinator Dennis "Danger" Madalone becomes animated. They've entered his arena. "And we can *slam* Dax to the floor, too," he says, "because we have a great look-alike double who likes this kind of stunt."

"Yes, that slam is important," Behr agrees. "But I don't want her spinning up there. No Busby Berkeley," he says, referring to the well-known director's elaborately staged dance numbers. "And no *Exorcist*," Behr adds, although whether he's referring to that film's levitation sequence or the "spinning" of the central character's head is not clear.

"Okay," Race summarizes. "We'll fly Terry and we'll drop her a short distance and then we'll have a stunt double do a longer drop."

Line by line, scene by scene, the group discusses the script. What does the burned-out Orb look like? Is there leaking nitrogen in the *Defiant*'s bridge? What is Jake doing during the battle? Is there interactive light on the ships' exteriors when the moon explodes? Finally, they arrive at Scene 83, the second scene that will feature little Sahgi, along with a host of other Bajorans.

"What level of vedeks and monks should we have among the Bajorans?" Race asks.

"They should be high-ranking," Behr says. "And there should be a lot of people."

"Forty-five atmosphere," Race says, referring the number of extras the scene will require. He writes it on his script page. Then he's ready for Scene 84. "Do we use a Steadicam here?"

"Yeah!" Kroeker confirms. He's already decided how he will choreograph Sisko and Kira's entrance into the Infirmary.

The script in each person's hands reads:

```
                From off screen, we hear Worf's bloodcurdling SCREAM of pain
                and rage.
    85          INT. SURGERY
                As Sisko ENTERS to see Jadzia's lifeless body on the bio-bed,
                Worf stands over her -- he's taken the braid out of his hair, allowing his hair
                to fall loosely over his shoulders.


                Sisko steps closer, takes hold of Jadzia's hand.


                The moment hangs in the air for a long beat, then Worf begins
                to SING a Klingon mourning CHANT.
```

Now Behr suddenly makes a statement. "We're going to change one little thing here."

Everyone in the meeting looks up, waiting.

"Dax is going to say one poignant line."

A murmur goes around the room.

Changes are to be expected, of course, and it's important to make the production staff aware of them as soon as possible, as they can affect multiple departments in any number of ways. But as changes go, this one is fairly significant. Since Beimler and Behr plan to rewrite the scene, the group won't be able to finalize their plans for this scene for a while.

The decision to add a final scene for Jadzia, allowing her to live long enough to say good-bye to Worf, was an important one. Beimler admits that he was a little worried about it. "I was afraid that we wouldn't do it justice," he says.

And Behr was on the fence. "There was never a total consensus among the writers," he says, "but one of René Echevarria's reasons for existence is because he tends to speak to the softer, gentler side of our natures, and he felt he needed to see her die."

Michael Piller was even more specific in his plea for Jadzia's last few moments of life. "I wrote them a note," Piller says, and begins quoting from it: "'I beg you to consider the following, and I've never been as sure of anything in my life. Let Dax live a little longer. Keep your audience interested in her survival rather than losing the tension by having her die in the fourth act. The battle raging and the Orbs failing will not have nearly as much audience interest as Dax's survival. You don't have to do any dialogue with her, although a couple of words may be touching.'"

So Behr and Beimler addressed the script's perceived shortcoming. Comments Behr: "I felt that as long as we kept it short and sweet and let the emotion come out of the moment and not just smack the audience over the head with it to the point where it becomes uncomfortable and unsavory, it was okay. So we gave her a line, and she died on camera."

The decision will cause a few scheduling problems. Oster reports that Terry Farrell has asked that her character's death be her last scene on *Deep Space Nine*. When Jadzia died in the Temple, this was doable. But with Worf involved in the death scene, it won't be. Michael Dorn is currently working double duty, playing everyone's favorite Klingon in both *Deep Space Nine* and the new motion picture. He has a limited window of

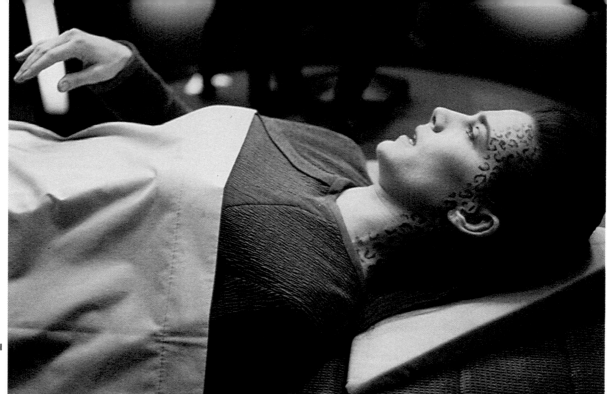

A lively Terry Farrell awaits her cue for one final take of her death scene. ROBBIE ROBINSON.

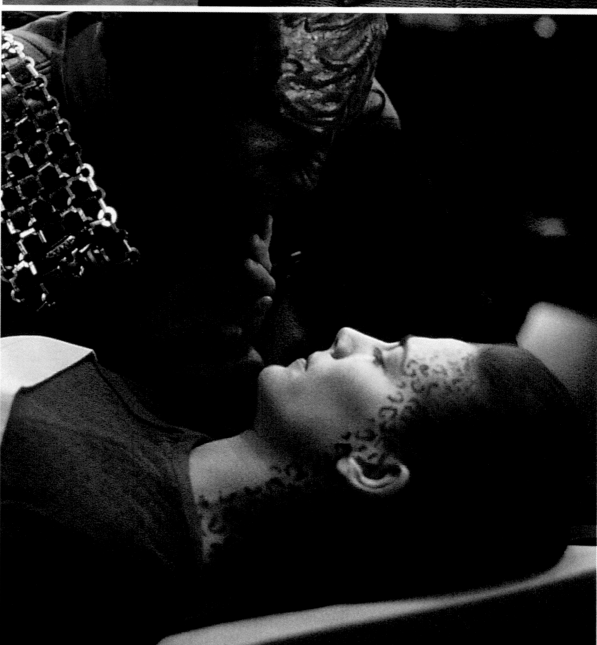

"Our baby would've been so beautiful." ROBBIE ROBINSON.

Reunited with his wife one last time, Worf kisses Jadzia's hand.
ROBBIE ROBINSON.

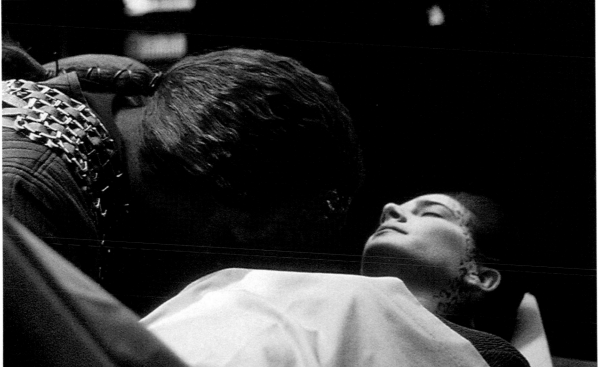

The final moment. Jadzia breathes her last, and Worf grieves.
ROBBIE ROBINSON.

MAKING A LIST AND CHECKING IT TWICE

THIRTY-ONE BAJORAN ADULTS.

    Four Bajoran children

    Two Bajoran monks

    One Bolian

    Two Klingons

    Two Ferengi

    Nine Starfleet personnel

    Two dabo girls

    One "Greenhorn"

    And Morn, of course. Not to mention Sisko, Kira, O'Brien, Bashir, Dax, Odo, Quark, Worf, and Jake.

    No, we're not going shopping for action figures. We're getting ready to start the day over in the hair and makeup trailers.

The unreal Worf (James Minor) sprints across the Promenade to the Infirmary, with the real O'Brien (Colm Meaney) hard on his heels. ROBBIE ROBINSON.

It is 4:42 A.M. on Friday, April 17, and the first of the hairdressing staff and makeup artists are arriving. More will arrive in a little while, and still more will actually have the luxury of rising *after* the sun does and still manage to get to work on time. Every one of the series's cast members and background players will need attention today, but fortunately, they are not all scheduled to arrive at the same time. Before the day is over, twenty-five makeup persons, thirteen hairstylists, and seven costumers, including some familiar faces from the *Voyager* team, will have provided support for today's scenes.

"On this show, makeup, hair, and wardrobe are so intensive that we spend lots of time just telling people in what order they will need to get actors made up and how many extra workers they'll need to bring in to help," says 1st AD Race. Because Race must spend the majority of his time on shooting days near the director and the camera, he leaves such organizational duties to his staff, led by Second Assistant Director Joe Candrella. "The paperwork on this show is a tremendous organizational challenge," Race continues. "The production report, which is the official record of a day's shoot, lists when the actors come in, when they go out, all of the time the extras spend on the set, whether they get any special adjustments for working in smoke or for putting on prosthetics. You can have a hundred extras in a scene and by the time you break down all of their functions, you may have ninety different categories. It is a massive bookkeeping support function."

Today, there are fifty-three extras. More than enough to keep everyone busy. The first scene up is number 83, the scene that precedes Dax's death in the script.

83   INT. PROMENADE
WORF AND O'BRIEN grimly emerge
from the airlock and make a
beeline for the Infirmary.

The call sheet for Day 5 indicates that Worf's photo double, James Minor, will fill in for Michael Dorn in the morning. The production has made arrangements to bring Dorn over from the feature set at 2:00 P.M. if they need additional coverage, but in the end, they don't call on him. Note the spelling of Sahgi's name in the character list; Bajoran isn't an easy language for humans. The last part of the day will be devoted to filming a missing scene from "Profit and Lace."

Just cross "*Star Trek* street," and you're back at *DS9*.
ROBBIE ROBINSON.

At least that's what it will look like to the audience. But in fact, the actor in Worf's Klingon makeup is not Michael Dorn, despite an astonishing resemblence to the actor. That's what makes James Minor a good stand-in and a boon to the production on days like this, when Dorn has to be in two places at once. On this particular day, he's on location filming *Star Trek: Insurrection*. *DS9*'s production team has tried to be very accomodating to the needs of the film crew, investing a great deal of time in working out a schedule utilizing Dorn that would be friendly to both productions. "They gave us a block of three days that he was free," says Race. That block was supposed to include today's filming, but...well, things can change rapidly on a film set.

"It turned out that they needed him today," says Race, "so they traded us back part of next Monday." But the 1st AD takes it all in stride.

Dorn's rescheduling has modified the way the scene will be shot. The master will be broken into two parts, the first showing Worf and O'Brien from a distance as they run ahead of Sisko and the others coming out of the airlock, the second showing Sisko more closely as he walks into the crowd. For the first part, Director Kroeker has chosen to place the camera on the overhead walkway that connects the two sides of the upper level. The set-up will provide a nice view of the airlock's entrance, the Promenade, and the gathering crowd of worried citizens. It will also provide sufficient distance to hide the fact that Worf isn't Dorn.

At 7:55 A.M., the AD staff begins escorting the fifty-three extras to the Promenade from where they have been mingling in front of Stage 17. At 8:10, they are assembled, and Race instructs them about the scene. "Be animated," he says. "Be very verbal about Sisko's arriving back at the station. I want you to ad-lib things like, 'Emissary, the wormhole has closed,' and 'Emissary this,' 'Emissary that.' He's the only guy who can help with this problem, so go to him."

Jerry Bono, a key costumer, joins Race and adds a warning. "And no wristwatches," he says sternly. The extras all check themselves for such anachronistic items.

8:18. "Action!" calls Race. The Promenade is lit at what Jonathan West calls "the standard level" that is provided by the set's permanent lights. The gearlike door to the airlock opens to reveal the actors inside. The shot goes without a hitch, and one take is all that's necessary.

"Moving on," Race calls out. It is 8:25.

Now Kroeker steps into the group of extras to block the second half of the master, in which Sisko walks through the crowd and speaks to Sahgi, the young Bajoran girl. The script says that Sahgi is an eight-year-old, but Michelle Horn, who plays her, is actually eleven. Standing near her are the additional children that Oster had approved during the production meeting.

Kroeker traces the path that he'll ask the cast to follow. The director trusts the Worf makeup; Minor will

Jonathan West supervises the lighting setup for part of Scene 83. The second team—stand-ins Clynell Jackson (for Avery Brooks) and Cindy Sorensen (for Michelle Horn)—"assume the position" at the actors' marks. To the left is an item you'd expect to find at any mall: the station directory. ROBBIE ROBINSON.

make a fast run past the camera. When he gets to the spot where he wants Horn to approach Avery Brooks, he stops. A camera assistant who is following him immediately puts a white tape mark on the floor at his feet, then an orange one at Horn's feet. "I want them close together, very tight," the director says.

He turns the set over to Jonathan West for lighting. "Second team," Race calls, and Brooks's and Horn's stand-ins take positions at the tape marks. Stand-ins, who usually share height and coloring characteristics with the actors for whom they fill in, are often used for lighting tests.

West first installs two 8K (1,000 watt) soft lights, one for Sisko and one for Sahgi, and a 2K soft light that will gently backlight the actors as they walk.

The camera is placed on the Promenade's overhead walkway for the opening shot of Scene 83.
ROBBIE ROBINSON.

Director Allan Kroeker shows Sahgi (Michelle Horn) where Captain Sisko will be standing, while Avery Brooks provides some pre-scene coaching from behind the lines. ROBBIE ROBINSON.

"I don't light sets," says West. "I light shots. Because every shot is different. You have to choose where the actors are going to be and then incorporate their lighting with the regular set lighting so that it all flows smoothly. The only thing that matters is what the camera, which represents the audience, is seeing at that specific moment," West continues. "That's your image. That's your painting."

Now West and Race walk off the shot, counting and timing their steps as they go. "We need seven or eight seconds before Michelle starts moving in," West says.

Race turns to one of his assistants. "Make sure that the extras aren't packed together too tightly here," he says. It's important to keep the path open for a variety of reasons, not the least of which is that Gavin Ames, who will photograph this segment of the master shot with a Steadicam, will be walking backward.

"I walk backward all day long, so it really doesn't bother me anymore," jokes Ames, who has been carrying the seventy-five pounds of equipment around sets for five years. He describes the task that lies before—or rather, behind—him. "I precede Mr. Brooks through the crowd of extras along a path that has been predetermined by the choreography of the shot. It should be interesting because there are some small children in it

Brooks looks on from his mark as Kroeker gives one of Sahgi's playmates her own set of instructions. ROBBIE ROBINSON.

and I'll have to constantly be aware of my eye height versus the camera's operating height versus the main child's height." This means that the six-foot-seven-inch Ames will need to "get into sort of a squat," he says. "It just takes me about a minute to learn the choreography."

As the Steadicam operator retreats along the chosen path, his camera assistant, Alan Gitlin, stands at the side of the set, pulling the Steadicam's focus and changing its aperture by remote control. Using the microwave signal, Gitlin says, "I could pull focus from a mile away."

The extras are called back and put into position. Then at 8:57 the actors step onto the set. Race announces a safety meeting before they get started. "The Steadicam will be backing up," he says, and explains the trajectory. "Let's have a half-speed rehearsal for the move. And...Background."

The rehearsal works fine. At 9:05 Kroeker calls for Take 1.

Race preps the extras again. "Remember, it's tense! This is not business as usual at the mall!" Then, "Action."

Worf and O'Brien very quickly run past camera, then the rest of the *Defiant* crew, led by Sisko, walks through the crowded Promenade. Suddenly the little girl approaches Sisko. Avery Brooks pauses. Michelle Horn delivers her speech. She leaves. Brooks follows. "Cut." Take 2. "That one was great," he says. "Print."

"Everybody remember where you were standing," Race reminds the actors and the extras. "We're gonna move in for coverage." The second half of Sahgi's speech will be done again, this time in close-up. Race turns the set over to West.

While waiting for the new setup to be completed, Avery Brooks stays near the set, engaging the children in conversation. He asks questions and they answer; they ask and he answers. Smiles abound. "I enjoy children," Brooks states emphatically. "That's a part of my nature, as well as Sisko's. Children are the future, after all."

9:21. There are two shots necessary for the "coverage," a term that means, very simply, close-ups. The two close-ups will be edited in to make the conversation more intimate for the audience and to emphasize sections of the dialogue. One shot is over Brooks's shoulder onto Horn's face, the other over her shoulder onto Brooks's

"Where everybody knows your name . . . " No, it's not Cliff and Norm. It's Script Supervisor Stuart Lippman and Key Costumer Jerry Bono taking advantage of a break in filming. ROBBIE ROBINSON.

face. Since the shots are tighter than the master, only a small number of the extras are required to be present; the rest relax in other areas of the stage, or just outside.

West is using a fifty-millimeter lens on the Panavision camera. The larger lens will easily capture the detail of the tight image. Kroeker is very happy with the first take, a close-up of Sahgi, and orders that it be printed. Then he walks from the monitor area and kneels down on the set. "Do your lines for me once," he says to Horn. "I want to hear your emphasis on the words." She does. "Good," he says. "I like that," and he returns to the monitors. After Take 2, he calls, "Cut. Excellent. Print that one too."

"Turnaround on Avery," Race calls. As the lighting crew makes some adjustments, several of the actors compliment Michelle Horn on her performance.

Horn, who has a recurring role on the television series *Profiler* and who plays the voice of the lead female character in Disney's animated *Lion King* sequel, was hired only two days ago. She received her script pages only last evening. And, she says, "I went over my lines outside of the stage with my mom this morning, and then I did them by myself in my head until I memorized them."

Seating for seven on the Promenade. ROBBIE ROBINSON.

Michelle's morning started early. She had to be in the makeup trailer at 6:00 A.M. to have her Bajoran nose prosthetic applied by Makeup Artist Karen Iverson. "This is the first time I've had makeup like this," Horn says, feeling her nose. "Putting it on took over an hour."

"People think that applying a Bajoran nose is the easiest thing to do because it involves such a small prosthetic piece," notes Makeup Artist Natalie Wood, who is on the set "maintaining" the four Bajoran background players that she transformed this morning. "But it's right in the middle of the face, so if you don't do the edges right and get the colorization just right, it really stands out."

"All of the makeup needs to be maintained," Race adds. "That's in addition to having people come in very early to make the actors up. Plus, people must be standing by at night to take the actors apart. They can't just rip off the prosthetics or yank off the heads. Appliances have to be carefully removed, partially to protect the skin of the people wearing them, and partially to protect the elements that may be reused."

Now Brooks, Horn, and a small number of extras are back in position, this time for Brooks's close-up. Two takes, both of which Kroeker decides to print.

"Moving on," Race announces. He turns to follow Kroeker, who is heading toward the nearby Infirmary set. The time is 10:27.

Scene 83 originally had a different ending. In the April 8 draft, after Sisko promises Sahgi that he'll do what he can about finding the Prophets, Kira says, "That's a big promise. Even for the Emissary." But Kira's line was eliminated in a revised script page dated April 13.

"Sometimes silence is better than words," Ira Behr explains, "especially in a loaded scene like this where you run the risk of seeming to reveal too much. Kira has many attitudes and emotions and values about the Prophets and about what's just happened regarding them." Given the choice of "playing Kira's attitudes or not playing them," Behr says the producers found a third choice. "We decided to let it all be unsaid and wait to find out how she's taking this stuff at the beginning of the seventh season."

Kroeker watches a somber Brooks rehearse his entrance into the Infirmary. ROBBIE ROBINSON.

CODE BLUE

JUST A FEW MINUTES LATER, AT 10:32 A.M., THE CAST AND CREW OF *DEEP SPACE NINE* **ARE ASSEMBLED ON THE INFIRMARY SET.** Avery Brooks, Nana Visitor, Colm Meaney, and Cirroc Lofton are dressed as they were in the scene on the Promenade. Armin Shimerman and Rene Auberjonois are still in street clothes, although they are already in full Quark and Odo makeup. Alexander Siddig is the last to arrive this morning, his makeup just completed.

Kroeker spends five minutes talking to Siddig and the others about "the emotion delivered in Bashir's lines." After the discussion, the actors retreat to finish dressing or reread the dialogue, and Kroeker turns his mind to the lighting and look of his first shot.

The POV (point of view) is from inside the Infirmary, with Sisko, Kira, and Jake entering through the door. This means that the Promenade, located—just as it seems in the show—right outside the Infirmary, must be fully lit. Two sets at once.

But before the lights can be set up and the camera set in place, a practical problem must be taken care of. All of the equipment—which consists of stacks of apple boxes, ditty bags filled with makeup and brushes, hammers and electric drills, a dozen cartloads of "c-stands," reflective flags, "stinger" extension cords, and mis- cellaneous wiring—is now in the shot. "Everything's gotta go!" Race says, simply. This flurry of housekeeping happens with almost every move from set to set. The equipment has to be kept nearby, "just in case," and just out of frame for every scene. It takes four minutes for a dozen people to push everything ten feet to the west.

Kroeker and Race block the shot and work with West to set up the appropriate lighting. "Put a four-foot by four-foot bounce card behind that chair," Jonathan West tells First Company Grip Steve Gausche. The card is in place and ready to be adjusted in less than a minute, a perfect demonstra- tion of why that mountain of equipment is always kept close at hand. Both the Promenade and the Infirmary are ready to be shot in about a half hour.

11:07. Allan Kroeker shouts, "Action!" from behind his monitor. The grips behind the wall man- ually pull on a chain and the door opens. The actors start to move, but the pacing of the scene feels wrong. They were supposed to be in action as the door opened. A quick conference with the actors gets to the root of the problem. They can't hear the director through the closed door.

They also serve who only stand and wait. Steve Oster and Nana Visitor. ROBBIE ROBINSON.

Beimler and Behr enjoy chatting with the couple they finally "got together" in "His Way." Beimler admits, "We love going down to the set, but normally during the year, with the scheduling, we just can't." During the last days of the final shoot the producer/writers give themselves permission to play hooky. ROBBIE ROBINSON.

"Reset backgrounds," Race orders. Take 2. Race makes sure the actors hear the command. This time they are in movement, but they're too spread out. The camera cuts it too close, leaving Nana Visitor partially out of frame.

Take 3. The actors walk in, the extras in the Promenade visible behind them. The dolly-mounted Panavision camera pans with the actors and stops when they reach their marks. The doors close. Brooks, Visitor, and Lofton show varying degrees of emotion as Siddig plays his lines. He is off camera, but standing at his mark for the benefit of the other's eyelines. Siddig's delivery is vitally important, since the actors on camera time their reactions to his words.

"Cut! That looks good," Kroeker says, his brow furrowed. Take 3 is the only complete take. But one is all that's needed. It is 11:15. Photographing the three takes took only eight minutes.

"Nana is wrapped. Cirroc is wrapped," Race calls out. The two actors say good-bye as they head for the makeup trailer to be cleaned up. They're going home. Lofton, in fact, might have gone home a lot sooner if not for a last-minute decision by Behr to insert him in the scene. The final script had Sisko enter the Infirmary with Kira only. But that suddenly seemed wrong. "He's the captain's son," Behr says emphatically. "And he was on the ship the whole time. So he should be there."

In a few minutes, the camera will turn around to show Siddig. He'll be delivering the same lines again,

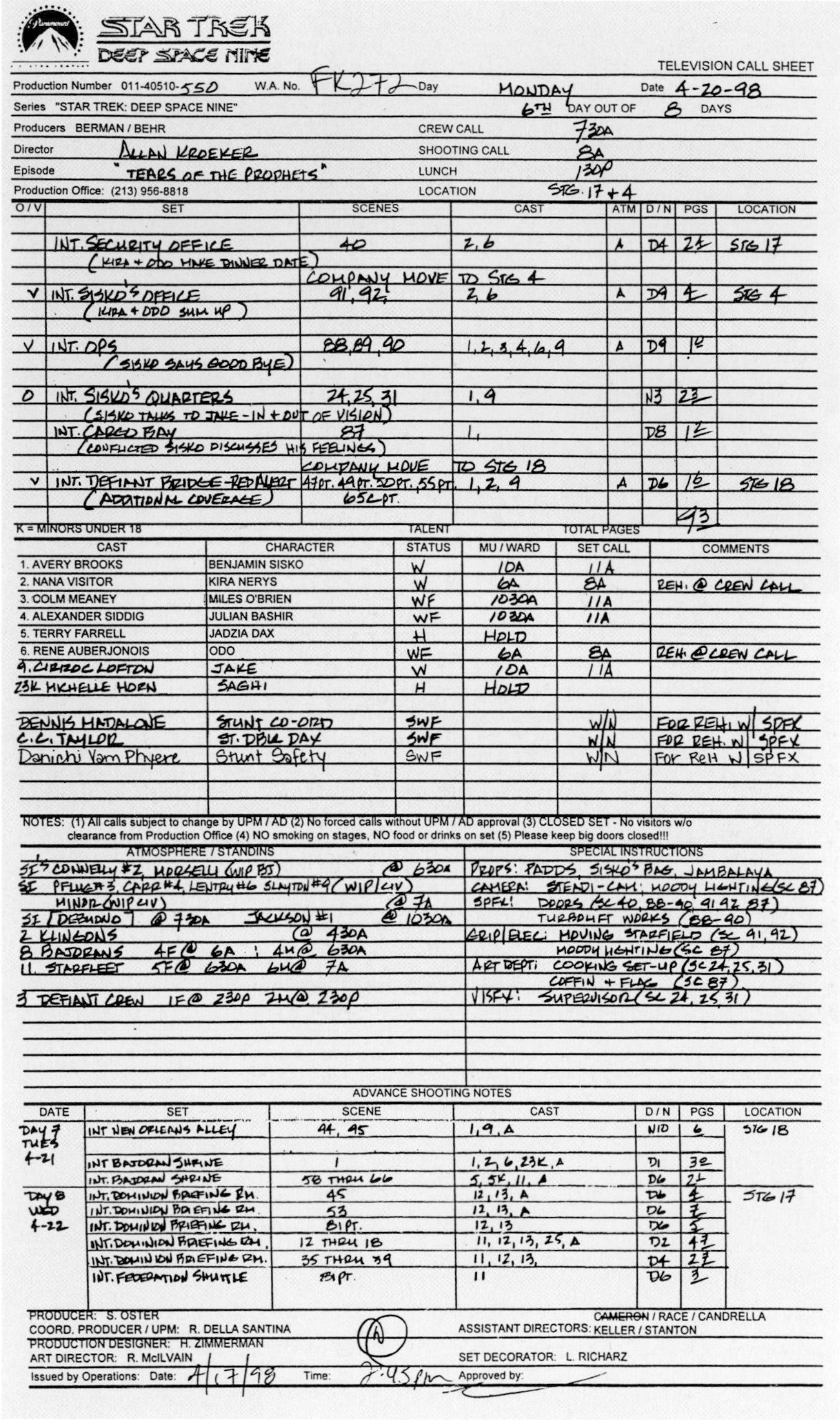

STAR TREK DEEP SPACE NINE

TELEVISION CALL SHEET

Production Number 011-40510-550 W.A. No. FK272 Day MONDAY Date 4-20-98
Series "STAR TREK: DEEP SPACE NINE" 6TH DAY OUT OF 8 DAYS
Producers BERMAN / BEHR CREW CALL 730A
Director ALLAN KROEKER SHOOTING CALL 8A
Episode "TEARS OF THE PROPHETS" LUNCH 130P
Production Office: (213) 956-8818 LOCATION STG. 17 + 4

O/V	SET	SCENES	CAST	ATM	D/N	PGS	LOCATION
	INT. SECURITY OFFICE (KIRA + ODO MAKE DINNER DATE)	40	2, 6	A	D4	2 1/8	STG 17
		COMPANY MOVE TO STG 4					
V	INT. SISKO'S OFFICE (KIRA + ODO SUM UP)	91, 92	2, 6	A	D9	4/8	STG 4
V	INT. OPS (SISKO SAYS GOOD BYE)	88, 89, 90	1, 2, 3, 4, 6, 9	A	D9	1 2/8	
O	INT. SISKO'S QUARTERS (SISKO TALKS TO JAKE - IN + OUT OF VISION)	24, 25, 31	1, 9		N3	2 3/8	
	INT. CARGO BAY (CONFLICTED SISKO DISCUSSES HIS FEELINGS)	87	1		D8	1 2/8	
		COMPANY MOVE TO STG 18					
V	INT. DEFIANT BRIDGE - RED ALERT (ADDITIONAL COVERAGE)	47PT. 49PT. 50PT. 55PT. 65CPT.	1, 2, 9	A	D6	1 6/8	STG 18

K = MINORS UNDER 18 TOTAL PAGES 9 3/8

CAST	CHARACTER	TALENT STATUS	MU / WARD	SET CALL	COMMENTS
1. AVERY BROOKS	BENJAMIN SISKO	W	10A	11A	
2. NANA VISITOR	KIRA NERYS	W	6A	8A	REH. @ CREW CALL
3. COLM MEANEY	MILES O'BRIEN	WF	1030A	11A	
4. ALEXANDER SIDDIG	JULIAN BASHIR	WF	1030A	11A	
5. TERRY FARRELL	JADZIA DAX	H	HOLD		
6. RENE AUBERJONOIS	ODO	WF	6A	8A	REH. @ CREW CALL
9. CIRROC LOFTON	JAKE	W	10A	11A	
23K MICHELLE HORN	SAGHI	H	HOLD		
DENNIS MADALONE	STUNT CO-ORD	SWF		W/N	FOR REH. W/ SPFX
C.C. TAYLOR	ST. DBL. DAX	SWF		W/N	FOR REH. W/ SPFX
Danichi Vam Phyere	Stunt Safety	SWF		W/N	For Reh W/ SPFX

NOTES: (1) All calls subject to change by UPM / AD (2) No forced calls without UPM / AD approval (3) CLOSED SET - No visitors w/o clearance from Production Office (4) NO smoking on stages, NO food or drinks on set (5) Please keep big doors closed!!!

ATMOSPHERE / STANDINS	SPECIAL INSTRUCTIONS
SI'S CONNELLY #2, MORSELLI (WIP BJ) @ 630A	PROPS: PADDS, SISKO'S BAG, JAMBALAYA
SI PFLUG #3, CARR #4, LENTRY #6 SLAYTON #9 (WIP/LIV)	CAMERA: STEADI-CAM; MOODY LIGHTING (SC 87)
MINOR (WIP LIV) @ 7A	SPFX: DOORS (SC 40, 88-90, 91 92 87)
SI [DESUNDO] @ 730A JACKSON #1 @ 1030A	TURBOLIFT WORKS (88-90)
2 KLINGONS @ 430A	GRIP/ELEC: MOVING STARFIELD (SC 91, 92)
8 BAJORANS 4F @ 6A ; 4M @ 630A	MOODY LIGHTING (SC 87)
11. STARFLEET 5F @ 630A 6M @ 7A	ART DEPT: COOKING SET-UP (SC 24, 25, 31)
	COFFIN + FLAG (SC 87)
3 DEFIANT CREW 1F @ 230P 2M @ 230P	VISFX: SUPERVISOR (SC 24, 25, 31)

ADVANCE SHOOTING NOTES

DATE	SET	SCENE	CAST	D/N	PGS	LOCATION
DAY 7 TUES 4-21	INT NEW ORLEANS ALLEY	44, 45	1, 9, A	N/D	6	STG 18
	INT BAJORAN SHRINE	1	1, 2, 6, 23K, A	D1	3 2/8	
	INT. BAJORAN SHRINE	58 THRU 66	5, 5K, 11, A	D6	2 1/8	
DAY 8 WED 4-22	INT. DOMINION BRIEFING RM.	45	12, 13, A	D6	4/8	STG 17
	INT. DOMINION BRIEFING RM.	53	12, 13, A	D6	7/8	
	INT. DOMINION BRIEFING RM.	81PT.	12, 13	D6	3/8	
	INT. DOMINION BRIEFING RM.	12 THRU 18	11, 12, 13, 25, A	D2	4 7/8	
	INT. DOMINION BRIEFING RM.	35 THRU 39	11, 12, 13,	D4	2 7/8	
	INT. FEDERATION SHUTTLE	81PT.	11	D6	3/8	

PRODUCER: S. OSTER
COORD. PRODUCER / UPM: R. DELLA SANTINA
PRODUCTION DESIGNER: H. ZIMMERMAN
ART DIRECTOR: R. McILVAIN
ASSISTANT DIRECTORS: ~~CAMERON~~ / RACE / CANDRELLA KELLER / STANTON
SET DECORATOR: L. RICHARZ
Issued by Operations: Date: 4/17/98 Time: 7:43pm Approved by:

The call sheet from Day 6. Today is a big day for good-byes. The "turbolift works" comment under special instructions is for precautionary purposes, letting crew members know that the lift will be operational this day (for Scenes 88 through 90), so naps beneath the ops set are ill advised.

since this close-up will be intercut with the master. The lines Siddig is speaking have been revised since the "final draft" of the script was written. That draft included a line that read, "I was able to save the Dax symbiont by immersing it in a neurotropic solution, but we need to get it back to Trill as soon as possible." But in the April 13 revised pages, the phrase, "by immersing it in a neurotropic solution," was eliminated.

"That was 'tech talk,'" explains Behr, who felt the need to sharpen the focus on what the scene is really about. "This was no time for tech talk."

At 11:29, Siddig, Brooks, Shimerman, Auberjonois, and Meaney return to the set. With the exception of Brooks, they are all in wardrobe; Siddig wears what looks like a bright red robe. "We have six of those surgery outfits," says Wardrobe Supervisor Carol Kunz. "They were created in the second season of *The Next Generation* for the episode 'Samaritan Snare,' when Picard had his open-heart surgery."

Something old. Now for something new. "Rene has a new sculpted face for this episode," reveals Makeup Artist Dean Jones. "Over a period of time, everyone's face changes, and we adapt our prosthetics to those changes. We've rounded out Odo's jawline slightly and added some texture to the bottom of the neck to match the texture of Rene's natural skin, so that it blends better." The new prosthetic is actually on a test run. "It's been approved for today only," Jones says. "We hope to use this all next season, but there could be changes."

For Siddig's close-ups, Avery Brooks will be off camera, so now he's wearing street clothes. After a short rehearsal, Race calls, "Final touches. Let's do this." It is 11:36. Then, "Roll please...and...Door!" The door opens, even though it, too, is off camera. Siddig delivers his lines perfectly, repeating the inflections he'd used a half-hour earlier. Kroeker likes it, but says, "Let's do it again."

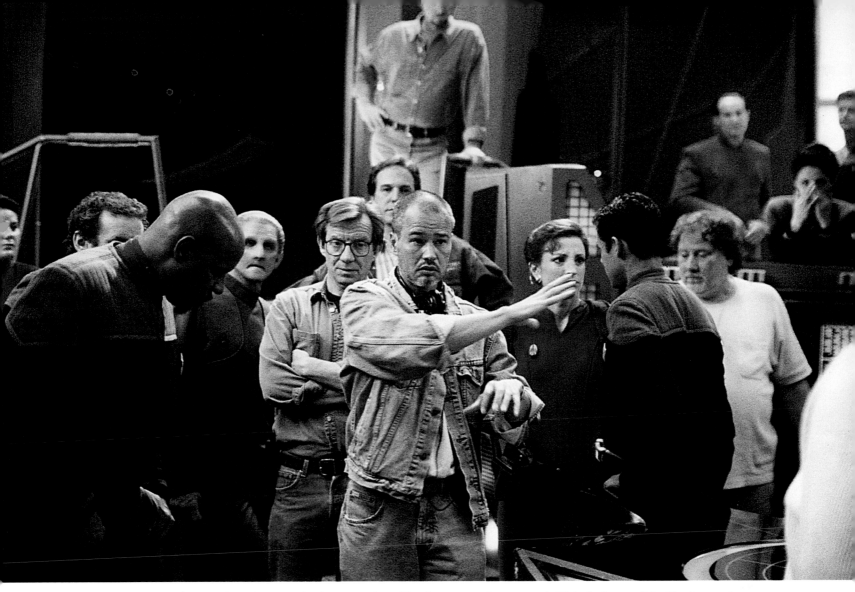

Before they can get to Sisko's scene in the cargo bay, Kroeker must choreograph Sisko's farewell to the troops in ops. Cast and crew gather round for final instructions as Kroeker describes the movement of the camera. ROBBIE ROBINSON.

Take 2. "Cut! Great!" Kroeker smiles and addresses the script supervisor, who is taking extensive notes. "Stuart, print both of those."

"Avery is wrapped. Colm is wrapped," Race announces. "That takes us over to Quark's." And at 11:42, exactly one hour after they stormed into the Infirmary, everyone is on the move again.

In truth, Scene 84 would have taken another half hour to shoot if it had been filmed as written. The scene originally had a tag on it. After Bashir has revealed that he can't help Jadzia, the script says:

Bashir can see that Sisko isn't himself.

BASHIR
Are you alright, Captain?

SISKO
I've been better . . .

The path less chosen. Steadicam Operator Gavin Ames makes a living out of walking backward. Here he begins to track Sisko's last walk through Ops. ROBBIE ROBINSON.

"The station's all yours, Major," Sisko addresses an unseen Kira. ROBBIE ROBINSON.

"This leave of absence you're taking, sir . . . how long do you think you'll be gone?" As usual, the blunt Bashir cuts to the chase, asking the question everyone in Ops would like to ask. The line also lets the audience in on the fact that Sisko has not resigned. ROBBIE ROBINSON.

"Good luck, sir," says O'Brien. Ames holds his position while Mark Overton moves the boom mike toward Colm Meaney. ROBBIE ROBINSON.

"Let's go home, Jake." Ames takes a step back as Brooks moves forward and Overton extends his arms backward to pick up the line. ROBBIE ROBINSON.

The eye of the hurricane. Rene Auberjonois is an isle of serenity in the chaos of "final touches."
ROBBIE ROBINSON.

"Bashir is a doctor, and Sisko looks like he's just been through the mill, so that seemed like a real doctor thing to say," explains Behr. "But the actors thought it took away from the feelings about Dax, so they didn't feel that they could do it." This time it was the actors, not the writers, who had made a script decision, which Behr okayed. "That's the way they felt," Behr says. "So I didn't push it."

A MAN ALONE

DEEP SPACE NINE'S CARGO BAY IS A BIG ROOM.

When it's in use on the series, it's a big crowded room, filled with cargo modules and station equipment. And when it's not in use, the space on Stage 4 is a big messy room, regularly housing stacks of plywood, cartloads of electrical equipment, and hastily relocated props.

But on the morning of April 20, 1998, the cargo bay is a big *empty* room.

At 6:00 A.M., a paint and cleanup crew arrives to do "final touch-ups," as if the room itself is one of the featured players. "This room really gets beat up," says painter Bob Fambry. "We're filling every little ding with putty and spackle. Then we'll scratch it all down and paint it." In addition, as mentioned at the Production Meeting, the old frayed carpeting has been pulled out, and at the last moment it was replaced.

Today's call sheet lists six scenes to be completed. Scene 87, Sisko's soliloquy over Jadzia's coffin, is scheduled as number five. Sometime today, this room will be bustling with activity as the production crew moves in. But even then, only one actor and one prop will occupy the space while it's being filmed.

"When I first read the script and saw that Sisko has a one-page monologue, I wondered how in the world we were going to put movement into the scene," Allan Kroeker says. "But then I got inspired. A scene like this breathes life into you, because we're not wading through a lot of technobabble."

Far from it. The words that inspired Kroeker demanded contact with very deep emotions, as much for the writers as for the character speaking them. And reaching those emotions was not an easy process.

"Ira and I wanted to find the anguish of the man and focus on what it really was about," Hans Beimler says. "The scene had to be about some deep, lasting inner truth about Sisko."

"We had a lot of questions to answer," Beimler continues. "Why is Sisko leaving the station? Why isn't he resigning? Why does he feel he has to go home? We felt that if *he* could answer those questions, he wouldn't need to go home, so we had to answer them for the viewer by letting them see through his eyes without being too specific as to where he is in his mind."

A soliloquy is defined as a dramatic or literary form of discourse in which a character reveals his or her thoughts when alone. With a little help, Behr and Beimler wrote four versions of the scene, starting with the one in the "final draft," dated April 8.

Some of the modifications between the four versions are simple colloquial changes. For instance, the first version's "I'm going to miss you more than you'll know," became, "And I'm going to miss you," in the revised pages dated April 13. "Sometimes less is more," Beimler says simply. "We wanted to get it tighter and more concise."

But other changes in the second draft took the meaning into a deeper psychological realm. "I need you, Jadzia. I need your advice," became, "Why aren't you here, Jadzia? I need you to help me sort things out." The word "advice" doesn't describe what is in the speaker's mind. It's vague. But "sort things out" is specific. The writers found the replacement phrase they were looking for near the end of Sisko's speech, where they'd ini-

Randy McIlvain sketches out some rough ideas for the episode in the *DS9* Art Department. The staff is split on whether or not the torpedo that became Jadzia's final resting place was the same as Spock's. ROBBIE ROBINSON.

tially placed it. After moving it up, they had to replace it with something stronger. They came up with "…so I can figure out a way to make things right again." Even more specific.

A less subtle change also came in the second set of revised pages. A line that stated, "…but without the Orbs, I can't even contact them," was eliminated altogether. "Rick Berman felt that this was opening a can of worms that we didn't need to open at that moment," says Behr. Behr ageed that the line might have made the audience wonder, "'Maybe Sisko can't contact them, but can they contact *him*?'" he says. "The scene isn't about that," he adds, so it was cut.

The last line of the first version was, "So I've made a decision. I hope it's the right one." The line would have made the audience anticipate hearing about that decision in Season Seven, but its replacement once again handled that in a more specific way: "I have to make things right, Jadzia. I have to." Now, the viewers' anticipation is not about "what," but about the more dramatic "how."

The third version of the soliloquy was distributed only hours after the second version, in the afternoon of April 13. In it were two changes, both of them intended as stage directions. "I should have listened to the Prophets, not gone to Cardassia," was changed to "I should have listened to the Prophets and not gone to Cardassia." In other words, there was just the simple addition of a connective conjunction, but it was there for an important reason. "Written pauses can backfire on you," Behr says. "Sometimes you get longer pauses than you want." The "and" tends to prevent the pause.

Although its moments on camera were fleeting, you can see the Art Department's meticulous detailing. ROBBIE ROBINSON.

WARNING : EPS GNDN SYS

IN THE EVEN OF RUPTURE OR BREACH OF TERATOGENIC COOLANT FEED, A CHEMICAL HAZARD ALERT PROTOCOL MUST BE INITIATED. ENVIRONMENTAL SUITS MUST BE DONNED BY ANY PERSONNEL REMAINING IN AREA.

WARNING : NANOPULSE MATRIX

IN CASE OF MAIN ODN FAILURE THIS UNIT CAN BE REINITIALIZED BY OPENING THIS PANEL AND PULLING THE RED LEVER SHARPLY TOWARD YOU UNTIL THE FIRST DETENT. REFER TO EMERGENCY PROTOCOL 554GF.

The labels created by Doug Drexler to be placed on the torpedo casing. COURTESY DOUG DREXLER.

The stark setting of the Cargo Bay set gives extra weight to Sisko's sense of loss. ROBBIE ROBINSON.

The second change transformed, "and I'm responsible," to "and *I'm* responsible." Behr explains, "Sometimes we emphasize how we'd like the actors to deliver lines." In the long run, though, the decision is frequently up to the actors.

An addition to the fourth version of the soliloquy is the most powerful change of all. It came about after a lot of discussions, a lot of group participation, and an epiphany. The added line was:

```
"I failed as the Emissary and,
 for the first time in my life,
 I've failed in my duty as
 Starfleet officer."
```

"That is a huge and important moment in the show," Behr says emphatically. "It came about because Ron Moore felt the speech was still missing a specific." The original idea for the story was to have Sisko feel crushed by the death of the Prophets. But Jadzia's death had reduced the impact of that tragedy. "So we had to draw back from our original plan," says Behr. "We needed something else. So Hans, Ron, and I just sat around talking. Finally we came upon this idea of acknowledging failure. I don't remember whether Hans or I said, 'For the first time in my life I've failed in my duties as a Starfleet officer,' but Ron immediately said, 'That's it!' At the beginning of the show he is a success in both of those things. He is the Emissary who is bringing children *peldor joi* even while he's the officer plotting the invasion of Cardassia. He's on a roll. But now he feels like a failure. We condensed all of that in a very simple line."

And today those lines, simple and not so simple, are being put onto film.

At 5:23 P.M., the filmmakers complete the shots of Jake and Sisko having dinner in their quarters. "Move to cargo bay," Louis Race says. When they enter the set, the only thing sitting on the new carpet is a torpedo tube on a stand. But the room looks different than it does on television. The west wall is actually a large stage door that rises toward the ceiling, like the curtain to a stage. At the moment, the wall is raised, effectively making the entire end of the set an entryway. Many of the crew members appear through it.

Allan Kroeker and Avery Brooks walk around the coffin together, circling it, looking for the best angle. The room is a rectangle; the torpedo tube sits parallel to the shorter walls. "Let's try it with the coffin flipped," Kroeker says, and the property staff rotates the torpedo tube and stand. Now it parallels the length of the room. It looks better.

The director and the actor converse. "Let us do the moving [with the camera] and you do the talking," Kroeker says. Brooks agrees, but suggests that he use both sides of the coffin by taking one step. Kroeker likes it. "So we'll do a one-eighty [degrees] with the camera," he says. "Let's rehearse."

At 5:29, Brooks recites the soliloquy for the first time. On the line "Why aren't you here, Jadzia?" he stops, then repeats the line, stronger this time. He stops and repeats it again, even stronger, hitting his fist on the coffin top. Allan Kroeker crouches on the floor, directly in front of Brooks, staring at him as if he himself is the camera. When Brooks finally stops speaking, three minutes have passed. But now both Brooks and Kroeker know what they want to do. Kroeker will put the Panavision camera on a dolly and roll counterclockwise, following Brooks as he moves from the end of the prop to its side.

As Brooks heads off the set, Kroeker talks with Louis Race as he resumes his low crouch so he can look up at the prop. "Second team, stand by," Race calls out and Brooks's stand-in, Clynell Jackson III, steps in. Since this is a one-man scene, Jackson is the entire team. "Lights," Race shouts. Jonathan West discusses the setting with Chief Lighting Technician Ronnie Knox. As a grip lowers the raised west wall, the room grows dark. Then suddenly some red lights are illuminated, and the whole look of the room changes.

"We're putting a very strong source of white light almost directly above and slightly behind Avery," says West. "And we're bringing in some red light from the door area. The rest of it is just a little bit of fill light so we can see into his eyes. I want to make sure that we get a dot of light in his eyes so that we can see 'into his soul.' Everything else is just dark background." West looks around. "It's very stylized," he says approvingly.

Tim Roller agrees. "Usually there's so much going on, with the Cardassian architecture and the graphics and the videos, that we hardly ever shoot anything that's this 'quiet.' I really like the perspective of this big room with the small coffin."

The coffin/torpedo tube *is* small, barely six feet long. That much everyone can agree on. They also can agree about the stand upon which the prop is sitting. "It's from the mirror universe," Scenic Artist Doug Drexler explains, laughing. "They built it so the mirror Bashir could roll it into engineering in 'Shattered Mirror.'"

The thing no one can agree on is, "*Which* coffin is it?"

A few days earlier, there had been an enthusiastic discussion regarding the mystery tube in *DS9*'s Art Department. As she mentioned at the Production Meeting, Laura Richarz thinks it's from the second *Star Trek* motion picture. "It's always been in the warehouse," she says, "and we've repainted it several times. I think we also used it in the episode, 'The Ship.'"

"And *Voyager* has used it," Art Director Randy McIlvain adds, unable to resist joining into the speculation.

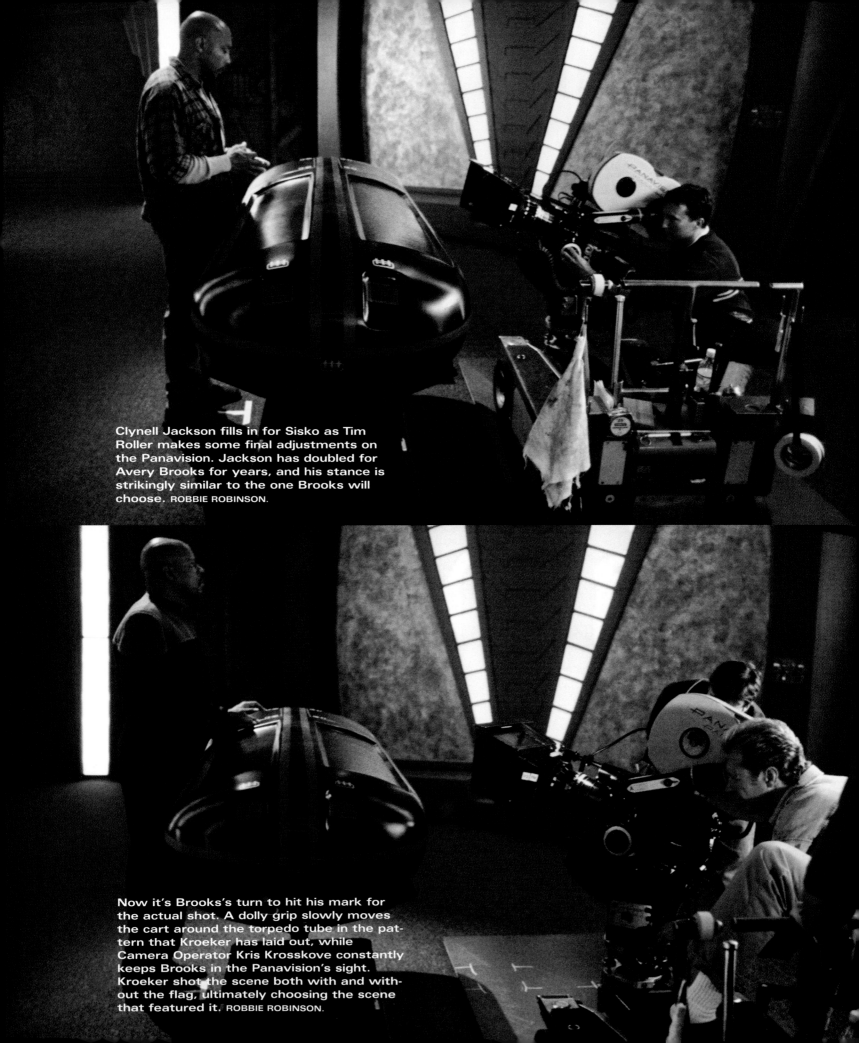

Clynell Jackson fills in for Sisko as Tim Roller makes some final adjustments on the Panavision. Jackson has doubled for Avery Brooks for years, and his stance is strikingly similar to the one Brooks will choose. ROBBIE ROBINSON.

Now it's Brooks's turn to hit his mark for the actual shot. A dolly grip slowly moves the cart around the torpedo tube in the pattern that Kroeker has laid out, while Camera Operator Kris Krosskove constantly keeps Brooks in the Panavision's sight. Kroeker shot the scene both with and without the flag, ultimately choosing the scene that featured it. ROBBIE ROBINSON.

Sound Mixer Bill Gocke gets ready to roll sound. Gocke uses an older Nagra analog recording system. It's not state-of-the-art, but it's the preferred equipment for many film and TV sound mixers. "This thing is like a tank," says Gocke proudly. "You can drop it and it still works. It's a great workhorse." ROBBIE ROBINSON.

"We *do* have the prop from the second feature," admits Scenic Art Supervisor/Technical Consultant Michael Okuda. "However, Herman Zimmerman had a bunch of new torpedoes made for *Star Trek VI: The Undiscovered Country.*" Okuda shrugs. "So it's really impossible to say whether the one in this episode is Spock's or not."

"This is *not* the one from *Wrath of Khan*," Drexler states definitively, closing the speculation. "That one's on Genesis."

In any event, Drexler should be able to recognize this particular coffin with no trouble the *next* time he sees it. He's spent many hours with it for "Tears of the Prophets." "I painted the detailing on it right outside of ops," Drexler says. "Lots of snazzy red pinstriping and vinyl lettering and numbers." Drexler also designed several small clamps and clasps on his computer, which were then printed, cut out, and painted in brushed aluminum by Paramount's Sign Shop. "I stick them on the torpedo so they'll catch the light and glint nice. We want it to look like real technology, and the detailing brings it to life," Drexler notes. "Otherwise it's just a black tube."

Back on the soundstage, four grips carry in four sheets of three-quarter-inch birch plywood. It is stiff and strong and will support the rolling dolly without sagging. But it may creak, and this scene demands total quiet,

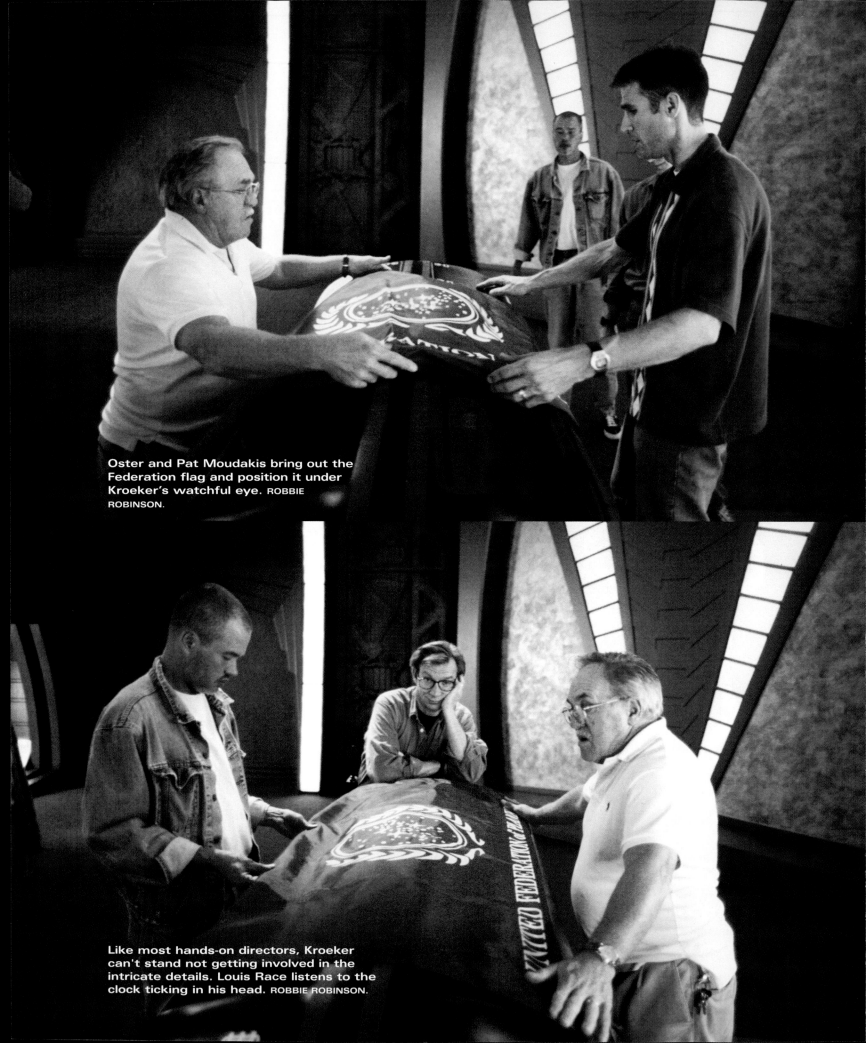

Oster and Pat Moudakis bring out the Federation flag and position it under Kroeker's watchful eye. ROBBIE ROBINSON.

Like most hands-on directors, Kroeker can't stand not getting involved in the intricate details. Louis Race listens to the clock ticking in his head. ROBBIE ROBINSON.

so the grips cover the plywood with sheets of one-quarter-inch Masonite and tape the joints with paper masking tape. "That gives it a good solid base to run on," says Steve Gausche, satisfied with the work. And Dolly Grip Alvin Simmons rolls the mounted camera rig into position.

At exactly 6:00 P.M., Steve Oster appears on the set. Jonathan West sits at the camera and looks through the lens, making last-minute adjustments. He asks for a second fluorescent bulb to be added to the "eye light."

While the light is being placed, Race looks around the set, vigilant in his search for distracting elements, reflections, or sounds. "This is a long and difficult shot for Mr. Brooks," he says. "And it's a key scene. So my job is to try to isolate the actor and keep good control of the set. I want to give him the best possible environment to perform in."

Steve Oster glances around the room, his eyes suddenly locking on the coffin. He disappears, and when he returns a moment later he is with Assistant Property Master Pat Moudakis, who is carrying a Federation flag. "The flag should be over the coffin, and it almost slipped through the cracks in the scramble to get things ready," he explains.

As Oster and Moudakis study the naked coffin, Allan Kroeker joins them. First they lay the flag along the length of the tube, then they change their minds and drape it horizontally over the tube's midsection. "It plays better when it drapes toward the floor," Oster decides. Horizontal it is.

West is still at the camera, and Simmons rolls him through the shot one more time. "That's beautiful, guys," Kroeker says. He's ready to shoot. Looking around at the sparse set and minimal lighting, he jokes, "It's a cheap shot." He exits toward the monitors.

"We're using a zoom lens," Roller comments. "Jonathan wants to hold the room in focus and do a sort of forced perspective on the coffin, so we'll do a slow dolly move, and when Avery walks toward it, we'll zoom from twenty-four milimeters to about fifty."

At 6:17 P.M., Avery Brooks returns to the set. Kris Krosskove is seated at the camera. Kroeker calls a rehearsal, and for the first time he sees the shot on the monitor. It starts on the lone torpedo tube. Then Brooks walks into frame, stops at the head of the tube, and talks. When he reaches the line, "I have to make things right," Kroeker whispers "Yes!" and beats his fist against the air.

The rehearsal over, Stuart Lippman announces, "That was exactly two minutes long."

Two minutes, but all in one take. That's never easy for an actor, particularly not if you're the only one talking. But Brooks's delivery is flawless.

"I've been at this thing a long time," he explains later. "My training allows me to submerge the language into my consciousness and then let it come. It's not a matter of just regurgitating the words."

Kroeker stands and paces into the cargo bay, then paces back to the monitor. He is excited, having fun, in his element. "Okay, let's start." he says. It is 6:23.

"Roll please," Race says. The expected responses follow his order like precisely spaced dominoes falling against each other, click, click, click:

"Speed."

"Marker."

"Action!"

Again, Brooks walks into the camera's frame and stops at the head of the coffin. The dolly begins to roll to the right. But a third of the way through his soliloquy, the actor stops. "Let me do it again," he says.

Krosskove is happy about the halt in action. It gives him the opportunity to convey a warning to the only people moving on the set. "I can see your reflection in the coffin," he says, glancing toward still photographer

"On *TNG* and *Voyager*, generally the torpedo shells have been a metallic gray color, "says Doug Drexler." But whenever we do them on *DS9*, we like to make them look the way they did in *Star Trek II*—shiny black with red trim. Sharp looking and kind of sinister too." Note the fluorescent lighting at the side of the setup. ROBBIE ROBINSON.

"I have to make things right, Jadzia. I have to."
ROBBIE ROBINSON.

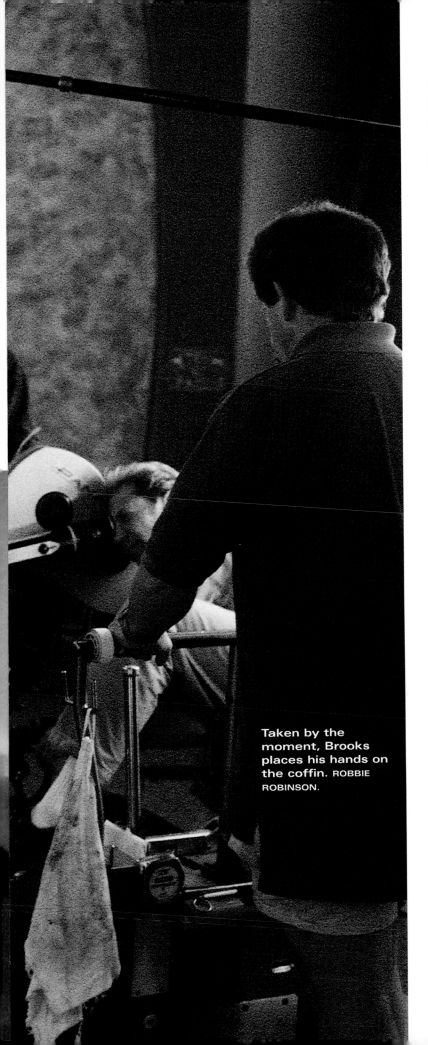

Taken by the moment, Brooks places his hands on the coffin. ROBBIE ROBINSON.

"I need to think . . . clear my head." ROBBIE ROBINSON.

A change of camera angle provides a close-up of Jadiza's last moments. ROBBIE ROBINSON.

for Worf and O'Brien to dash to the Infirmary while the others follow more slowly, Farrell feels that the two pass through the crowd in the Promenade *too* far ahead. "I'm looking for Sisko here," Farrell notes. "So when they run ahead, I kind of forget about them and for a second there's only the Promenade crowd on screen. We lose Sisko for too long, and it's disorienting."

Farrell cuts the head of the second part of the shot so that it starts on Sisko. It works better, tracking smoothly from the initial overhead shot.

Scene 87 also receives the same "head trimming" technique, although this time the cut is the result of a decision by Kroeker. As a result, we lose Sisko's entrance into the cargo bay. "Allan just felt that he wanted to come in directly on the soliloquy," explains Farrell. After viewing the revised scene, the editors confirm that the opening has more of an emotional punch this way, but they also appreciate the original version. "When you see the coffin sitting in that room by itself, and then Sisko walks in," Farrell says, "it's a pretty strong statement." But it's a statement the viewers will miss.

A subtle problem is now detected by the editors. In Scene 85, as the camera lingers on a close-up of Terry Farrell's face, "Her eyelids have just a little bit of flutter," notes Ramirez. That'd be fine if Jadzia were sleeping, but by this point in the script she's expired. No problem, says Ramirez. "We'll freeze her eyelids with an optical fix."

"I like to get a preconception of what a story is really about," says Composer Jay Chattaway. "I read the scripts to get insight into what the writers are trying to achieve. Then, when I see the on-line version of the show, I know whether it's true to the original ideas."

The typical *Star Trek* scoring session doesn't take place until approximately a month after photography on an episode ends. Usually the composer is so busy scoring earlier episodes up until that point that he has no time to read an unrelated script. But "Tears" had a twist that required Chattaway to read the storyline to the episode much earlier than normal.

Blame it on Vic Fontaine. "We needed to do a 'prerecord' of James Darren's song, 'Here's to the Losers,'" Chattaway says. Just as television shows may be prerecorded for later playback, so a singer will often prerecord a song for lip-synching during a later performance—in this case, a scene in "Tears of the Prophets."

So Chattaway received a copy of the script in order to prepare himself for a recording session with Darren. And once he got over his initial impression—"I found it rather bizarre that in a season ender where we lose a major character we should also go into the holosuite to hear Vic Fontaine sing"—Chattaway was ready to rock.

The best actors you never saw. It may look like a scene from *Radio Days*, but it's the ADR session for "Tears of the Prophets." The group holds the distinction of having worked looping sessions with the cast of every *Star Trek* incarnation, from the *original series* (during the making of *Star Trek V: The Final Frontier*) to *Voyager*. Left to right: Richard Penn, Carlyle King, Charles Bazaldua, Paige Pollack, and Gary Schwartz. ROBBIE ROBINSON.

Terri Potts (*left*) and April Rossi (*center*) at the ADR session. Their focus is on the bar patrons behind Dax and Worf.
ROBBIE ROBINSON.

"We have the track from 'His Way,'" reminds Gersh. "It's all bottles and setting up glasses."

"That'll work," Matiosian says.

Suddenly the screen goes to a series of black slugs—the missing visual-effects shots. A note on the screen refers to "OWPs." "Operations Weapons Platforms," Potts translates. "You'll have fun with them. They're Cardassian, but different from anything that we've ever done before."

"They're state of the art," Adelman adds, and the editors each write themselves a note.

"We'll need a big group ADR session," Potts says as they watch the start of Scene 83.

In Scene 84, Williams questions, "Is everyone okay with Sid talking so quietly?" Williams can't tell if he says, "There was nothing I *could do* for Jadzia" or "*can do*." Potts replays Bashir's speech and makes a note. Perhaps the line will have to be rerecorded.

Of Jadzia's death scene, and Worf's subsequent scream and chant, Potts says, "We won't have any sound effects at all here. The music will tell us everything." The same is true for the scene over the coffin.

"There's an electronic cycling sound in the final alley scene," Potts notes. Clearly it's something that *wasn't* supposed to be on the soundtrack.

"We'll mask it," Matiosian says. "Or maybe we'll just put in a cricket sound every time there's a 'whoosh.'"

"Avery is already in New York," Potts says. "I've faxed him a list of the lines we want him to loop. He'll do the work there and we'll do a telephone line tie-in."

As the editors leave the room, Potts continues working on her looping notes, talking quietly as she writes—"I'll bring in seven people for the 'walla' session . . ."

"'Walla' is an old ADR term," Potts explains at the looping session. "It's called that because background crowd dialogue always sounds like, 'wallawallawalla.'"

It is 10:00 A.M. on May 28, and a group of three women and four men is arriving at Modern Sound, a state-of-the-art recording facility several blocks from the Paramount lot. Potts knows each of these voice-over artists well. They've been meeting at this studio to record background dialogue almost weekly since the first *TNG* episode, "Encounter at Farpoint," eleven years ago. Each of them holds a notebook filled with both general and very specific *Star Trek* information.

Sound Editor Ruth Adelman annotates the ADR spotting notes while ADR Mixer Al Ferrante keeps his mind on the sound levels. Ferrante has worked on the looping session of every *TNG*, *DS9*, and *Voyager* episode. "Once I even set back my vacation plans so I wouldn't break my streak," he says. ROBBIE ROBINSON.

"We have pages of technobabble about different parts of starships, like the engineering section and the bridge," says Gary Schwartz. "We know dabo terms, sickbay terms, ops terms. And we all make our own individual notebooks. That allows us to play off of one another's research."

As the actors look over the script notes that Potts gives them, Al Ferrante, the engineer who will record the session, prepares the recording board. While he works, he provides a mini-tutorial on ADR. "Automated Dialogue Replacement has actually only been automated since it became a programmable function in the mixing and editing consoles in the late sixties. Before that it was called 'Loop Only Dialogue Replacement,' or 'looping.'"

Why looping?

Ferrante smiles as if he's been anticipating the question. In the early days of dialogue rerecording, the actor didn't look at a film image when he redid his line, he explains. Instead, the sound editor would take a

Nice day for a walk. The voice-over actors circle in front of the microphones, moving in synch with Bajoran strollers on the upper level of the Promenade. The sounds will provide a backdrop for the scene in which Bashir tells Dax she can have a baby, as seen on the monitor. ROBBIE ROBINSON.

piece of film with the original line on it and splice it to make a loop out of it. "Then the loop was hung on a reproducing machine and it would go around and around. The actor would listen to it until he felt that he could mimic the line just as it was on the loop, and then they would record it," says Ferrante. "After a loop was used, it was discarded, but there was never time to properly dispose of them during the session. We'd take them off and throw them on the floor and load another and take that off and throw that on the floor and load another." He chuckles at the memory. "When the process was over, there used to be two or three hundred pieces of film just covering the floor of the machine room."

Since each scene requiring background dialogue noises is different, Barbara Harris, the voice-casting specialist who books these sessions, chooses which members of this group will be gathered for each scene. For the opening Temple shot, they need adult and child voices. One of the actors, Paige Pollack, has been chosen specifically for her ability to do children. *"Peldor joi,"* Pollack quietly rehearses in a youthful voice. *"Peldor joi."* The others ad-lib lines that relate to the happy Bajoran holiday: "Did you bring a gift?" "I saw you in the Temple." "We're going to have decorations and a cake this evening."

The actors display their improvisational prowess as they go from scene to scene. "Okay, who wants to be in the band?" Potts asks when they reach the Las Vegas Lounge sequence.

Rossi explains what this scene is about as the men step toward the microphones. "You're a musical group playing in an outer-space lounge," she says.

The actors immediately get into character. As they reach the imaginary bandstand, Charles Bazaldua looks at his fellow "musicians" and asks, "Do we know how to play 'I Want To Hold Your Claw'?"

When they get to Scene 83, the large crowd scene, Rossi explains that the lead characters are rushing through the Promenade to Dax's death. The collective mood of the actors drops to one of serious concern. "Shall we drop to a murmur when the child speaks to Sisko?" Bazaldua asks.

"Yes," says Terri Potts as she plays the scene on the monitor. The seven actors watch it three times before they're ready to play it. They will do it in motion, walking around the microphones, as if they were rushing toward the Emissary.

"Make it big at the beginning," Harris says. "Then take it down to a slow buzz." After two takes, everyone is satisfied.

"Now let's do another take with only four people," says Potts.

"It'll give us an option in editing," Ruth Adelman explains, "depending on what the music is doing."

Options are important to Potts. She next asks for a take with the actors doing only "heavy breathing." "The scene is probably covered by the low buzz," she says, "but I just want to make sure we have it." And then she asks for one more, with Schwartz and Bazaldua speaking only in Spanish.

By 5:28 P.M., the walla session is complete. But the ADR phase of postproduction is far from over. Every principal actor in the series has some looping duties. The requirements covered by this group took up less than three pages of Potts's "looping list." The entire list is twenty-one pages long.

REQUIEM

"WE HAVE TO BE VERY SERIOUS HERE, BECAUSE THIS IS A VERY EMOTIONAL SCENE," JAY CHATTAWAY BEGINS. "It is a scene where a husband is watching over his wife as she is dying."

It is June 8, at 10 A.M. The forty-two musicians listen quietly. Most of them are regular participants in *Deep Space Nine*'s scoring sessions, and they have grown accustomed to hearing Chattaway tell them something about each episode. But this is the first they've heard of Jadzia's death. If he's trying to set a mood, he's succeeded.

Several dozen highly sensitive microphones hang overhead, waiting to deliver every sound to the ears of the engineers and producers behind the glass of the control booth. Yet the only sound is Chattaway's voice.

"But this is not a death moment," the composer continues. "The symbiont inside of her lives. And it will be transported back to Trill . . ." Chattaway waits only a fraction of a second before spinning on his heels to make a mock preemptive strike against the clarinet section. "Don't do it!" he warns.

Now a low giggle erupts from the orchestra. Chattaway is serious about conveying the scene's weighty subject matter, but he wants the musicians to enjoy playing the upcoming cue. Hence the bad pun about trilling, which, in musical lingo, means using a vibrato.

Composer Jay Chattaway practices two-fisted conducting. "I labored with how to end the show musically," Chattaway says. "Then I realized that using a trumpet over Sisko's soliloquy and then moving to a New Orleans flügelhorn would be a really cool tie-in." PETER IOVINO.

He starts to move on. "Jadzia is still alive at the beginning of the cue," he says, "but we could say that the Trill is nearly gone."

A moan arises from somewhere in the room. The composer's efforts to prepare his musicians are one step shy of going over the edge. He reins himself in. "Remember the last show we did," he states. Since Chattaway primarily does the even-numbered episodes, that would be "Time's Orphan." "Worf and Jadzia really bonded. They were talking about having a baby together. Obviously, that won't happen now." His musicians are right where he wants them. "So," he says slowly, "let's try to get through this. Very *rubato*. And one, two, three, four, five." And the room fills with music. Even though it is a rehearsal, it is beautiful, rich, and melodic. Afterward, Chattaway suggests only a few note changes for some of the instruments. "Let's record it," he says.

The musical direction *rubato* calls for a free tempo, allowing the musician to lengthen certain notes and make up for the time by shortening others. The effect makes the music more expressive. And that's exactly what Chattaway wants on this musical cue for the death of Jadzia Dax.

Of course, there's more to this cue, titled "Sad Homecoming," than just the death. It is two minutes and fifty-eight seconds long and begins with a shot of the *Defiant* docking at the station.

"When they come off the ship, the music has a bit of urgency," Steve Rowe points out. Then, for each of the scenes that follow, it changes in coloration."

Each section of instruments is individually miked. Four microphones handle the violins, four handle the cellos, and two capture the basses. Each woodwind has its own microphone, while the electric guitar, bass, and keyboards feed directly into the recording board. The mikes on the high stand above Jay Chattaway are for "ambiance"; they pick up the overall sound of the room. PETER IOVINO.

Chattaway is familiar with every hue. "I write from the point of view of the principal characters," he explains. "When the music is Sisko-related, it's a little bit more Federation sounding, with solo horn and solo trumpet on a string background. It's Americana music that relates to his personality.

"Then when we get to the Worf section, the timbre changes considerably. I use big open fifth chords in the low brass and some percussion things that are more readily associated with what we've musically defined as the Klingon culture. So when Worf does his scream and his chant, it's very Klingonesque."

Chattaway also added a layer of digitally synthesized choral voices to Dax's bedside scene. "I use snippets of Gregorian chant," he says. It's Chattaway's interpretation of what Klingons would sing if they were less prone to arias. "It's voiced the same way, all in open fifths," he says. "When that's doubled with the low brass, it has a religioso feeling, but harmonically it doesn't go where you would expect it to. If it were a true dirge or a somber funeralesque thing, it would be more tonal. But I think that by nature Klingons would not be all that tonal when they conduct vigils." Chattaway pauses, as if he's hearing himself for the first time. "Actually, I don't really know," he says laughing. "We make all this stuff up, you know. I mean, there's no way I can research this."

From inside the booth, the recording mixers can view the conductor, the orchestra, and the episode itself on three monitors. PETER IOVINO.

A keyboard player's-eye-view of the composer in action. Jay Chattaway conducts a contingency of forty-two musicians who play instruments ranging from classica violas and French horns to state-of-the-art digitally-programmable keyboards. PETER IOVINO.

At the exact moment of Dax's death, Chattaway plans to use a cadence, a series of notes or chords that ends a section of music to give the listener a sense of finality. "And then it goes into a unison, a big low note, right after she closes her eyes, to show that she's really gone."

At this point, the episode moves on to Scene 86, a simple optical shot of the station, sitting alone in space. The shot is designed to reinforce the isolation that Sisko is feeling, but Chattaway finds his own use for it as a transitional point in a long music cue. The last seven minutes and twenty-two seconds of the episode are literally nonstop music. For a number of reasons, Chattaway has divided that music into two pieces. The simplest, he explains, is that "seven minutes would be too long a cue for the endurance of the musicians."

There's also a technical reason for the break. "When I was writing, the show was still not in its final edited form," says Chattaway. "If I had written the entire seven minutes as one cue, and the editors had trimmed that optical shot for length, the music would have been out of sync when we came back into the station to see Sisko over the coffin. But with the break, if the music has to be adjusted, the editor can just let the first part sustain over the station shot and simply move the second part to overlap it as much as necessary, and then come up out of it when we go into the cargo bay."

DEEP SPACE NINE   40510-550 (06)

"TEARS OF THE PROPHETS"

Studio: "M"
Date: 6/8/98 (MON.)
Time: 10:00 A.M.

Composer: **JAY CHATTAWAY**

Total Time: 23:30

* ORCH. BY GREGORY SMITH

M-	Cue Title	Reel	Part	Timing	Violins	Violas	Cellos	Basses	Flute	Bb CBC	EWI	Horns	Trumpets	Trombones	Tuba	Keyboard	Synth.	Harp	Guitar	Fender Bass	Percussion	Drums	Total	Pages
41	LET THE BATTLE BEGIN *			3:33	14	6	4		1	1	1	6	3	2	1		1				2		42	24.5
42	PATH OF DESTRUCTION *			3:08	14	6	4		1	1	1	6	3	3			1				2		42	18.5
51	TABLES ARE TURNED *			2:21	14	6	4		1	1	1	6	3	3			1				2		42	17.5
52	SAD HOMECOMING			2:58	14	6	4		1	1	1	6		3			1				1		38	14.5
53	GOODBYE OLD SOLDIER			4:24	14	6	4		1	1	1	6	1				1				1		36	18
31	O.W.P.			:05	14	6	4		1			6		3			1				1		36	1
32	YOU CAN'T BE BOTH			:22	14	6	4		1			6		3			1				1		37	2.5
33	OLD RED EYES			:43	14	6	4		1	1	1	6	1	3			1				1		39	4.5
35	MARCHING TO CARDASSIA			:46	14	6	4		1	1	1	6	1	3			1				1		39	5
15	DOWNTOWN CARDASSIA			:06	14	6	4					6		3			1				1		36	1
11	PELDOR JOI			:06	14	6	4					6					1						31	1.5
12	POINT MAN			1:21	14	6	4		1	1	1	6	1				1				1		36	6.5
13	PLANNING PARENTHOOD			:05	14	6	4		1	1	1	6					1						34	1
14	BABY BLUES			:18	14	6	4		1	1	1	6					1				1		35	2.5
16	NEW MAN			1:21	14	6	4		1			6					1				1		33	6
21	HECKLE AND JACKAL			:10	14	6	4		1			6					1				1		33	1.5
22	ROMULANS			:09	14	6	4					6					1				1		32	1.5
23	THE PROPHET ZONE			1:08	14	6	4		1	1	1	6					1				1		35	6
34	LOVE LESSON			:25	14	6	4		1	1	1	6					1						34	2.5

The "cue sheet" assembled by Steve Rowe shows that Chattaway has written twenty-three minutes and thirty seconds of music. The final timing is 23:21:40, over half of "Tears of the Prophet's" forty-two minute and thirty seconds' broadcast time.

"You don't hear the segue," notes Steve Rowe. "When you see the episode, it'll sound as if it's all one piece. "

The cue that makes up the second half of the long piece of music is titled "Goodbye Old Soldier" on the cue sheet. As frivolous as the titles sometimes sound, they represent more than simple reminders for the composer. Since any of the cues could be reused in the music track of another episode or could be used on another episode's "temp track" for screening purposes, the cues are copyrighted. "The titles get locked with that piece of music for copyright, and for worldwide distribution," Rowe says. "And it sticks with the cue all the way down through ASCAP [American Society of Composers Authors and Publishers] and the Library of Congress."

At 2:00 P.M., Chattaway prepares the assembled orchestra for the final cue of the show, "Good bye Old Soldier."

"The piece opens with a soliloquy from Sisko as he says good-bye to Dax in her coffin," he explains to them. "As he's talking, he decides that he's not done a proper job as a commander, so he takes his son and they

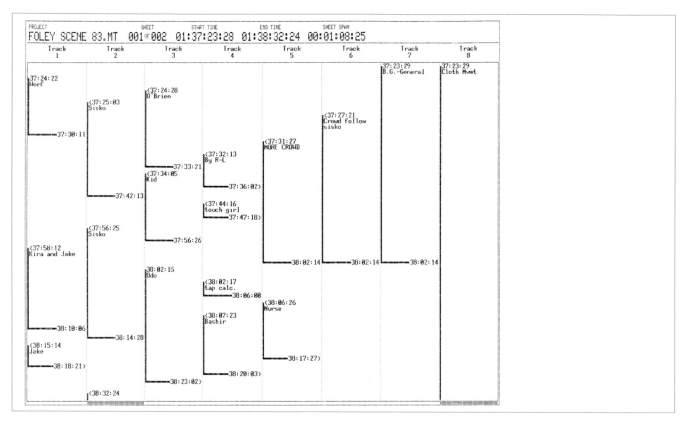

The "Foley sheet" from Mace Matiosian's computer shows the sounds of Scenes 83, 84, and 85, starting with Worf's footsteps out of the airlock to Sisko gently touching Jadzia's face. "We rerecord every sound," Matiosian says, "because the set is miked for dialogue so the sounds don't get picked up very well." The process, called Foley, is done by a team of people who manipulate props, etc. in front of a microphone.

mal for *Deep Space Nine*. We start out by doing a 'write pass,' as we call it, viewing the show and automating all of the sound levels as we pass through it. On our second pass, we record. Then we do a third pass so Terri Potts and Steve Oster can listen to it and point out any changes that still need to be made."

As they work, the three mixers concentrate on their own contributions to the track, while at the same time maintaining an awareness of what the others are doing. "I'm listening to the dialogue and effects as much as to the music," Morrison says. "It's a time-share thing. The dialogue, of course, is king. We can't all play maximum levels at once. So we weave in and around the dialogue. I know where the music is laying back, because that's the way the composer wrote it. So if the music's low, we'll feature an effect. We've got to hear the words, so everything else kind of fills in the holes underneath to keep it all moving."

"It's like putting together a jigsaw puzzle," adds Chris Haire. "One angle of a shot may have been filmed early in the day and the coverage was filmed hours later. The background ambiance may be entirely different, so it's part of my job to smooth that all out and make it flow."

"Once everything's mixed together, we may find that a music cue comes in a little early or a little later, so we'll move it a few frames," says Steve Rowe. "Or I might suggest that we're missing something, a certain sound. In Dax's death scene, we have an oboe playing over a beautiful little string section. It sounded a little busy to me, so I asked Terri if we could play the oboe a little lower."

"What's important is that the dialogue is clear and understandable and that there's a sense of emotion,"

Potts notes. "At the music-scoring session, I wear a headset that gives me the dialogue in one ear and the music in the other, so I get that sense of the music's emotion playing against dialogue. And that's what I do in here, too. Richard, Chris, and Doug do listen to each other's work, but they have to focus on their specific areas because that's what they're supposed to do. Overseeing the dub comes under my jurisdiction. I'm the ears that take it as a whole. I have to make sure that everything falls into place, and I try to finish it as a complete emotional piece."

At 5:00 P.M. on the session's second day, Steve Oster arrives to review the dub. His initial interest is in the hundreds of sound effects incorporated into the space-battle sequences. But he isn't so focused on them that he fails to notice something completely different when Worf begins his Klingon chant. "Bring the Klingon drum down a little," he says. "I don't want it to sound conspicuous, as if some Foley thing is going on."

A few seconds later, Oster nods. Better.

"Because I haven't been sitting there for two days, I provide a final set of ears," Oster says. "I come in fresh and sometimes hear things that the others might not because they're immersed in it. I listen for a balance. It's true the dialogue has to be heard, but we want to sell the effects. We want to make everything sound big and exciting. And of course," he adds, "we want to have the music just carrying us along."

CODA

DEEP SPACE NINE CAN OCCASIONALLY SEEM FRIVOLOUS—WITH HOLOGRAM LOUNGE SINGERS OFFERING SAGE (BUT HIP) COUNSEL IN BETWEEN OLD SINATRA TUNES, AND FERENGI BARTENDERS HAVING TEMPORARY SEX CHANGES TO SAVE THEIR PLANET'S ECONOMY—BUT THE SHOW'S EXECUTIVE PRODUCER TAKES HIS JOB VERY SERIOUSLY.

"I've said this many times, but I can't say it enough," says Ira Behr. "We want to make good television. We want to do shows that can stand as decent hours of television. One of the things I have to do as 'leader of the pack' here is to make sure that everyone working on the show, especially the writing staff, knows how seriously I take it, so that *they* will take it seriously as well."

That said, Behr can express his hopes for "Tears of the Prophets."

"I'm very excited about this show," he says, just prior to its airing the week of June 15. "There's so much going on, and I mean that in a good way. Everything from the invasion of Cardassia to lovely scenes with Weyoun, Damar, and Dukat, to Pah-wraiths and Prophet visitations. All this and Vic Fontaine, too. And a song! It's an amazingly busy show that seems to be bursting at the seams. Usually, when we do something like this, it's a setup, and we pay it off later on. This time, because of Dax, in a way, we had to set it up and pay it off all in one episode. But that means you'll get a lot of bang for your buck. I think it's a wonderful entrance into the seventh and final season."

ROBBIE ROBINSON.

STAR TREK:
THE NEXT GENERATION
INSURRECTION

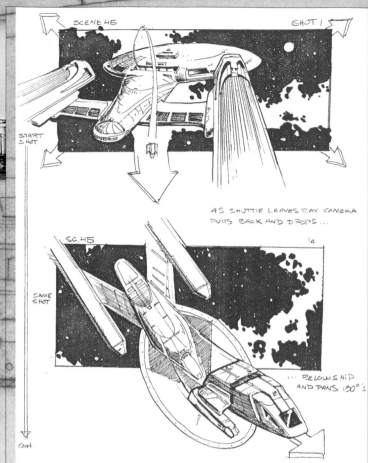

SCENE 45   SHOT 1

AS SHUTTLE LEAVES BAY CAMERA
PULLS BACK AND DROPS...

SC. 45   1A

START
SHOT

SAME
SHOT

CONT.

...BELOW SHIP
AND PANS 180°'s

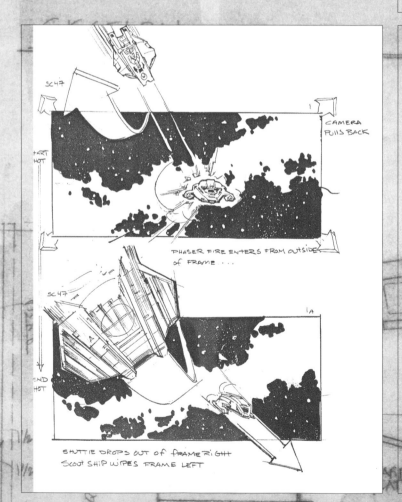

SC 47

CAMERA
PULLS BACK

START
SHOT

PHASER FIRE ENTERS FROM OUTSIDE
OF FRAME ....

SC 47   1A

END
SHOT

SHUTTLE DROPS OUT OF FRAME RIGHT
SCOUT SHIP WIPES FRAME LEFT

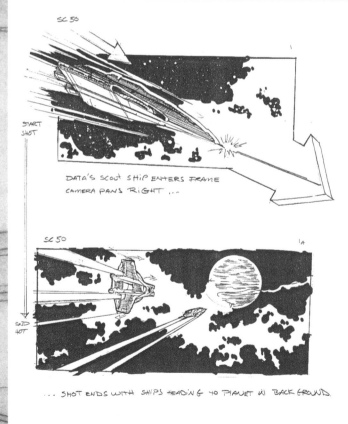

SC 50

START
SHOT

DATA'S SCOUT SHIP ENTERS FRAME
CAMERA PANS RIGHT ...

SC 50   1A

END
SHOT

... SHOT ENDS WITH SHIPS HEADING TO PLANET IN BACKGROUND

SC 54 — START SHOT — 2 — CAMERA LOCKED W/SHUTTLE. DATA BEHIND ZIGZAGGING. CAMERA PULLS BACK FROM SPACE THROUGH ATMOSPHERE

SC 54 — SAME SHOT — 2A — SPACE BEGINS TO CHANGE INTO BLUE SKY

SC 54 — SAME SHOT — 2B — SHUTTLE BEGINS TO HEAT UP FROM REENTRY — CONTINUED

SC 54 — CONTINUED — SAME SHOT — 2C — SHUTTLE CLOSES DISTANCE TO CAMERA

SC 54 — SAME SHOT — 2D — CAMERA PANS SHUTTLE TOWARDS PLANET

SC 54 — SAME SHOT — 2E — SHUTTLE IN DISTANCE SMOKING — CONTINUED

In the preceding sections, I attempted to convey every element involved in the creation of the final product. For this sequence from Star Trek: Insurrection, an "aerial" dogfight involving Picard, Worf, and Data, I've left out the dialogue and some of the action. That's so you'll still have lots of surprises in December.

Movies are different from television. On average, a Star Trek episode takes one hundred days from story sessions to aired show, a Star Trek film over five hundred. Everything is bigger. Story. Production values. Budget. Crew. The number of people involved in every decision.

Some decisions, of course, involve only one person....

FIRST CONTACT

EARLY 1997. HE DOESN'T REMEMBER THE DATE, BUT HE REMEMBERS THE PLACE. "I was in my office at Paramount, writing," recalls screenwriter Michael Piller. "The phone rang and Rick [Berman] asked if he could come over and see me."

The two offices are located in neighboring buildings, Piller's in Dietrich (as in Marlene) and Berman's in Cooper (Gary). The buildings themselves are just yards apart, separated only by a road leading to Stage 19, where the sitcom *Wings* was shot for many years. So it was just a matter of minutes until Berman arrived.

"I didn't know what it was about," Piller admits, "but the first thing he said to me was, 'Don't say "no" until I finish talking.'"

Now Piller was really intrigued. Although he had returned to the *Star Trek* fold as a creative consultant for *DS9* and *Voyager* following a stint on his own non–*Star Trek* projects, he was no longer acting as executive producer on either *Star Trek* series, nor actively writing *Star Trek* episodes. He was hardly prepared for the next words out of Berman's mouth.

"I felt personally that I needed to write something that would make people feel good," observes Screenwriter Michael Piller. "I wanted to go to the movies and feel the way that I did when I was growing up—to be roused and come away from the experience having had a *good* time." ELLIOTT MARKS.

"How would you feel about writing the next *Star Trek* movie?"

Although Piller was surprised, he had a quick response. "I hope you didn't think I *would* say 'no'!"

"It was a logical step," states Berman, who serves as producer on the film. "Michael and I have worked together for nine years. We worked together for five years on *The Next Generation*, and we created *Deep Space Nine* together, and then *Voyager* [with Jeri Taylor]. So it was not at all an unusual choice."

A few days later—the log of Piller's assistant, Eric Stillwell, pinpoints the month as February—Piller went over to see Berman and run some ideas past him in what became the film's de facto pitch session (a term that describes the process wherein hopeful scribes toss out their ideas to producers in the hopes of snaring a writing assignment). He remembers describing it to Berman in this manner: "We open with Picard at Starfleet Academy, and he's antiestablishment, a young, rebellious figure. Everything he's not as an adult," much the way young Picard was established in the *TNG* episode "Tapestry." "At the Academy," Piller continues, "we meet Picard's friend Duffy, and we establish a wonderful, terrific relationship between the two of them. Then we cut to the future, which is the present of our franchise, and Picard is called into Starfleet Headquarters by an admiral, who says, 'We need you to go into the unknown, where we have a Starfleet officer who is attacking Romulan ships.' And Picard is horrified to learn that this officer is his old friend, Duffy."

A simple suggestion of, "Why not Data?" sets the stage for *Star Trek: Insurrection*. ELLIOTT MARKS.

Berman liked the idea, so Piller began working on it, meeting regularly with Berman to discuss various plot points. By the time Picard's alter ego, Patrick Stewart—serving for the first time as a producer as well as the lead actor in a *Star Trek* film—came in a few weeks later, the pitch had been fleshed out a bit more, including the fact that at some point in the past there had been a falling-out betwen Duffy and Picard. "Patrick responded quite well to the initial pitch," recalls Piller.

While Berman went off on vacation, Piller began to sketch out what he describes as, "a very, very verbose version of this story with big holes and gaps and questions." Then Berman came back and read it. And immediately he saw problems.

"Rick thought that it was just too political on too many levels," notes Piller. On a large scale, there were the uneasy politics between the Federation and the Romulans. On the more personal level, there were the political conflicts between Picard and Duffy. "I was sort of pulling something out of the Sixties radical movement," admits Piller in retrospect, "with Picard having become more conservative [since his academy days] and Duffy having become more radical."

At this point, just as he has done innumerable times in the past for the *Star Trek* writers, Berman came up with a possible solution. "He looked at me," says Piller, "and he said, 'What if Duffy were Data?' And I knew a good idea when I heard it."

Patrick Stewart felt that Picard should continue along the path he'd forged in *First Contact* by further exploring the dynamic nature of his character. ELLIOTT MARKS.

Story writing, however, is such a collaborative process, that Berman modestly confesses he's not sure *whose* idea it was. "I haven't the slightest idea," he says hesitantly. "Those kinds of suggestions come continually from both my mouth and Michael's mouth. Every once in a while one of them sticks."

Now the story was about Picard versus Data. Regardless of who said it first, the notion inspired Piller. "Suddenly you could see half of the movie in your head," he says. "Picard going after Data. Picard battling Data. Maybe even Picard *killing* Data. I really liked the idea."

And in fact, in an early version of the story, "Picard 'killed' Data halfway through the script, only to find out that he had killed his friend for the wrong reason," Piller conveys. "We became quite enamored of this story. It was powerful drama with great action sequences. We really thought we had it."

But they didn't *quite* have it. "The first reactions to that story were terrific," Piller recalls. "Many people at the studio just loved it. It was relevant, it was topical, it was dramatic. We could already see the [theatrical] poster in our minds." But that was only the first round of reviews. There were more.

The first word of discouragement, notes Piller, came from an executive at the studio, who felt that the story was still too political. "But the crushing blow," he says, "came from Patrick Stewart. He wrote a letter to Rick from Australia, where he was shooting [the made-for-cable movie] *Moby Dick*, saying that he was very unhappy with the story."

Stewart enumerated several points that he felt the screenplay needed, chief among them more physical action for Picard. "I thought that Picard's involvement in the action line of the story in *First Contact* had been very successful," explains Stewart, "and I wanted to continue that. My feeling was that the captain should be in the thick of things. While we were shooting the series, when Gene Roddenberry was still alive, he often expressed the belief that the captain's life shouldn't be put at risk. You send the first officer. You send Worf. But in recent years, we've put that thinking to one side. You've *got* to have the captain in jeopardy."

"I was mostly interested in rediscovering the moral and intellectual leadership that Picard had demonstrated in the television show," says Piller. "But Patrick really felt that going back to the television show was a mistake. He thought that one weakness of *Star Trek Generations* was that there had been too much effort to be true to the television show. One of the reasons that *First Contact* had been more successful was because they had created a new Picard, one who was much more action-oriented and stronger. He wanted to pick up where *First Contact* had left off with Picard.

"We exchanged letters," says Piller. "Quite passionate letters. But it's very hard to get a meeting of the minds that way."

Piller laughs at the memory now. "Rick and I said, 'What are we going to do? How are we going to fix this story? And how can we save the parts we really like?'"

BATTLE IN THE AIR

IN THE END, THERE WOULD BE SOME COMPROMISES. Piller would spend the next full year working out another version of the story with Berman, one that contained only a few of the original elements, and then writing the screenplay based on that story. But he did manage to salvage the idea of Picard versus Data, although to a different degree than he'd first imagined. "The plot is still driven by Picard going after Data," he observes.

In line with Stewart's wish for more activity, Piller came up with something much more physical for him to do while he's pursuing Data than direct the actions of others from the captain's chair.

He created a *Star Trek* "dogfight."

During the two world wars, and for a long time thereafter, a dogfight meant an epic battle conducted between two airplanes of different nations, frequently resulting in the death of one or both pilots. Those aviators sat in exposed cockpits, making them vulnerable to the enemy. Because of those dramatic qualities—visibility and courage—dogfight battles became staples of uncountable Hollywood war movies. Unlike today's *Top Gun*-style fighter pilots, stuffed into tight cockpits and hidden behind tinted visors and feature-concealing breathing apparatuses, pilots in earlier films could show audiences their faces and let viewers read their expressions as they moved in for the moment of truth.

That requisite visibility is exactly what Michael Piller had in mind for his dogfight: an old-fashioned airborne battle between two men who could look each other in the eye. In fact, in the script, he introduces the concept to the audience a full ten pages before the chase sequence begins:

34: EXT. SPACE—IN THE FOREGROUND: THE SCOUT—(OPTICAL)
...the scout zooms right by our view as it moves at us and we clearly see the face of Data through the window...

The day before filming begins, the scout sits alone, resting on the inactive gimbal. COURTESY JOHN EAVES.

HOT SET

The realized scoutship. ELLIOTT MARKS.

Brent Spiner will spend the better part of four days seated in this tiny set. ELLIOTT MARKS.

The call sheets, like everyone else, "talk" about the weather. Or rather, they include a forecast of the day's anticipated barometrical highlights, important information for the schedule planners amongst the crew. The call sheet for April 14 notes "High 60 degrees—Low 40 degrees—Chance of Rain in A.M." It also indicates that Brent Spiner has a 5:00 A.M. makeup call. Hornstein has been lucky this week; he had an idea of what the weather was likely to be early enough to influence Spiner's schedule. A conversation with the film's producers over the weekend freed up Spiner on Monday (April 13), thus allowing the actor to get a good night's sleep in preparation for this early Tuesday call. Monday's scenes, in Riker's quarters and in sickbay, were also cover sets that did not require Data's presence.

The scenes inside the scoutship are being shot on Stage 5, and there, at 7:30 A.M., is the recently gilded Brent Spiner. With golden skin and yellow eyes, he has been transformed into his android counterpart. Frakes prepares to start shooting, and Spiner braces himself. The chair he sits on is bolted inside a wooden box that is mounted on a hydraulically powered gimbal balanced several feet above the soundstage floor. The floor, of course, is not expected to move. But the box, and Spiner, will move a lot.

From a distance, the setup looks like a scene from a Russian fairy tale, like the hut of the old witch Baba Yaga, perched precariously on the leg of a chicken. In order to talk to Baba Yaga, one was required to get the chicken leg to stand still long enough to enter the hut.

Hydraulics are much more reliable.

"The gimbal sits on a giant knuckle that's capable of going in four directions, and a ram to make it go in those four directions," explains Special Effects Coordinator Terry Frazee. "It can tilt four feet up or four feet down, so there's an eight-foot slant. These hoses running along the floor lead to a big hydraulic pump parked outside the stage that supplies the power. It's pretty simple."

In fact, the toughest thing about it was probably getting it into the soundstage. "The gimbal alone weighs about eight thousand pounds, and now with the set on it, it weighs about twenty thousand pounds," Frazee says. "So before we could bring it into the stage, we had to go down into the basement and shore up the floor." Frazee laughs. "It's always something. And we certainly couldn't carry that weight in here on a forklift, so we assembled the set outside and then got it in the way they say the Egyptians built the pyramids. We pushed it [into the soundstage] by hand, putting one block under it and then putting the next block under it and then putting the next block under it. It took us about two hours to get the whole megillah from the door over there to over here where it sits, but we got it in." The distance covered? About forty feet.

"Hydraulic...," Jonathan Frakes shouts, "...gimbal...and...Action!"

Special Effects Foreman Geno Crum mans the controls to the gimbal, making him the *real* pilot of Data's scoutship. ELLIOTT MARKS.

Across the stage, Special Effects Foreman Geno Crum pushes the control rod that regulates the hydraulic pressure. The rod is an oversized joystick, but without a measurement gauge attached, it is not a precision instrument; exactly how many feet the gimbal will tilt depends on the operator's agility. Crum is the perfect man for the job. After several decades performing as a professional rock 'n' roll drummer, his wrists are strong and his control is precise.

Suddenly, Stage 5 is filled with the sharp hissing sound of air rushing into the hoses. The wooden box makes a series of jerking drops, first tilting fifteen degrees to the left, then jolting back up to its original position, then dropping fifteen degrees again, this time to the right. Spiner rides the jolts as if he's a passenger

The boxes suspended on ropes are lighting equipment called "far-cycs." The lights, along with the electrical cables connected to them, will be raised to the rafters during shooting. They will rake the bluescreen with an even light wash all the way to the floor. Here they have been lowered for the convenience of the lighting technicians. ELLIOTT MARKS.

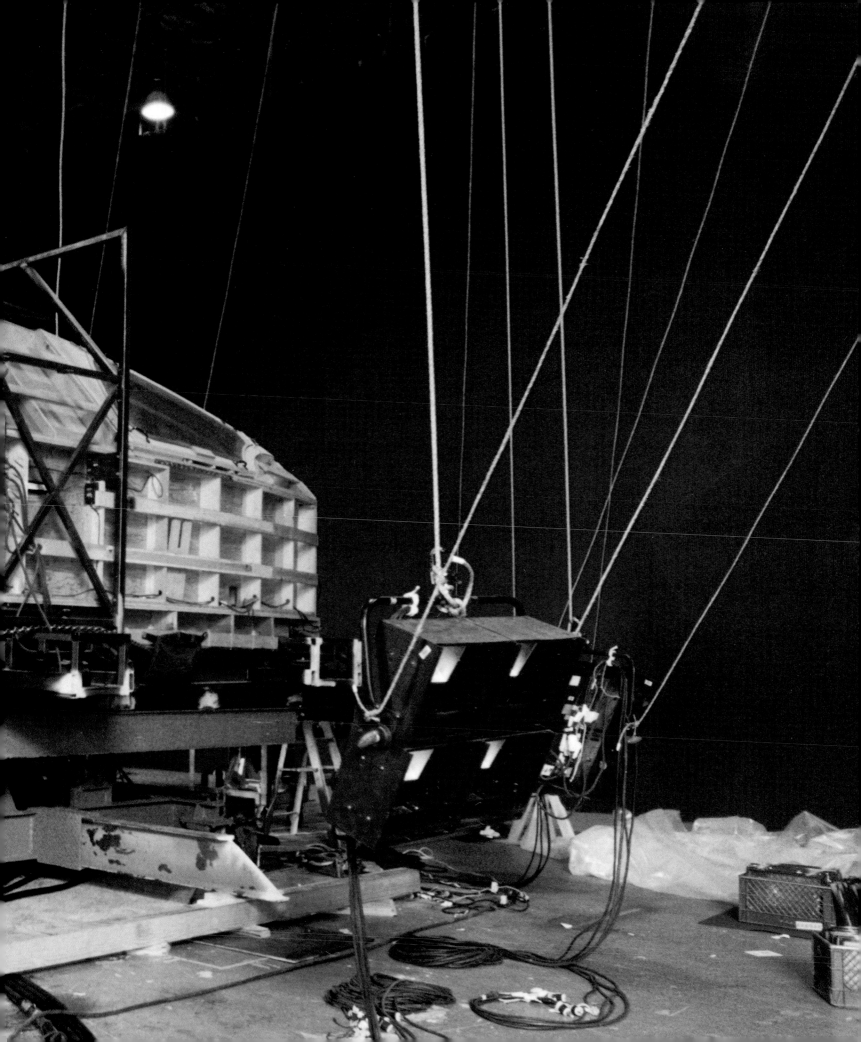

In order to get the right angle for the shot, the camera is underslung from the crane's arm. ELLIOTT MARKS.

Concealed behind the camera equipment, an unseen boom operator picks up Spiner's dialogue. The metal handles attached to the exterior of the cockpit will come into use when the grips lift away that section of the scout for a later scene. ELLIOTT MARKS.

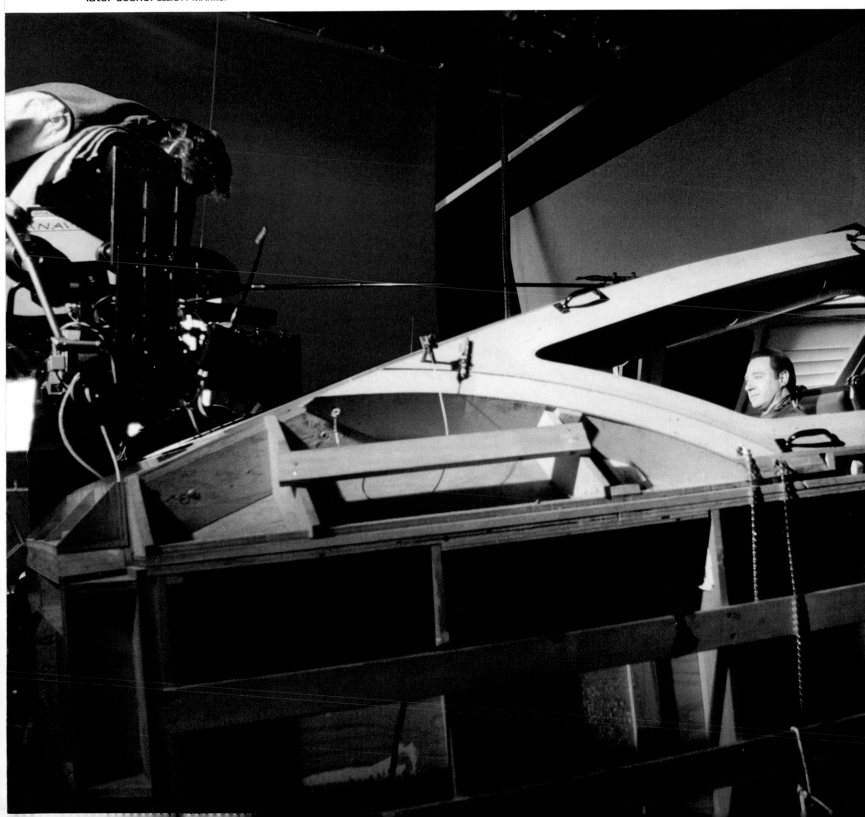

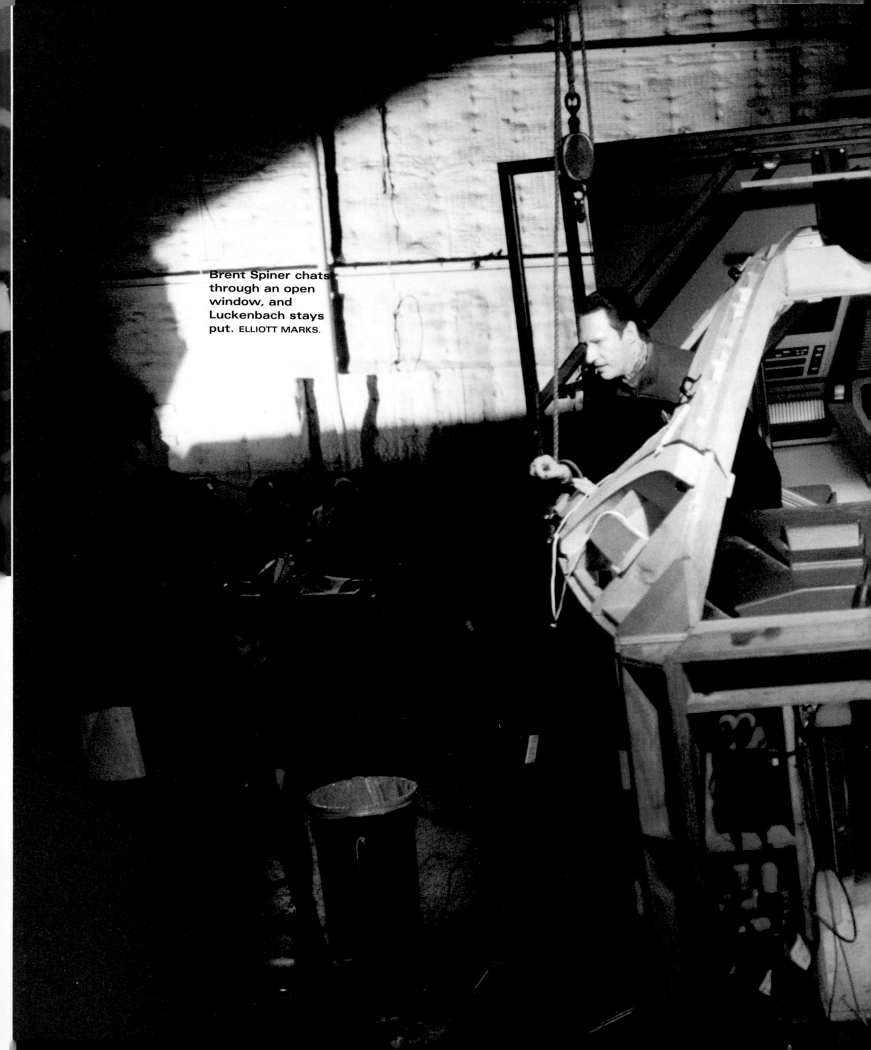

Brent Spiner chats through an open window, and Luckenbach stays put. ELLIOTT MARKS.

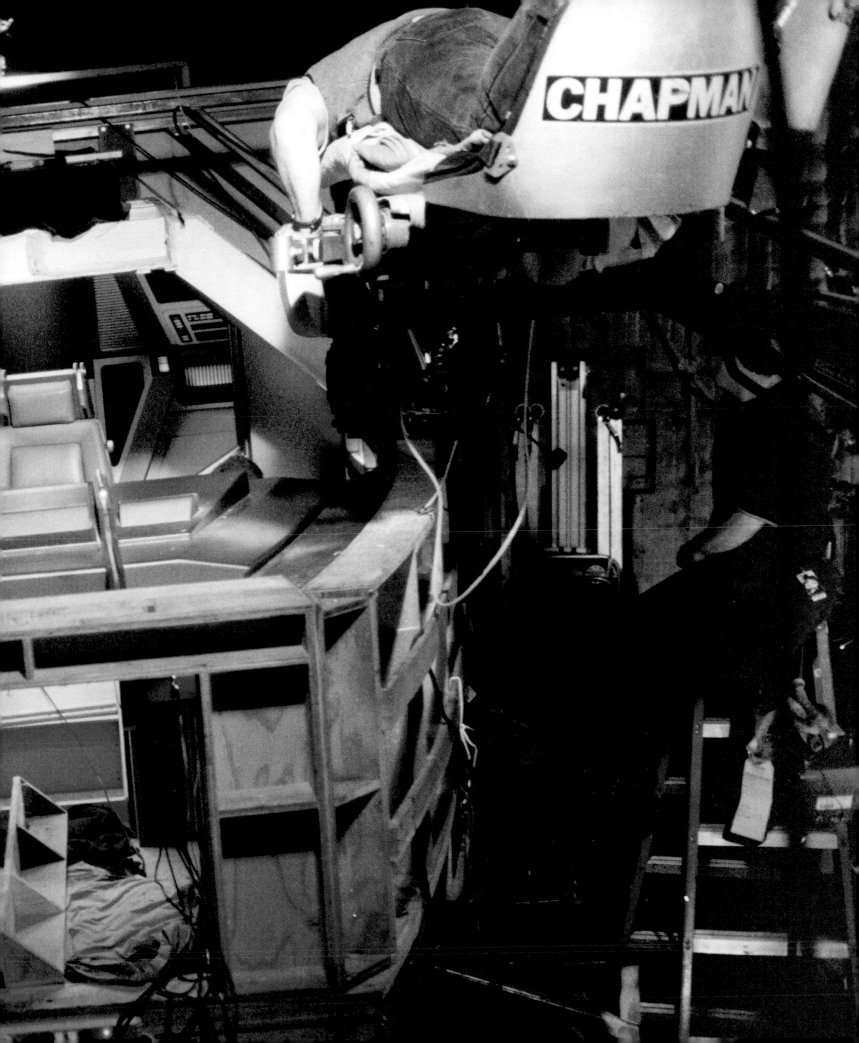

Causey examines his audio equipment while waiting. "I'm recording entirely in digital on a two-track Stella DAT," he explains. "It uses a tiny minicassette that looks amazingly fragile, and in a sense it is. It has such a high level of sophistication that it's always worrisome, because the slightest bit of error, recording error or computer error, could make us throw the whole recording out."

Causey used the same digital audio transfer machine in recording *Generations* and *First Contact*. "I've been into DAT for quite a while, since *Lethal Weapon III*, and then *Hoffa*, and every film I've done after that. But I still protect my backside with this analog machine." Causey laughs as he looks down at the the lower shelf of his sound cart. "It's an old mono Nagra. If for whatever reason we have some failure in the digital link, we have this. But it's really just a security blanket. The DAT is utterly reliable. We could shoot with it 365 days in a row and not have one problem."

CAPTAIN TO THE BRIDGE

AT 9:25 A.M., PATRICK STEWART AND MICHAEL DORN ENTER LAUGHING.

Stewart is in street garb, sans theatrical makeup, wearing a purple sweatshirt and casual slacks, reflecting the note on the call sheet that clearly states the actor's performance today will be "Off camera only."

Dorn, on the other hand, has arrived at the soundstage decked out in a Starfleet uniform and full Klingon makeup. Yet he, too, will be performing off camera. Dorn is working double duty today. He's spent the morning working on Stage 4, an attendee at a ceremony honoring Captain Benjamin Sisko, who has just received the Christopher Pike Medal of Valor. The scene will be part of the opening teaser in *Deep Space Nine*'s sixth season finale, "Tears of the Prophets."

That Dorn's potentially conflicting shooting schedules complement each other so perfectly is a testament to the scheduling abilities of the assistant directors working on each of the productions. When Dorn was required for scenes on the television episode, they made sure that his appearance would not be needed by the motion picture company, and vice versa. On some days, that meant working on one soundstage with one group of co-stars for part of the day, and then on another set with another group of actors for the rest. Although it's early in the day, Dorn has just been released by *Deep Space Nine* (his day there began at 6:00 A.M.), and the film company is ready and waiting for him. It goes like clockwork, and the actor didn't even need to go through a wardrobe change. All he had to do was walk directly across the street to Stage 5, two minutes from space station to scoutship.

Patrick Stewart and Michael Dorn stand on the semilit *Enterprise* bridge recording part of their vocal track on a remote microphone. ELLIOTT MARKS.

Luckenbach, with his feet at the top of the chair on the crane, explains, "Laying down across the top of the crane is the only way I can get my eye to the eyepiece to see what the camera is seeing." He spent several hours of several days in various contortions. ELLIOTT MARKS.

As the two actors near the set, Jonathan Frakes spots them and launches into an impromptu serenade, his voice ringing across the soundstage during a momentary break in the hissing and clanking. "It's Paaaaa-trick. And Miiiii-chael," he intones to no discernable melody. No one on the set is surprised at the behavior, and in fact, most of the crew just keep on doing what they've been doing, without looking up. The entire entourage is used to it. Clearly at ease with his position, Frakes sings much of the time, whether he's grabbing a cup of coffee, thinking out scenes, or directing.

"We are a *very* musical cast," Stewart observes as he walks past the director toward a colorful array of melon and pineapple that Craft Services Manager Sam Arroyo is setting on a table. "Brent has just come off a musical on Broadway, and in September I'm going to be singing at the Hollywood Bowl." Not a word, however, is said about Frakes's spontaneous performance, an omission that the director seems to notice.

"We're really blessed that we still laugh at each other's jokes," Frakes says.

A few yards away, Director of Photography Matthew Leonetti and Gaffer Patrick Blymyer test the set's master light, a salmon-colored 1300-watt halogen bulb shining down from above the action. When the sequence is finally composited, it will appear that the interior of Data's ship is tinged by light penetrating the

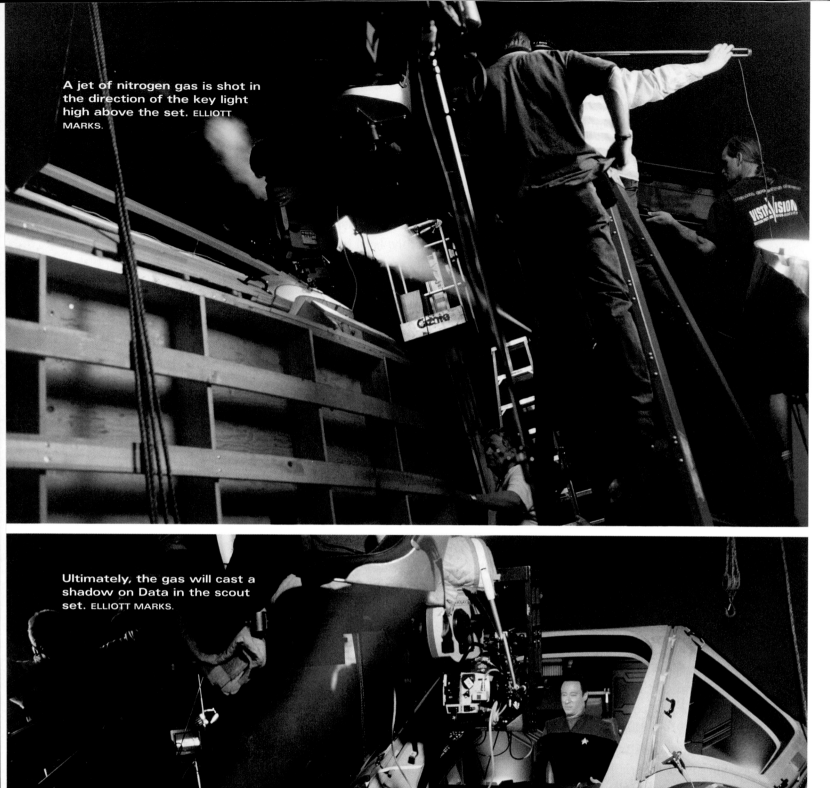

A jet of nitrogen gas is shot in the direction of the key light high above the set. ELLIOTT MARKS.

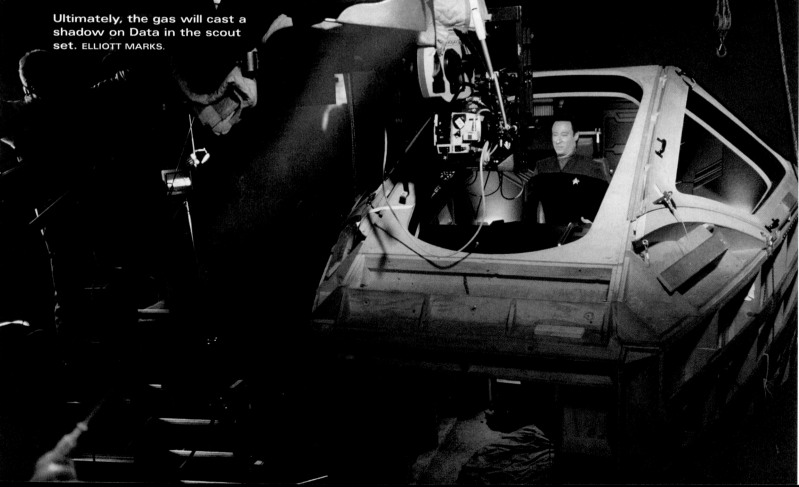

Ultimately, the gas will cast a shadow on Data in the scout set. ELLIOTT MARKS.

"Scene Sixty-Eight is up," Fleck announces. Then he glances at his watch and realizes that the crew must break for lunch in just a few minutes, at 12:00 noon. Should they break a few minutes early, thereby allowing the crew to return to work a little before 1:00 P.M., or should they use the remaining minutes to fit in a little prep for the next scene?

The setup for the scene is somewhat complicated and will take a while to prepare. Fleck goes over the story elements in his mind. Although it won't be obvious to those who haven't seen the storyboards, the scene calls for Picard's shuttle to pass directly above the scout. The ships will be created by the Visual Effects Department, of course, but part of the scene—the shuttle's shadow passing through the scout's windshield and crossing over Data's face and the scout's interior—must be completed today, in live action.

Fleck decides that there's time for one component of prep: rolling in a large tank of nitrogen gas.

"We're using nitrogen for this effect," explains Terry Frazee as he attaches a hose to a c-stand raised high above the windshield. "As the nitrogen goes between the light and the set, it'll cast a shadow. We don't photograph the nitrogen, just the shadow, so it'll actually appear as if there's an off-camera cloud passing by." Or rather, a speeding space shuttle for which the cloud is standing in. "This will shade the whole master light, so it should shadow the entire booth that Brent sits in," says Frazee. "That'll be a pretty good effect."

He joins his crew to roll in the two hundred-gallon nitrogen tank. But he'll have to wait to attach the hose to the tank. "That's lunch," Jerry Fleck shouts to all within hearing distance. "Be back in sixty minutes."

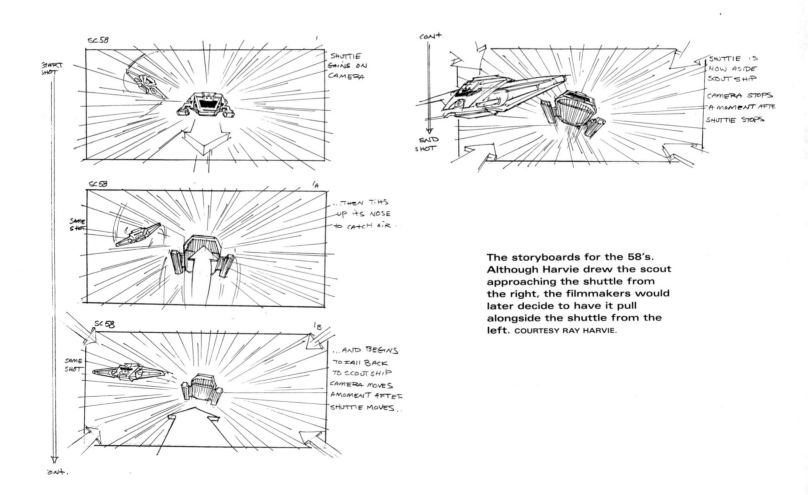

The storyboards for the 58's. Although Harvie drew the scout approaching the shuttle from the right, the filmmakers would later decide to have it pull alongside the shuttle from the left. COURTESY RAY HARVIE.

Joe Brennan, David Luckenbach, and 2nd Camera Assistant Harry Zimmerman squeeze inside the scout to shoot over Data's shoulder.
ELLIOTT MARKS.

SPIN CONTROL

AT 5:00 P.M., AFTER A FULL DAY OF SHOOTING, FRAKES IS READY TO FILM THE MOST MECHANI-CALLY INTERESTING SHOT OF THE DAY, SCENE 74.

74 INT. SCOUT--(OPTICAL)
Over Data toward the approaching ground...

Actually, the most interesting thing about this shot is its relationship to Scene 71, which the visual-effects team will create in post production:

71 EXT. SCOUT AND SHUTTLE--(OPTICAL)
They begin to spin and spiral downward...

That's right, *spin*. As written, Scene 74 does not "ask" for the camera angle Frakes is about to shoot. The script simply says the shot is "over Data," calling for the camera to look over his shoulder and out through the windshield at a bluescreen. But because the lights are all set up to shoot from the front, Frakes has planned an additional shot to take advantage of the current angle, one that will provide the editor with more material when he's assembling the sequence for Scene 74.

"This is a reverse of the shot that's written," David Luckenbach explains. He is holding a hand crank that is attached to a long axle. This, in turn, is attached to the camera mount. The specially concocted rig will allow

The crew moves off to film other sequences but they haven't finished with the scoutship. While the set sits idle, a note is posted declaring it off-limits to passersbys, which is what "hot set" means. ROBBIE ROBINSON.

The twenty-two-foot arm extending towards the scout is part of the "Bulldog," the largest motion-control rig in Hollywood. The 3,500-pound unit often is taken on the road. "We just back it onto a stage, unhook it from the truck, drop the legs, level it, and we're ready to go," Hurley says, "after we hang a camera on it, of course." ELLIOTT MARKS.

By studying an animatic supplied by Santa Barbara Studios, Image G's Adrian Hurley can program his computerized camera to shoot live-action footage of Data that will match the movements of the vessel being created in CGI.
ROBBIE ROBINSON.

rolls and how it comes into frame," he says. "I can get perspective changes on the north, south, and tilt, and I can track and pan their rotation change. By moving my rig around, I can match what the animatic is doing and save the moves in the computer here."

A portable computer cart is in front of Hurley, but the more impressive part of his equipment is a computer-controlled rolling camera, hanging from a track installed on a crane. "This is the Bulldog," Hurley says fondly. "It's our biggest motion-control rig, and it gets used a lot because of the length of the arm. It's twenty-two feet long."

Hurley referes to the camera as a Fries-Mitchell. "Actually," he explains, "it's a Mitchell camera that was made in the l930s. When it was manufactured, it didn't have a very good viewing system, but a fellow named Doug Fries modified it. It has very good registration, so when we do repeat passes, the film lines up perfectly and we get the shot every time."

Seated a few feet away, Hurley's associate at Image G, Motion Control Operator Paul Maples, runs a videotaped image of Straus's animatic on a series of screens. At first glance, Maples appears to have doubled up on the various pieces of equipment laid out in front of him. As it turns out, he has. "I have two monitors, two keyboards, and two computers, all running through the video system… which has two recorders," Maples says.

"The three-quarter-inch video recorder and the half-inch video recorder can each talk to each of the computers, and both of the computers can talk to anything else. It's a good system," he explains. "As long as I have two recorders together, I can do real-time video capture and compositing on the fly. If I had only one system, I'd have to go into some other compositing software, and that would take time.

"We got this system because of the *Deep Space Nine* episode, 'One Little Ship,'" Maples continues. "In that show, a runabout had been shrunken down by a subspace phenomenon. We actually went to the stage and hooked the computer up to the Panavision camera to encode some of its moves. Back at Image G, I was able to go frame by frame through the moves and figure out exactly how to put the little ship into each shot."

"It was absolutely frame perfect with the live action," Hurley confirms. And now that they have the equipment, he says, "we can do a multitude of things that we couldn't do before with just our video decks."

The equipment may be upscale, but assembling the system still requires a good deal of old-fashioned electrical know-how. Hundreds of wires hang loosely from the board on the back of Maples's equipment. "Of course, we've spent hours labeling every wire so they'll all match up," Hurley says, chuckling.

Brent Spiner has a 12:00 P.M. set call, and shooting will begin sometime after that. But the crews from Santa Barbara Studios, Image G, and *Star Trek* have been working on these shots since the previous morning. "We came in yesterday and built the rig," Hurley explains. "We leveled the crane, and then I looked at the animatic to decide where the crane needed to be positioned to achieve the angles the animatic showed. Then I programmed to match it."

On Maples's video monitors, pictures of the scout set and the animatic version intermittently flash, replacing one another in a kind of strobing effect, so that the two images seem to be one. The scout's image is being fed live from the camera only a few feet away, while the animatic's is from the videotape playing on the three-quarter-inch recorder. "Right now we're mixing the animatic and the live picture back and forth to try to set up the move," Maples reveals. "Adrian has some numbers that he's trying to go by."

"There are frame counts on the animatic tape, and I'm matching those frames," Hurley explains. "I pick the first position, and then I pick about every tenth frame. The computer figures out all of the in-between frames for the camera to go through. After I finish, I'll play it back in real time and we'll look at it to see if it works." Hurley watches a monitor as the camera follows its programmed move. "And it does," he says, happily.

At noon, Jonathan Frakes steps into Stage 5 to take a look at the progress. With Lauritson running this show over here, Frakes is free to work across the lot on Stage 16, where he is directing a different interior, a stunt-driven sequence.

The call sheet's weather prognostication for the day says, "Cloudy. 30 percent chance of rain." But in fact, Frakes is dripping wet—100 percent wet. When Brent Spiner arrives, he is dry, but only because he was carefully covered by rain gear and an umbrella to prevent his makeup and costume from being rendered unfilmable during the brief but soggy walk from his trailer. After a quick conversation with Lauritson and Spiner, Frakes pulls his coat collar tight around his neck and steps out the door, back into the pouring rain.

"It's Cinco de Mayo," says John Grower in disbelief. It doesn't usually rain in Los Angeles after early April, but this, as everyone has stated, is a most unusual year. He walks over to study an illuminated area of the bluescreen located near the scout missing top. It doesn't seem like enough light to adequately cover the extensive bluescreen that surrounds the set on three sides, and it isn't. But Grower is concerned only about the section near the top of the scout. In other words, he wants to be able to shoot the area of set where there is nothing and where the screen behind it can be interpreted as nothing. That's understandable; it is, after all, a space movie.

At 12:25, Mark Oppenheimer announces, "Five minutes." Oppenheimer's title is a mouthful: first assis-

After Data's scenes are completed, the set is dismantled and the front portion is sent off to be restored to its earlier incarnation as the *Voyager* shuttle. ELLIOTT MARKS.

STAGE 5

tant director, second unit, visual effects. He's been monitoring the efforts of each separate group of technicians all morning. Now, at last, everyone seems ready to begin actual filming. Oppenheimer glances toward Spiner, who has been casually conversing with various crew members since his recent arrival.

"Oh!" Spiner states in mock surprise, as if he'd just noticed that everyone is in position and ready to roll…except for him. "I'm just gonna go get a real quick touch-up."

Everyone laughs, and the actor heads not for the stage door, but for the scout. He circles around to climb up the steps. His task in this shot will be to stay perfectly still.

Lauritson stands before a color monitor, examining the composition of the shot. He knows that everyone has their cues. "Action!" he calls. The red alert lights begin flashing in the shuttle. The crane whirrs loudly as the motion-control camera makes a two-foot drop, then a three-foot forward move along the overhead track. Four seconds later, Lauritson calls, "Cut," and the camera rolls back to its original position.

Spiner had sat motionless during the shot, and he continues to hold the pose now.

"Brent, that was perfect," Oppenheimer tells him.

"I can do it better," the actor ad-libs, not moving. "Do you see blinking lights?" he asks, tongue-in-cheek.

"Yes." Oppenheimer rejoins. The red alert lights are impossible to ignore; the entire set is filled with blinking lights. "Take Two."

When the second take is completed, Lauritson asks to look at it, so Maples gives him an instant replay. "That's great," Lauritson comments. "Let's do the next one. Brent, this time you're looking at Picard."

Hurley runs the camera through its motions for a short rehearsal so that everyone knows what the shot will be. "Should I turn my head when I see the camera turn?" Spiner asks.

"Yes," Lauritson responds. Everyone is ready. "Take One…Action!" Again the second unit director waits four seconds before calling, "Cut." But Spiner's head turn isn't right. Lauritson consults with Hurley, and together they decide that after two and a half seconds, they will cue the actor to begin slowly moving his head to the left. They try it one more time—and it's good. "Print that," Lauritson says. "Let's do another."

After two more takes, Lauritson says, "That looked good. Let's play that one back." He likes the shot, and says so to Oppenheimer.

"Work lights!" Oppenheimer calls, and the overhead stage lights flash on. "Brent, you can get down. We'll shoot some clean reference passes."

Now the Santa Barbara crew reaches up through the open cockpit. Using pieces of rolled duct tape, they hang white balls around the edges of the opening. The balls will serve as "reference points" when they track the computer-generated cockpit over the plate of the live set. In the midst of this activity, Bruce Jones notices some of the Art Department's graphic-design markings on the scout's console.

"Someone put these nice geometric shapes here, probably for some other reason than helping me," Jones comments wryly, "but they'll work to my advantage. I'll just track the corners of those things, and that'll be my reference, so I can put the simulated cockpit in as if it's right in that console. It'll be like a miracle."

By 5:00 P.M., all of the Data material needed for two of the 58's is on film, and Oppenheimer calls, "Wrap." Tomorrow they will film the last of the 58's and Scene 34. The call is set for 9:00 A.M. Similar shots. Same time, same place.

"Last week we had an extremely hectic day on location," Peter Lauritson comments as he moves toward the exit. "But the kinds of shots that we did today happen at a different pace because the motion-control requirements take time to get the precision that we're aiming for.

"Actually," he says with a big smile, "for a director, this is pretty easy duty."

HURRY UP AND WAIT

MAY 14. For nearly two weeks, principal photography has concentrated on other scenes at other locations. But now, Stage 5 again resounds with a cacophony of hammers, drills, and shouted conversations. In the midst of all this controlled chaos, Jonathan Frakes relaxes comfortably in his director's chair, legs crossed, reading a section of the *Los Angeles Times*. Tall and handsome, if a bit frayed around the edges from too many days with too little sleep, Frakes is obviously at peace with the world. His lips are pursed and he is whistling softly, the familiar melody barely audible against the wall of noise that surrounds him.

"I'm Popeye, the sailor man..."

Everyone around Frakes seems to be in a hurry. That's usually a sign that people are trying to make up for lost time. A glance at the call sheet seems to confirm this possibility. Patrick Stewart and Michael Dorn were due to appear on the set at 8:30, but they're nowhere to be seen. They are, however, in their trailers, ready, willing, and waiting.

It's the set that's late. An hour and a half after call time, stage preparations are still under way.

The stage setup looks a lot like it did back on April 14, except that the box sitting on the gimbal is bigger. That's because it isn't the scoutship. It's a shuttlecraft from the *Enterprise*-E, which will soon be making its debut on the silver screen.

Of course, it's hard to tell what it is by looking at the unfinished exterior. Like the scout's, the shuttle's distinctive look will be realized in the world of computer graphics. On the interior, however, the shuttle already bears a resemblance to a typical Starfleet vessel. In fact, the set resting above the shored-up stage floor looks suspiciously like *Deep Space Nine*'s runabout set—which it is. The feature film production has "borrowed" another set from another *Star Trek* series. But because the series makes heavy use of the set, the shuttle sequences had to wait until *DS9* wrapped its season on April 23 before the production could begin filming the shuttle scenes.

"We've done a whole lot to it," Marty Hornstein comments. "We've taken out the support struts and put them someplace else. And we've put in a new window because Peter Lauritson needs a side window for the camera to look through, and the runabout doesn't happen to have a side window that's big enough for that."

It costs money to change an existing set—the price of construction *plus* the cost of *de*construction as the set is returned to its original condition must be taken into consideration—but Hornstein is quite pleased that they were able to use the runabout. "It's a lot less expensive than building a new ship from scratch," he says. "Production is always pure compromise."

Besides the "bigger box," there is another noticeable change to the setup. The visual-effects screens hanging around three sides of the ship are no longer blue. They're green. "The screens are interchangeable," observes Bruce Jones's assistant, Dan Munez. "Sometimes color choice is just an issue of whatever's available."

Like many other specialized items on a movie set, the screens are usually rented, which explains why the bluescreen was removed when it was no longer needed, following the prior week's work. "Besides," Munez adds, "green is a lot more fun, I think. And it's a little bit more high-definition."

At the base of the greenscreen, the Grip Department has been working on constructing a platform that will hold a second camera. Lloyd Barcroft is balancing a wooden two-by-four brace under the platform while another grip drives a nail into it. Art Director Ron Wilkinson notices the activity as he walks by. "Do you need more support?" he asks.

In response, Barcroft only shakes his head. But from somewhere nearby, underneath the set, a disembodied voice mumbles, "Moral support."

Frakes has not been idle all morning, of course. At 9:00 A.M., he and Matt Leonetti looked at a copy of the cut footage of the dogfight sequence so they could compare what they already had with what they planned to film today. Obviously, a large number of the scenes in the sequence were missing, their positions made conspicuous by the"black slugs" or "holes" edited between the elementary animatic visual-effects footage and the live shots of Brent Spiner. Nevertheless, although rough, the timing of the sequence looked correct, and already the dramatic effect of the action was evident. The director and the director of photography were both happy.

The two men also had time to make an interesting decision in their choice of camera for some of the shots. Leonetti has ordered a Steadicam mounted onto the head of the crane. The camera itself rests on a system of springs, balance points, and bearings, and they feel it is just the tool for the job.

"We're trying to convey the feeling of floating in space," explains David Luckenbach. "The Steadicam will let me roll the horizon a little bit, so I can get that feeling of 'floatiness,' left and right and up and down. It adds a third axis that we wouldn't have in conventional mode. And with the Steadicam mounted on the crane, we can float the crane up and down as well, to give us that additional motion. I think this'll give us just the feeling we're looking for."

Finally, at 11:15, the set is ready for a lighting test, and the two actors are given a "heads up" in their trailers. In the meantime, stand-ins James Minor (for Michael Dorn) and Dennis Tracy (for Patrick Stewart) step

Originally created for *Star Trek V: The Final Frontier*, this ship was briefly considered as a candidate for the E's shuttle. But it had badly deteriorated during its years on the lot, so the producers chose to "cast" a re-dressed *DS9* runabout. PENNY JUDAY.

The realized shuttle set, complete with transporter pad, located in the aft section. ELLIOTT MARKS.

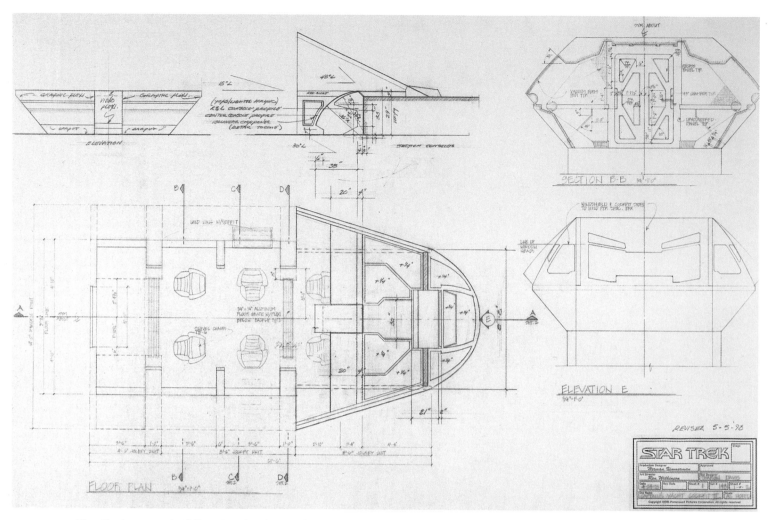

The final concept of the shuttle shows the necessary modifications, including the important windshields. COURTESY NANCY MICKELBERRY.

into the set to complete the picture, and for ten minutes Leonetti and the lighting technicians tweak the settings on their equipment. Then Stewart and Dorn themselves arrive in full costume.

"Rehearsal's up!" Jerry Fleck announces, and the actors exchange places with their stand-ins.

The first shot up is Scene 46, the first live-action scene of the dogfight sequence. It starts with shuttle occupants Picard and Worf almost casually looking for the scout, when, suddenly, they are hit by a phaser blast. Frakes has designed the shot to have camera number one, "A-camera," the Steadicam, concentrating on Picard, while "B-camera," the standard Panavision, follows Worf. The separate photography will allow the editor to make numerous cuts during the fast action. And shooting both of the actors at once guarantees that the lighting will always match up, simplifying the editor's task. Geno Crum is ready at the controls to the gimbal, but during the rehearsal, the machine will stay quiet.

The actors do their lines. After the rehearsal, Frakes has a question. "Should he continue shooting until the end of the scene, or should he stop in the middle, where an edit from Worf's face to Picard's has been planned?" The director holds a quick conference with Bruce Jones.

The hallmark of the *Star Trek* Art Department is careful attention to detail, from the smallest Starfleet ID label to the countless backlit graphics. ELLIOTT MARKS.

"We're gonna go '*blam*,'" Frakes elaborates, "and then the ship will go—" He wags his arms like a shaking ship "—'*shumpa, shumpa.*'" The two men examine the storyboards, but they can't come to an immediate decision about the moves.

They run the animatic on a monitor while comparing it to the storyboards at the same time. Both men want to know the shot clearly in their minds. "Let's rehearse it once with the gimbal," Jones suggests. At this moment, Peter Lauritson comes onto the set and Frakes asks him to join in their discussion.

By 11:35 they've made up their minds. "Let's try it."

As Crum starts the generator, smoke immediately begins to waft from inside an electical switch on the side of the cart. Crum turns it off quickly as the sharp smell of burning wire fills the area.

Obviously there is a problem. Gaffer Patrick Blymyer and Paramount's Best Boy Electric Patric Abaravich leap into action and dismantle the switch while the rest of the electricians gather. One of the assistant directors radios the problem to Paramount's fire marshal, who arrives less than a minute later.

The prognosis: the switch is fried. Someone will have to build a new one from scratch in the studio's Electrical Department, a task that obviously will take a few minutes.

Step inside, out of the chaos of the soundstage, and
for a moment the shuttle seems real. ELLIOTT MARKS.

Dozens of graphics fill the interior. Sit down in any chair and you would think that this ship could fly.
ELLIOTT MARKS.

Matt Leonetti does a final walk-through to make sure all the lighting elements are correct. ELLIOTT MARKS.

Gaffer Patrick Blymyer is the man in charge of all electrical equipment on the set, from the smallest lightbulb to the longest cable. ELLIOTT MARKS.

"Let's try one *without* the gimbal," Frakes says, and everybody moves back to their positions. It is now 12:09 P.M. Rehearsal. The camera shakes at a point in the script that says, "Suddenly, *wham*—a blast…"

"Let's cut just after the camera shakes for the first time," Frakes decides. Now a question is relayed to the director from the actors. Frakes thinks for a moment, then shouts, "He's shooting you guys in the butt, so throw yourselves back!"

Now they try it again. "Dive, dive, dive," Frakes shouts during the rehearsal. Then, "Cut," and he circles the shuttle, climbs the small wooden staircase leading into it, and disappears inside.

A moment later he emerges, shaking his head, a touch of a smirk on his lips. "Actors," he mumbles, in pseudo–sotto voce. "I'm gonna be really tired by tonight," he says, and he stumbles down the eight steps, missing each one slightly, in a short series of pratfalls. Frakes's smile as he reaches the bottom reveals how much he's enjoying himself, and the smile grows even bigger when Ron Wilkinson shouts, "The gimbal is ready to rock and roll!"

Instantly, Jerry Fleck takes up the clarion call. "Okay! Ready! Picture's up!" And for the first time today, he calls, "On a bell!" It is 12:38 P.M.

James Minor and Dennis Tracy "stand in" for the principal actors during a setup. Minor also stands in for Michael Dorn on *Deep Space Nine*. Because actors frequently are required elsewhere while camera and lighting tests are performed, stand-ins are essential. ELLIOTT MARKS.

The gimbal works perfectly as Crum rotates it five degrees to the side and twenty degrees downward. The monitors show what the cameras are seeing, two men who really appear to be flying in a spacecraft, albeit a spacecraft adrift in front of a sea of green.

Jonathan Frakes calls, "Cut," and then stands motionless. "Wow," he says at last.

"I think we're cool," says Fleck.

"Yeah," Frakes responds.

"It was worth the wait," Fleck notes enthusiastically.

Stewart and Dorn join the others behind the monitors to look at the shot. They all like it, so the diretor makes the only statement fitting the situation.

"Take Two!" he says.

And everyone returns to their positions. It is 12:45.

Then, at 12:50, it's "Take Three."

"Cut. Print number one."

There are times in any production, regardless of all efforts, where *everyone* has to hurry up and wait. ELLIOTT MARKS.

Now Fleck asks for the cameras to be moved to slightly different positions; Dorn will be more promi-nent in shot 46 Apple. While this work is being done, Crum approaches Frakes. "I'd like to anticipate the move," he says. "The controls on the gimbal are sluggish." Frakes agrees to Crum's plan of action.

A director is something like the proverbial wise old man on the mountain. He is constantly being approached by members of the crew who need answers, and as the man in charge, the director is expected to have those responses on the tip of his tongue. Thus, Frakes isn't caught off guard when Property Master Bill MacSems approaches him carrying a complicated mechanical prop that has nothing to do with today's scenes. The device will play an important role later in the film.

Frakes plays with it for a moment, manipulating several of its moving parts. "This whole gag should take only a second," he comments. "There's almost no time for any of this to happen...."

The two discuss exactly how the prop will be executed for its scenes. Then MacSems leaves and the direc-tor turns back toward his monitor. "Alacrity!" he shouts. "Action!"

Somehow everyone is ready and the shot goes off without a hitch. "Cut," Frakes says.

Then: "One more."

Then: "Very lovely. Moving on." Turning to the script supervisor seated next to him, he says, "Print one and two, both cameras."

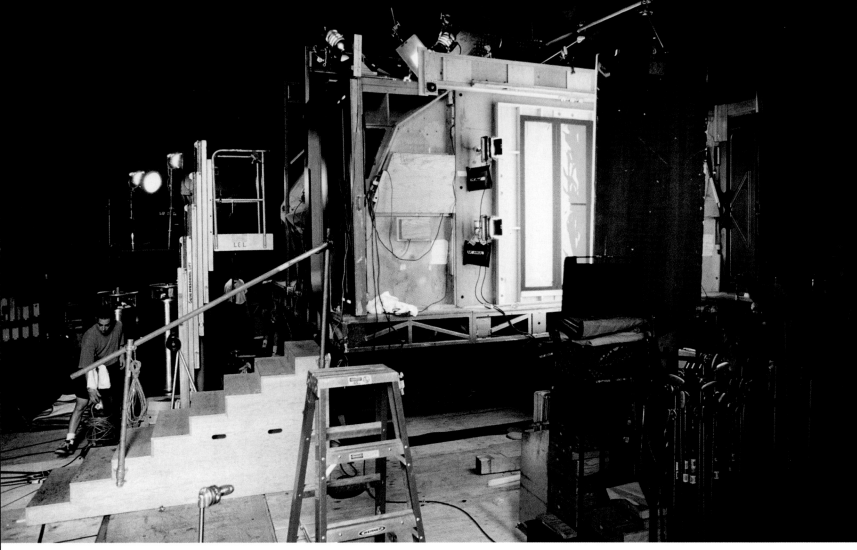

The "service" entrance to the shuttle. ELLIOTT MARKS.

The setups for the next two scenes, 48 and 49pt (that part of Scene 49 which corresponds to the 49pt that Brent Spiner shot on April 14, exactly a month ago) are similar, and they go quickly. After lunch, Scenes 51, 54, and 55 also speed by.

But eventually, things get a little harder.

Or, at least, louder.

5:30 P.M., Scene 57.

Per the script, "Picard works hard to stabilize the ship...." The special-effects team sets the scene by hooking up a hydrogen tank to shoot the steamlike gas through the shuttle, near the actors. The sound of the gas shooting out of the hoses is extremely noisy. The ADs pass out foam plugs for the workers on the stage to stick into their ears. Some people who are working farther back from the action don't accept the plugs, but seem to regret it later; they cup their hands over their ears while the gas is running.

Through it all, the actors gamely deliver their lines. Obviously, their dialogue here will need to be looped later on. But Tom Causey cannot count on that. He works hard to capture whatever remnants of the dialogue he can. The microphones that are planted on the walls inside the set are ineffective under these extreme con-

Worf leaps into action to stop the cockpit from filling with a lethal gas. ELLIOTT MARKS.

ditions; now he's entirely dependent on the boom mike. "If nothing else, the editor can use this as a cue track for when the dailies are assembled," Causey explains. "Or if the actors are good now, this will serve as a cue track for them when they loop the scene."

Time passes, footage is filmed, and at 8:00 P.M., Fleck announces to the cast and crew that they are wrapped for the night.

Stewart exits the box for the last time that day, looking no worse for wear than he did in the morning, despite the fact that he's been bounced around for hours. "I'm used to gimbaling," he says with a smile. "This is very straightforward by comparison to what I went through on the *Pequod* in *Moby Dick*," says the actor. "That ship was huge. They built it specifically to float in a large tank, but it also had hydraulic pumps so it could pitch and roll, and it could *really* pitch and roll, especially during the storm sequences. It never stopped moving."

Watching his steady gait as he heads for the exit of the soundstage, there's no doubt that the captain still has his "sea legs."

Joe Brennan plants a boundary layer microphone on the dashboard of the shuttle. ELLIOTT MARKS.

May 15. The next morning Rick Berman joins Matt Leonetti in front of the monitor to watch an image being transmitted, once again, from the spinning camera rig. They have just rehearsed Scene 70, which appears to be the most difficult shot of the day. Jerry Fleck has scheduled it to shoot "first up," thereby applying the greatest amount of time and the crew's freshest energy to the task.

"Patrick," Jonathan Frakes alerts the actor nearest the lens, "the camera will begin to spin just after you say your line."

But this time, much more than the camera will be spinning. Right next to the camera, a flat circle of wood with many holes drilled through it is slowly turning. The lights shining behind the circle spill through the holes, sending a mixed splattering of shadow and light that speckles the shuttle's interior and the actors. The effect brings to mind the sun shining through fast-moving broken clouds, which is, not so coincidentally, essentially the look they're going for. A few feet away, a set of blades, reminiscent of a windmill, spins in front of a lamp, adding additional shadows to the moving luminous mixture.

Now the gimbal starts rocking side to side and the camera starts spinning, capturing the undulation of the shadow and light.

Jonathan Frakes watches this orchestration with a smile. After the gimbal has once again been quieted, he climbs up onto what might be considered the "hood" of the shuttle, just outside the missing windshield, next to the camera. "Lloyd," he calls to the key grip, who is watching from below, "this is a wonderful setup!"

Lloyd Barcroft invented this moving camera mount only hours before testing. "I took the springs off the rocker arms for the valves on a 456 Oldsmobile that was parked on Paramount's back lot," Barcroft says. "The airbag (in the middle of the springs) is a leveler for an RV, the kind you use to keep it from rocking." ELLIOTT MARKS.

"Yes," Barcroft answers matter-of-factly. "*And* it's safe."

"You know," Frakes continues, "this shot may even be *in* the movie."

The work is completed, and at noon, Frakes calls for Scenes 53 and 58, two pieces that are both shorter and easier than the complicated scene they've just completed. There are no lighting or camera changes between the two scenes, so the director wants to shoot them as one. The two parts can easily be separated in the editing room.

In each of the scenes, Michael Dorn has one line of dialogue that contains made-up technological information: technobabble, as it is frequently referred to by *Star Trek* writers, directors, and actors. Since the words in this kind of dialogue generally have no correlation in our limited twentieth-century vocabularies, reciting them must be done by rote, a situation that generally offers ample fodder for comic outtake reels.

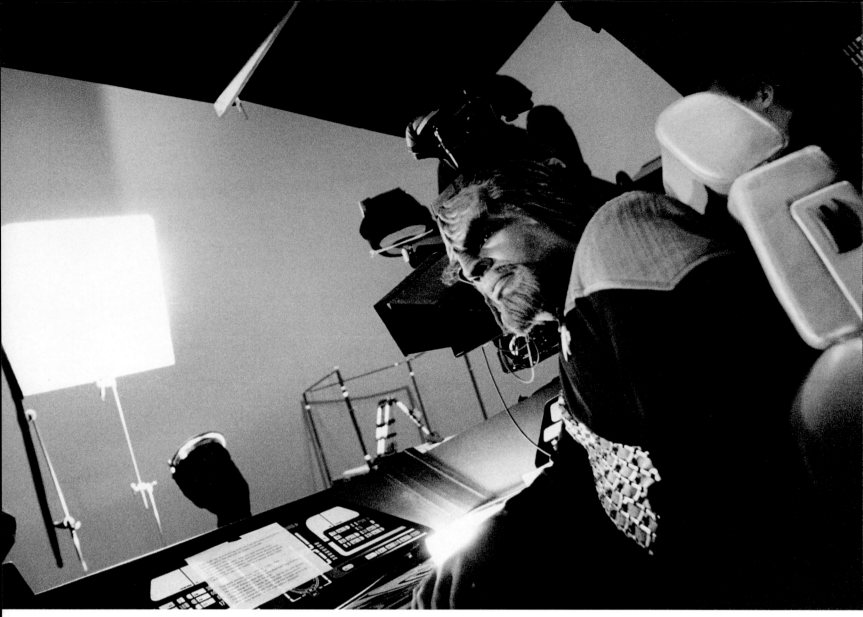

After portraying the character for eleven years, Michael Dorn seems perfectly comfortable in the persona of Worf.
ELLIOTT MARKS.

And sure enough, as Dorn delivers his lines, he mixes them up, saying part of the second line first.

Jonathan Frakes is seated in front of his monitor, holding a microphone. Frakes has come to enjoy using the mike, and the cast and crew are getting used to hearing the director through any of several speakers set up on stands around the set. As soon as Dorn garbles the line, Frakes calls, "Cut," into the microphone. Then he looks at the people gathered behind the monitor and tells them, straight-faced, "You know, that's the first time he's ever done that."

They go to Take 2, and this time, it's perfect. But Frakes wants one more take. He's not worried about eating up a few minutes of additional production time, despite the fact that he already has the material he needs. Somehow, he is running slightly ahead of the projected schedule. "Let's get this shot before lunch," he says. "That'll be a real bloom in our bonnet."

But Take 3 is not as good. Frakes goes into the shuttle to talk to the actors. Before long, they're at Take Eight.

A few minutes later, Frakes's voice emerges again from the speakers. "Let's cut. You don't want anybody to see that."

Maybe going to lunch early would be a good idea. Now Frakes starts humming a low moan into the mike. He sounds like a dog waiting for a crumb to fall. "MmmmmMMMmmmmMmm." He's having fun with his friends—and with his new toy, the microphone.

"Take Nine. Action."

This time the lines flow perfectly; the camera is right on target. "Yes!" Frakes shouts happily. "That's perfect! Thank you everybody."

"Shall I print that?" the script supervisor asks.

"Yes. Print nine only."

First Assistant Director Jerry Fleck waits patiently while Makeup Assistant Mary Kay Morse completes final touches on Michael Dorn and Camera Assistant Suzanne Trucks checks the focusing distance. ELLIOTT MARKS.

After lunch, the group returns to the sixties. That is, the series of scenes numbered in the sixties, not the decade. And in yet another parallel to those earlier scenes, Brent Spiner arrives, to take *his* place in front of a microphone on the semidark *Enterprise* bridge. It's Spiner's turn to read his half of the lines from off camera, and for Stewart and Dorn to be filmed reciting the same lines they'd read into the mike on the bridge the month before.

The shots go perfectly, and Spiner is released in exactly forty minutes. Unfortunately, he can't go home, so it's off to makeup and wardrobe. He has another scene scheduled for the end of the day. In fact, he will be in a shot that's actually *filmed* on the lit *Enterprise* bridge. As Spiner leaves the stage, an advance crew moves in to begin preparing the set, despite the fact that filming is going on nearby.

Before the production company can desert the shuttle for the final time, they need to complete several pieces of footage that Santa Barbara Studios needs, including the shuttle crew's portion of the 58's. Bruce Jones joins Jonathan Frakes at the monitors to watch the shots. One of the monitors is receiving three pictures, shown side-by-side on a split screen: an animatic of Data in his scout; a live feed of Patrick Stewart from the shuttle set; and the third shot, a composite of the first two screens, with a "live" Stewart separated from the Data animatic by a window. The composite looks almost real, as normal and matter-of-fact as if the characters were the drivers of two cars located in adjoining lanes on the freeway. Except, of course, for the fact that one of the images is Patrick Stewart and the other is a beigey-gray stick figure.

Now Stewart must look out of the window of the shuttle, act as if he sees Data in the other ship, then turn and talk to Dorn. Take 1 is very good. Jones asks to see it played back on the monitor on top of the animatic shot, but for some reason the "mix" component won't work. He must make do with seeing Stewart's take alone, with the animatic playing alongside of it. But it is still fine. The fifteen-degree drop of the gimbal seems to have matched the fifteen-degree drop of the animatic ship.

"We should do it again," Jones suggests. But before they roll, he converses with Luckenbach about capturing the same angle a second time. To assure himself that he can, Luckenbach looks at the animatic one more time.

Take 2 again goes fine, and they're ready to move forward.

"Moving on," Jerry Fleck calls, looking at his watch. It is now 5:05, and he still has a company move ahead of him, although it isn't far. They're only moving around the wall to the bridge set.

The visual-effects producer needs one more shot, 46 Baker, which is a side view of Patrick Stewart clearly positioned against the greenscreen. Jones knows the camera angle he needs in order to track this shot into his eventual composite. Now he climbs a ladder to place a number of pieces of tape, Xs, on the greenscreen. "When the camera is moving, the Xs will show us the parallax difference between the window frame and specific points in the screen," Jones explains. "We'll use those as tracking points to build our geometry out there, so we can lock our matte painting, or planet, to the greenscreen and give a correct sense of the ship's motion."

But placing the space background correctly behind the ship is even more complicated than that; the subject now turns to higher mathematics. "The inverse also is true," Jones continues. "By having those Xs out there when the shuttle is gimbaling, we can see how the ship is moving against those marks, and we can come up with a formula to give the illusion of reality when we put it all together."

While Jones is on the ladder, Patrick Stewart watches him thoughtfully. He knows the drill. Pretending that Data is out there among those marks is practically Acting 101. "We've been acting with things that aren't there, or that we can't see, like creatures or space phenomena, for eleven years," Stewart says. "The director usually gives us a detailed description of what we're looking at, or occasionally the artists will give us an artist's impression of what we're seeing. It's a process of the imagination," he says, "as a lot of acting is."

Bruce Jones carefully places taped Xs at specific spots on the greenscreen. The marks will serve as "tracking points" when the visual-effects team tracks Stewart's close-up into the final composite of Scene 58. ELLIOTT MARKS.

The film crew swarms over the shuttle set like an army of ants, each member with its own particular mission. A production crew is like a community unto itself, complete with carpenters, electricians, hairdressers, painters, caterers, and people who just walk around telling other people what to do. ELLIOTT MARKS.

Jonathan Frakes choses to exit the set via the window rather than disturb the group working inside the shuttle.
ELLIOTT MARKS.

By 5:32, Frakes, Grower, and Jones have the footage they need to complete Piller's dogfight sequence. The difficult live-action eye-contact scenes between Data and Picard are in the can.

Lloyd Barcroft sums the experience up: "It's a lot of work for a little bit of film. But that's the way this whole business is."

It *was* a lot of work, but somehow in the end, it didn't seem all that difficult to shoot. And *that* didn't happen by chance. "Part of it was just the result of good writing and good acting by Michael and Patrick and Brent," says Frakes proudly. "Some of the looks between the guys have thrown the scene far above what was on the page. But the technical details, all of that was the result of working the storyboard stuff out ahead of time with the folks from Santa Barbara."

Of course, much of the credit must go to Frakes himself, who has faith in his own instincts and in the knowledge of the people who report to him. That faith inspires his team to give their all for him, even those people who've known him long enough to tease the heck out of him. But when it comes to the respect of his peers, there's no joking at all. As Patrick Stewart observes, "He's the director, he's the boss, he's in charge—and all of us acknowledge that."

POSTPRODUCTION

EL NIÑO HAS DRIZZLED HIS LAST. During the first week of August, the temperature on the Paramount lot hovers around a smoggy ninety-five degrees. Two hours away, directly northwest via Highway 101, the temperature outside of Santa Barbara Studios reaches a high of eighty. Here, a quarter mile from the Pacific Ocean, the perfect air is refreshing and relaxing. But inside the visual-effects facility, relaxation is the farthest thing from anyone's mind. For the eighteen staff members assigned to *Insurrection* there is only one thought: space, the final frontier. And how to create all of the elements that will make it seem like a real place to the millions of people who go to see this movie.

And, of course, how to make the delivery deadlines.

"Eighteen people is a small team to create close to a hundred shots for the film," admits Visual Effects Line Producer Diane Holland. Fully twenty-nine of the shots specifically pertain to the dogfight sequence. And a number of those elements will be used in other parts of the movie as well.

Holland counts down just a few of the elements her company is developing for the production. "The scout. The shuttle. The *Enterprise*. Tachyons. The Starfield. The Briar Patch. The rings. The planet." Her voice trails off. There's a different combination of effects for each of those elements in each shot. To figure out exactly what each element is capable of (Do the rings move? Does the planet rotate? What the heck does a tachyon look like, anyway?), every person on the team is responsible for conducting an incredible amount of research and development (R and D) before he or she can begin to create the elements necessary for the final shot.

"Of course," Holland adds with a smile, "they'll need to deliver what the shot needs at a particular time, so that it can all go into compositing at the right time."

No pressure.

How do they do it? The concept of teamwork, of being a good "team player" may sound like a cliché—but it means survival in Santa Barbara. "With as many as fifty different things going into each shot," Holland says, "communication is extremely important."

The company has worked out its communication needs in both high- and low-tech ways. "All of our computers are hooked together through the network," explains James Straus. "On top of that, we have our entire project going through a program that tracks the status of every single shot and element the company does. Not only does it find the information that I'm looking for, but it will hunt down stuff that the other people are doing and actually decide, 'I think this is one of those elements he needs,' and it'll tell me about it."

Straus chuckles. "Of course, we're a small company, so I could just as easily walk down the hall and yell, 'Hey, is that comp ready?'"

When the comp for the chase sequence is ready, it will contain three types of shots.

"There's the type that Jonathan and Peter shot on stage," Straus notes, "with live-action elements that we have to match together with the computer elements. Then there is another type where the environments are live-action but the elements in them are computer-generated, like actual clouds with little CGI shuttles flying through them. The third kind of shot is completely digitally created. When we approach the planet, every single thing you'll see will be CGI: the starfield, the rings, the planet, the ships, even the actors."

Even the actors. For several digital space shots where the ships are far in the distance, the heads in the windows will be animated in the final film. The task of creating the digital people fell to Technical Director Eric Saindon, and they'll be of a much different caliber than the crude figures used in the onstage animatics. "I did models of Picard, Worf, and Data," Saindon says, his hands never leaving his favorite artist's tool, his keyboard.

"Of course, I started real simple, for the animatic. Then I went back and added skeletons and put skin on them. Now I'm rendering the facial features."

"Eric has put a lot of effort into those characters," Straus says. "I've seen CGI actors in movies before, but you can usually tell they're CGI. But when Eric drew Worf, I couldn't stop staring at it—it looked so *real*. The characters can even move their fingers and move their heads around because of the controls he wrote."

The fact that Saindon's work is so good makes Straus's job easier. "If the digital actors are completely convincing, then I can make these spaceships come closer to camera."

While Saindon's job was to make his subjects look extremely familiar, Art Director Richard Kriegler was asked to make *his* subjects look very *un*familiar. He was given the assignment "to seek out strange new worlds," including a ringed world that looks new and fresh, and nothing like Saturn.

"That's where I started," Kriegler says. "I found a picture of Saturn and I said, "I don't want our planet to look like this." The artist laughs at the memory, but he was very serious about the work. "I did seven different concepts for the rings, until the producers chose one," he says. "The concept is based on ideas from the script that lead me to make the rings soft, not hard-edged like Saturn's. I actually wanted to have some of the ring's material blowing off, like in a solar wind, and leaving a trail, so I went with this soft, fuzzy look."

"I'm also the concept artist for the movie," Kriegler adds, "so I had a free hand to start what I pictured in my mind after reading the script." Kriegler came to the job well versed in the level of art expected by the *Star Trek* producers and fans. "I spent twelve years working with Paramount's advertising department," he says, "and we did posters for dozens of movies, including all of the *Star Trek* ads. I used to be a painter," he relates. "But now I just work in the computer."

After Kriegler completes each matte painting, he says, "It stays in the computer, and then it just surfs over to the Three-D department where other artists work on them."

One of those artists is Technical Director Dave Witters. "I'm building the rings by adding striations that will give them a sense of scale," he says, noting that he works with a shader program, a rendering tool that defines levels of transparency, color, and density. "The shader utilizes a texture map that has a lot of striated detail and also adds a very fine granular detail that will add depth without looking computer generated."

Witters isn't finished, of course. After all, he's only been working on the rings "off and on for six weeks" since getting the matte painting. But he thinks he's using the correct colors for the final textured finish—a blue-green shade that the producers seem to like. "They've asked for a little more highlighting, so I'm blending that in now," he says. At the same time, he spreads a faint sparkle across the image. "There's a subtle camera move across the rings in one view, so you'll see matter in them, like rocks, that glint and move through an iridescent color spectrum, much like that of an abalone shell. At least, that's one of the things I'm *hoping* they'll do." Witters can't be sure, of course, because once the element is out of his hands, it will be, well, out of his hands.

The planet that will be encircled by the rings is being rendered in 3-D by Technical Director Virginia Bowman. "We just divided up the work, and Dave ended up with the rings," she says. "Of course, he's really good at particles." And did she get the planet because she's good at…

"No," she laughs, "I'm not sphere gal. It's just that the rings and the planet were both going to take up a lot of R and D time. So to have one person do both just wasn't going to work out."

Like Witters, Bowman started from mattes rendered by Kriegler. "Richard took a variety of scans from all over Earth, bays and lakeshores, and he composited them to produce new continents," she points out.

"I used aerial photographs shot from satellites in part of the building of it," Kriegler reveals. "Then I mapped twelve different pentagon-shaped matte paintings as sections of the planet. As they

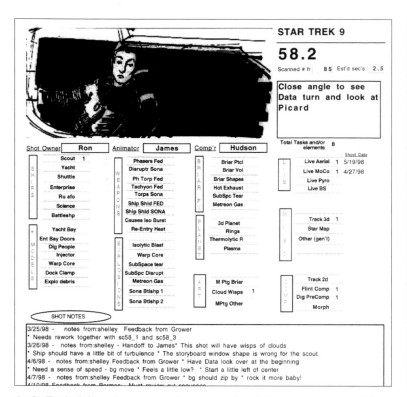

Left: Technicians keep complete records of their progress while creating each shot. Note that this redrawn story-board for Shot 58.2, like the original, remains, flipped. COURTESY SANTA BARBARA STUDIOS. *Right:* Straus's animatic was carefully matched by the motion control team when Scene 58 was shot in live action. COURTESY SANTA BARBARA STUDIOS.

wrap around the planet, each pentagon overlaps the other ones to tile the whole planet, and we end up with a sphere.

Bowman's 3-D goal is to, "nest a variety of increasing resolution texture maps so that we can fly right down to the surface and see really crisp mountains, and then water, and then flowers. The images will always be there," she explains, "but each doesn't cover the whole surface. As the digitized camera goes closer, certain parts will be revealed with really high resolution maps."

"There will be something like twenty-two different texture maps just for the surface of the planet," adds Scott Liedtka, who also is manager of the 3-D Department. "And Virginia will have as many layers for the clouds and the shadows of the clouds."

"We started with photos of clouds for the realism," Bowman says, knowing that a layer of actual image would sell the effect to the audience. "We've scanned them in and then composited all the scans." Those scanned photos became the cloud-layer texture maps, but Bowman wasn't satisfied. Now she has overlapped each map, which gives the clouds a new variety of texture, as befits a new alien world.

Gathering original cloud footage is not in Bowman's job description, of course. Accomplishing that job was up to John Grower himself. Grower can't help but laugh as he relates the effort.

"We decided to shoot clouds for the plates we needed," he recalls. "So we hired Clay Lacey and went up in one of his Lear Jets. Lacey is a very famous jet pilot, with world records for speed and around the world flights. He's a real *Right Stuff* kind of pilot.

"I had a snorkel imaging camera system that would give us full aperture thirty-five-millimeter film," the

STAR TREK NINE PROPERTY PARAMOUNT PICTURES
08:00:41:19.2   058   3062+07

7 1998 16:25

As shot on the soundstage, Brent Spiner and the scoutship's interior will next be compositied into a completely computer generated ship. COURTESY SANTA BARBARA STUDIOS.

visual-effects supervisor continues. "It was a brand-new periscope-mirrored system mounted on the bottom fuselage of the Lear Jet. The camera system was stuck in the middle where there normally would be seats."

The sequence from the film was supposed to take place at sunrise, but because some airports won't let planes take off in the predawn hours, Grower and Lacey decided to take off in the afternoon and shoot sunset for sunrise—a common practice in motion-picture production.

"We wound up shooting the San Luis Obispo area, because some of the planet's ground plates had been shot out in Santa Ynez, just outside of Santa Barbara. We needed the same kind of terrain from the aerials.

"We had to reschedule several times until we finally decided, 'This is it,'" he says. "And we did luck out, because that day there were clouds nearby. Of course, we were running against the clock. The sun was going down and we only had so much time left with useable light. We kept the cameras going until we'd shot about ten rolls of film, about four thousand feet."

So what was it like?

Grower shakes his head at the memory. "When we were at maximum cruising speed, we were going three hundred and some miles an hour. When we were diving, it got up to about four hundred miles an hour. And I was supervising, so I was sitting in the very back of the jet, behind the camera operator, and I couldn't really see what was going on on the outside."

If one has ever been stuck in the backseat of an automobile that is hitting hairpin turn after hairpin turn, one can begin to empathize.

"It was kind of a nauseating experience," summarizes Grower. "Particularly when the jet banked, like when we would be racing across the clouds, rolling camera, and then at some point we would 'cut.' We didn't have much time, so we'd have to bank to come around to do another take, and we wanted to tilt the camera a slightly different way as we were racing across the clouds. We were trying to do that as fast as possible, so we were *really* racing.

"I was holding on in the back there with cold sweat on my forehead. It wasn't a real pleasant experience. But somebody had to to it."

COMING SOON TO A THEATER NEAR YOU

AS I WRITE THIS, I HAVE NO WAY OF KNOWING WHAT THIS SEQUENCE WILL BE LIKE WHEN THE FILM IS COMPLETED—OR EVEN IF THE SEQUENCE WILL BE INCLUDED IN THE FINAL CUT. *Peter Berger is in the midst of editing. Jerry Goldsmith has yet to write the music. The members of the visual-effects crew aren't getting much sleep as they work around the clock to perfect the artistry that will make this and other sequences in* Star Trek: Insurrection *so breathtakingly natural that it will never occur to the audience that humans do not yet have the ability to zip through space or a planet's atmosphere at speeds that have not yet been recorded, in vessels that remain a mere dream in an illustrator's fertile mind.*

But if I had waited for all those chores to be completed before I sat down to write this, you wouldn't have been able to read this today. Still, going this far has been a privilege. Most writers don't get to spend so much time on a Hollywood movie set. Not even the screenwriter for Star Trek: Insurrection.

"Generally, I don't go on the set," says Michael Piller. "I have too many other things to do. And really, the screenwriter's job is more or less done when he hands the script to the people who produce it. The only thing that could happen when I go on the set is that somebody would come up to me and ask, 'Can I change this?'" Piller laughs.

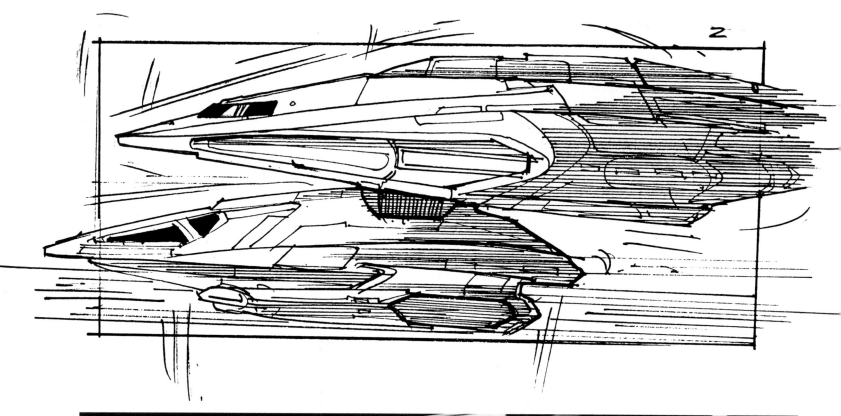

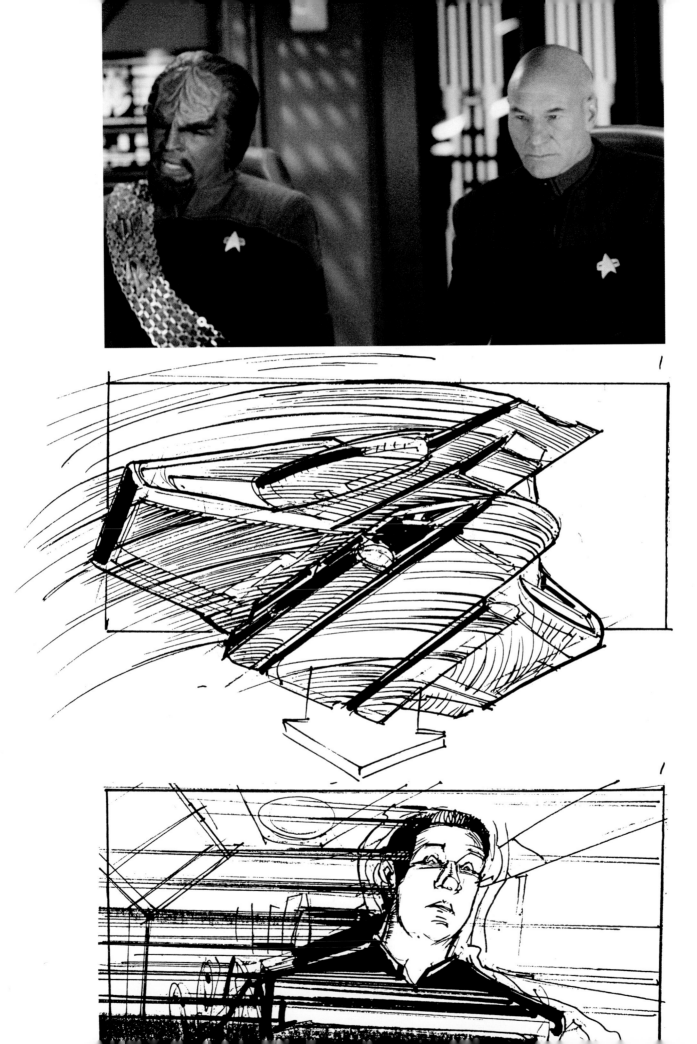

ACKNOWLEDGMENTS

IN WRITING THIS BOOK, I SPOKE WITH HUNDREDS OF WONDERFUL PEOPLE WHO GAVE OF THEIR TIME FREELY, DESPITE THE FACT THAT THEY HAVE THEIR WORK CUT OUT FOR THEM EVERY DAY— AND THAT DOESN'T TYPICALLY INCLUDE ANSWERING QUESTIONS FROM AN OUTSIDE WRITER. But there were many more people working on these productions whom I *didn't* talk to, people whose efforts are as important as those whose names are mentioned. I apologize now for any credit that I have inadvertently omitted. It was not deliberate, I promise. And to those people, I'm terribly sorry. This paragraph is just for you.

Very special thanks to: Rick Berman, Jeri Taylor, Ira Steven Behr, Brannon Braga, Michael Piller, Winrich Kolbe, Allan Kroeker, Jonathan Frakes, Monique Chambers, Rosemary Cremona, Maril Davis, Jackie Edwards, John Grower, Chandler Hayes, Christine Heinrichs, Ellen Hornstein, Marty Hornstein, Lillian Laouri, Peter Lauritson, Molly Mandell, Denise Okuda, Michael Okuda, Dave Rossi, and Robbin Slocum.

At Paramount, my thanks to: Patric Abaravich, Riki Leigh Arnold, Terry Betts, Gabby Cantero, Chip Carter, Paul Fleck, Terri Helton, Gary Holland, Cece Karz, Lili Malkin, Tony Materazzi, Pam Newton, Blaise Noto, Paul Ruditis, Phyllis Ungerleider, and Jennifer Weingroff.

At *Star Trek: Voyager*: Kate Mulgrew, Robert Beltran, Roxann Dawson, Robert Duncan McNeill, Ethan Phillips, Robert Picardo, Tim Russ, Jeri Ryan, Garrett Wang, and Ray Wise. Also thanks to: Daryl Baskin, Alan Bernard, Greg Berry, Ken Biller, Bob Blackman, Dick Brownfield, Randy Burgess, Chris Culhane, Michael DeMeritt, Rob Doherty, Louise Dorton, Wendy Drapanas, Bryan Fuller, Jerry Fitzgerald, Cosmo Genovese,

Gardner Goldsmith, Charlotte Gravenor, Greg Hooper, Merri Howard, Dennis Ivanjack, Richard James, Lisa Klink, Douglas Knapp, Bradley Look, Dennis McCarthy, Jim Mees, Joe Menosky, Tom Mertz, Janet Nemecek, Eric Norman, Josee Normand, Michael O'Halloran, Bill Peets, Lemuel Perry, Marvin Rush, Gerry Sackman, Sandra Sena, Adele Simmons, Alan Sims, Al Smutko, Rick Sternbach, Wil Thoms, Willie Thoms, L. Z. Ward, Steve Welke, Bill Westrom, James Van Over, Dawn Velazquez, Michael Westmore, Scott Wheeler, and Brad Yacobian.

At *Star Trek: Deep Space Nine*: Avery Brooks, Rene Auberjonois, Michael Dorn, Terry Farrell, Cirroc Lofton, Colm Meaney, Armin Shimerman, Alexander Siddig, Nana Visitor, and Mark Alaimo. And also thanks to: Gavin Ames, Andre Bormanis, Hans Beimler, Earl Binion Jr., Jerry Bono, Valerie Canamar, Camille Calvet, Joe Candrella, Jay Chattaway, Barbara Covington, Robert della Santina, Doug Drexler, René Echevarria, Russ English, J. P. Farrell, Bob Fambry, Lolita Fatjo, Steve Gausche, Michael Gerbosi, Julie Gesin, Alan Gitlin, Bill Gocke, Nicole Gravett, R. J. Hohman, Michelle Horn, Clynell Jackson III, Dean Jones, Phillip Kim, Ronnie Knox, Kris Krosskove, Stuart Lippman, Joe Longo, Randy McIlvain, Dennis Madalone, Mike Mistovich, Gary Monak, Ronald D. Moore, Pat Moudakis, Steve Oster, Mark Overton, Terri Potts, Louis Race, David Ramirez, Laura Richarz, Tim Roller, April Rossi, Stephen Rowe, Alex Shapiro, Heidi Smothers, Cindy Sorensen, Bradley Thompson, Mike Vejar, David Weddle, Jonathan West, Karen Westerfield, and Natalie Wood.

At *Star Trek: Insurrection*: Patrick Stewart, Brent Spiner, Gates McFadden, Marina Sirtis, and LeVar Burton. And also thanks to: Brian Armstrong, Tom Arp, Sam Arroyo, Rick Avery, Lloyd Barcroft, Ted Bayard, Peter Berger, Donald Black, Patrick Blymyer, Joe Brennan, Thomas Causey, Eugene Crum, Steve D'Errico, Bill Dolan, John Dwyer, John Eaves, Jerry Fleck, Terry Frazee, Greg Jein, Jerry Goldsmith, Christine Haas, Lumas Hamilton Jr., Kurt Hanson, Ray Harvie, Alan Kobayashi, Matt Leonetti, David Luckenbach, Bill MacSems, Geoffrey Mandel, Dennis McCarthy, Nancy Mickelberry, James Minor, Mary Kay Morse, Dylan Morss, Mike Olguin, Sandy O'Neill, Mark Oppenheimer, Billy Parrish, Buz Presock, Samuel Price, Keith Rayve, Kim Steinert, Eric Stillwell, Yolanda Toussieng, Nancy Townsend, Dennis Tracy, Suzanne Trucks, June Westmore, Monty Westmore, Ron Wilkinsons, Harry Zimmerman, and Herman Zimmerman.

At Modern Sound and related areas: Ruth Adelman, Charles Bazaldua, Doug Davey, Al Ferrante, Chris Haire, Barbara Harris, Don Hahn, Carlyle King, Mace Matiosian, Richard Morrison, Richard Penn, Paige Pollack, Gary Schwartz, and Paul Wertheimer.

In that very specialized world of visual effects, I wish to thank: Elizabeth Castro, Dan Curry, Ronald B. Moore, and David Stipes at Paramount Pictures; Koji Kuramura, Adam "Mojo" Lebowitz, Brandon MacDougal, Emile Smith, and John Teska at Foundation Imaging; Paul Hill, Greg Rainoff, and Ken Reichel at Digital Magic; Adrian Hurley and Paul Maples at Image G; Sandra Alvarado, Virginia Bowman, John Carey, Mark Fattibene, Janet Grower, Diane Holland, Bruce Jones, Richard Kriegler, Alison Learned, Scott Liedtka, Darren Lurie, Ron Moreland, Dan Munez, Matt Rhodes, Eric Saindon, Hudson Shock, James Straus, Mark Wendell, and Dave Witters at Santa Barbara Studios.

The task of shooting photography for this project turned out to be much more demanding than anyone had expected. My thanks to Scott Gibson, Peter Iovino, Penny Juday, Harry Lang, Elliott Marks, Ron Tom, and Robbie Robinson for their valor.

For their contibutions to this project and to humanity in general, my thanks to Steve Aboulafina, C.V.M., James, Maria, and Matthew Block, Louis Block, Greg Chastan, Susan Comara, Cyra and Michael Cowan, Vincent Eugene Craddock, Gordon and Susan Erdmann, Joyce Kogut and Jeff Erdmann, Carl Fortina, Sharlette

Hambrick, Charles Hardin Holley, Dan Madsen, Dave McDonnell, Lanie Miller, Germaine Morgan, Kenny Myers, Dan Newman, Riley Newton, Jim Oldsberg, Steve Palmer, Ellen Pasternack, Chet Prewie, Marcia Rand, Jill Sherwin, Society Chrleston Chew and Pookie, KathE and Steve Walker, Jeff Walker, Tom Weitzel, Robert Hewitt Wolfe, and Steve Wroe.

I thank, too, Paula Block at Paramount Pictures; without your daily guidance and support, this project would not have been accomplished. To Margaret Clark at Pocket Books, thank you for your patience and tenacity. I greatly appreciate the work of book designer Richard Oriolo and cover designer Joseph Perez, who surprised and pleased me at every turn. And also at Pocket Books, thank you to Gina Centrello, Kara Welsh, Donna O'Neill, Donna Ruvituso, Erin Galligan, Scott Shannon, Lisa Feuer, and Twisne Fan.

And finally, to Gene Roddenberry, the brightest light in that distant starfield, thank you for your dream and your creation. You have been thanked before and you will be thanked again. It never will be enough.

TERRY J. ERDMANN
Los Angeles, California
1998